BRUCE CROWN
CHRONIC PASSIONS

Printed in Canada and the United States.

First Edition printed in 2013.
Second Edition printed in 2015.

AP Publications

ISBNs of the first edition:
      978-0-9918883-0-6 (Print)
      978-0-9918883-1-3 (eBook)

Library and Archives Canada information:
Crown, Bruce, 1989—
Chronic Passions / Bruce Crown
FICTION / Mystery & Detective / Hard-Boiled
[Toronto, Ont]: AP Publications, 2013.

I've observed the desolate tundra us zombies call 'home,' and realized that my story is as forgiving as a tired mother and as bright as a burning star.

CHRONIC PASSIONS

We will easily forgive a child who is afraid of the dark; the real tragedy is when men are afraid of the light.

~

Arguably attributed to PLATO

PREFACE

Prefaces are for suckers who don't mind being buttered up before being served to the wolves. I will show you the respect of not buttering you up before serving you to the wolves.

We will at some point, after all, all be served to wolves.

BC. October 2012.

PREFACE TO THE SECOND EDITION

I have to write another one of these?
Come on. I have better things to write.

BC. August 2015.

NIHIL
INFERNAL TRUTH

WE ENTER THIS UNIVERSE alone in search of microscopic beauty—and while we love or are loved by others—we leave this world completely alone having only found infinite sorrow. Despite our vast numbers, we are each on a solitary journey. The tragedy is we realize this too late. No one else can see what we see, hear what we hear, feel what we feel. All we have of each other are glimpses of moments, whispers of experiences, memories of the past we wish we could make eternal, but in the end, we become a faint memory in the minds of a few good people.

* * *

We often see or read about catharsis in mediums like film or novels. The hero is usually a white, young-to-middle aged man who suddenly undergoes an epiphany. A divine or spiritual power suddenly bestows him the knowledge or courage to do what he must do and he does it impeccably by overcoming the impossible-seeming obstacles in his path. In the end he scores a babe on his arm and usually lives on the coast he mentioned in passing earlier in the medium. It is a mystery how he acts against his nature, his character, and his personality hitherto. This battle is usually for the ideal he's fighting for, be it justice, equality, love etc. In the course of the narrative he becomes a 'reluctant' hero, he doesn't want to do it but *someone has to*. If only life were that simple.

Man is as toxic as Chechnya and as cold as Finnish winters. He spends every second remarking the past, his mistakes, revelations, memories, feelings. Remarking these until he comes to a realization like a Zen Master at the top of a mountain: the past bares resemblance to conceptual Zoroastrian philosophy, good battles evil, and with enough persistence and courage good will win.

In times of yore, the good guy fought for some over-bearing and exaggerated principle of fairness or equality while the bad guy fought for the opposite: blasphemous cruelty, elitist societies, unequal distribution of resources, tyranny. That's the past. In modern times, evil is fought with lesser evils.

There exists so little good that even if one slithers beside it with a faint touch over its essence, its barely recognizable ideal is usually so weak and degraded that it is of no practical use.

* * *

A practical example is a speech given by the leader of the most powerful country on our miserable planet. Imagine, if you can, a speech about justice, somehow justice will be warped to rationalize our numerous invasions and involvement in affairs that we have no jurisdiction in. People listen attentively. They bask and rejoice in bringing democracy to parts of the world that makes absolutely no difference to their own lives within their particular corner of the globe. In front of this iron curtain of deception, our leader will make claims to equality, justice, fairness, and belief in a supernatural deity where nothing is hidden. The absolute truth lies behind the curtain. Not one hair on this leader's head gives a damn about equality, democracy, fairness, or justice. All the leader wants is control, control over a community, a city, a state, a nation, and finally, the world.

The roots are rotten, the leader treats the Good as his own personal looking glass like *all* those before him. We are shown only one side while others steal and plunder resources from the countries he's justified in invading three minutes prior to stepping down from the podium. We have faith in our leader and our freedoms. Our "leader" ought to win an Oscar.

Sometimes there are small subsets of people who are clever enough to cast the curtain aside and observe what average intellects cannot. People of this kind are often cast aside or ostracized for not being social enough or not understood by the elite hierarchy of the political realm. This is the tragedy of the human condition. This subset is actually thought to be stupid for not understanding said hierarchy, not understanding *the way things work.* By the time these cultivated individuals navigate the leader's house of mirrors, they'd much rather live out the rest of their days in solitary peace.

Truth is ugly yet attractive, everyone says they admire it but won't hang out with it at the cocktail party. It's forced to drink solemnly in darkness, wondering why people constantly talk about it but hate it when it makes a rare appearance. Ignorance is bliss, because knowledge is a spherical blade, cutting you viciously as you attempt to lift it. All you can do is gape at it in awe, circling it like a tiger, unable to quench your thirst.

* * *

Humans cannot withstand loneliness; the thought of dying alone frightens us. This is why we believe in nonsense like *soul mates* and paradise where your loved ones keep you company.

We are lonelier now than ever before.

I
MONTE CRISTO

It was colder than a politician's heart, thundering icicles as if heaven were losing its battle with hell. Decadent hopefuls were indoors, afraid of the storm like a man of his past. Behind the sound of the vicious thunder amongst the empty streets, an attentive ear could've heard footsteps. A man appeared to displace the water as if he didn't notice the storm. A reddish piece of ember lit up his lips. An older gentleman sat on his porch beside his dog and watched the drenched mystery-man for a while. He turned his head down the road when he thought he heard a wolf howl. *There's none of those in the nearby woods,* he thought. A murder of crows dissipated in the distance. Hell was winning.

The young man noticed the birds too. He looked with dampened eyelashes,

Do I love her? If you've never cared for anything or anyone, have you lived?

Is love preordained?

The old man kept his gaze towards the young man, who in that period had neared him. The old man addressed him as he walk past,

"Hey son, be patient, it has to die down sometime," his voice barely carried over the sound of the cyclone.

The young man turned to the sound addressing him. He stopped in his step and stared into the direction of the old man.

"You can wait with me until it dies down."

The young man stood as still as a statue for a few moments before finally gliding towards the porch. The old man was baffled by his appearance. His stride was confident and his, wet, lit cigar hazed around his burned, cracked lips, his curly hair twirled in front of his eyes and he slicked it back to reveal black eyes that appeared to constrict or dilate on demand. His tuxedo was snapped to the top of his broad shoulders, drenched with rain and sleet.

"I thank you for your generosity but I'm not headed anywhere," his sonorous voice easily carried to the old man's aging ears.

"Not headed anywhere? You look like you're going to party like it's 1999," the astonishment in the old man's wrinkled cheek only ceased when he looked down and pet his best friend.

"We're all headed somewhere I guess," he whispered, "But bad luck brings me here now at this exact moment."

"Why is that?" The old man asked with a raised eyebrow. Only Clark was an expert on Kant's *Transcendental Aesthetic*.

"I have a standing tradition. Midnight, Greenwich time, I walk for a mile or two, sometimes three. It just so happens that I am currently in this cold and cruel city…."

"Some traditions are meant to be broken," the old man seemed to give this claim considerable thought.

"Not mine!" the young man growled in a sort of effortless ferocity that appeared out of nowhere.

The old man thought he shouldn't pursue the matter and tried to change the subject, "Why Greenwich?"

"It's the most accurate time on the planet, makes us connected to the universe doesn't it?" the young man's voice progressively fell into a whisper. "0:00 o'clock, makes it... ominous."

A pseudoscientific moment, some psychic telling you the future in vague abstract terms that you couldn't really relate to but could somehow apply directly to your life if you gave it a second thought.

"What's your name son?"

"Clark," The cigar smoke was a smooth addition to the dampened porch.

It caught the old man's attention, "That's a well lit cigar in such a storm. Lit while it's drenched. What kind is it?"

"Only Monte Cristo cigars touch my lips," more smoke and ash filled the dewy air and the man's dog slumped and laid down.

"Couldn't wait until the storm died out before you lit it? Patience... ah to be young again," the old man joked.

"I doubt this storm will die out. Besides, patience is for Tuscan counts."

The old man's wrinkled neck gave way to a mechanical nod. He didn't understand the reference to patience and a count of Tuscany. He gazed at Clark just as a black sedan sped through the neighborhood towards the direction Clark had been walking. The young man glanced at his watch, politely nodded to the old man and continued with his walk.

The streets were empty. Clark's cigar was nearly smoked to the point of burning his cold, still lips. He wanted to stop, to think about his choices, to wonder about his place in the universe, why *was* he there at that exact time?

He could see police lights in the distance ahead of him. Looked like an ambulance and some onlookers at the intersection of *Grave St* and *Mort Lane*. He turned onto an alley as the officers used their crime scene tape to caution off the few bystanders whose morbid curiosity of death had dragged them out of their houses in one of the worst storms of the century. Unfortunately, or fortunately depending on the perspective, Clark's curiosity of death had long been satisfied that his brash attempt to turn away from the scene was stopped by an overzealous officer.

"You!" the officer howled.

"Yes?" Clark replied firmly but politely as he faced the badge. His cigar still had some life left in it and he saw no reason to put it out. *A cigar must be finished.*

"What you are doing here? Did you know the victim?" the officer took a step closer towards Clark, presumably to invade his personal space and make him feel uncomfortable.

Macho cops think they're men, soldiers, strong warriors. They must think they're samurai.

It's about power. They love it, that's what they thrive on. Take away the badge and all they are is a thug with a gun. Take away the gun, all they are is a man with a useless tin cut out in an obscure shape referencing a perverted form of justice. Take them both away and all they are is a scared little boy afraid of the corrupt world. They think the gun and the badge will protect them. They use it as their solace. They're wrong.

"Officer, I have no idea what you're talking about, I'm just a man on a walk."

"On a stroll... in a tuxedo... in this storm? You look like you're coming from a party," the officer had to scream since the sound of the thunder made it difficult to hear any outside noises.

Clark had yet to submit his gaze to this ridiculous questioning, "That's inconsequential Officer..." he read the nametag hanging off the officer's chest, "Johnson," what an average name, "Besides, you are also outside in the storm without raingear, am I to assume you are a suspect as well?"

"I'm going to need some ID," Johnson raised his voice more than he needed to.

Clark reached inside his dinner jacket without breaking the officer's aggressive gaze and handed the officer his license. As Officer Johnson wrote down the necessary information on a small piece of paper, Clark said,

"I'm late for something officer. Am I under arrest?"

The roided-out *officer* rattled back, retreating a step and submitting his stare after the ensuing silence, eventually he nodded to a man behind him who looked like a detective.

"No, you may leave," the tone of his voice fell back into a socially acceptable volume.

"Thank you Officer; you have been most cordial," Clark took a drag from his cigar and walked away from the scene.

Johnson thought about the kind of voice control the young man had displayed. While he had to scream to be heard, his suspect appeared to whisper. He finally shook his head.

"Cordial?" Pffft. Did he just step out of a time machine from 1604?

Clark's behavior aroused suspicion. The officer pulled out his notebook in fear of forgetting this strange encounter. His notebook was drenched in water within seconds. Nonetheless, he wrote down:

Suspicious character walking towards scene. Attempted to turn away into a side alley as soon as he spotted me. Spot interview and questioning yielded nothing. Further investigation is required.

The suspect was wearing a tuxedo. Vic is wearing a mid-length dress, red in color. They could have been at the party together. Intel on page 17 of report to follow. Request surveillance.

Much to the dismay of Officer Johnson, Clark continued with his walk as if nothing had happened and in fact didn't even sneak a glance back to see the beautiful victim lying in a pool of blood and water.

The medical examiner put the victim on the stretcher and loaded her into an ambulance. Clark suddenly leaned against the grungy, graffiti-ridden alley wall. He looked as if he would have fallen had the wall not been there to catch his balance. He reached into his left pocket and pulled out his phone, neglecting the damage the storm would do to it. He pushed the water aside on the screen and highlighted a name in his contact list. Looking to the downpour for a sign, he shook his head and the water in his hair dripped out before instantly becoming wet again. He shimmered but not from the cold. He didn't place the call. He dropped his phone in a small puddle to his left and stumbled forward.

Fate is cruel, she'll eventually give you what you desire before demanding payment. Unfortunately she doesn't take cash, credit, or debit; but rather pain, aching hearts, and abysmal thoughts of melancholy.

II
CONSTRUCT I

It was the kind of false start a track runner would get disqualified for in the Olympics. That storm wasn't the beginning, it was past the point of no return. Mortal choices had already been made. Dreams had previously spiraled out of control and became nightmares.

The smoke from Clark's cigar filled the *air* as he looked around. He was in a completely black room. The room seemed endless when he tried to walk from one side to another. It felt like an infinite place of darkness or some sort of creative space; the alpha and omega of the void. He stood still for a moment to think it through.

A path abruptly appeared before him. He gently stepped on the path. As he took each step, pavement appeared and extended to accommodate his stride. His cigar stung his lip and he allowed it to fall into the void over the edge of the catwalk.

His confidence increased with each step in this Matrix-like construct. He reached inside his jacket and pulled out another one of the Monte Cristo cigarillos he'd become accustomed to smoking. He lit it with determination that he'd finish it; there are no stalemates in his mind.

He continued walking until a sharp pain ached his left lower back. He turned around as the color drained from his face. He stared at a ghost while his mastery of facial neutrality—stemming from his interest in Ancient Stoicism—allotted him the luxury of controlling rebellious expressions with flawless ease. His stare was fixed on the knife plunged into his back and his fingertips pulsated as he stared at the blood. Why wasn't he afraid? Blood was order in chaos. Everything bleeds and everything dies. This was simple truth. He was dead; he died at the moment of birth. He'd accepted this and in fact embraced it.

The knife pushed him to the edge of the void. Blood was a confirmation of this truth and calmed him rather than unsettled him. He turned and looked at the assailant with his dark, constricted pupils feeling a little like Pyrrho, not believing his eyes. It was like looking into a mirror: a reflection of another man who looked and behaved exactly as himself, right down to the last curl on his head. The only difference between the stabbed Clark and the Clark who'd held the knife moments earlier was a sinister and sadistic smile on the part of the latter. He was weakened but knew what had to be done. Taking a couple of steps back, he gathered all his might and threw a lightning fast left hook. His hand hit nothing.

Finally he turned around with the knife in him and grasped his wound and continued down the path. His mind tried and went through thousands of deductions based on his current situation. With all his brilliance, the best possible solution he was able to offer himself was that this was a dream. The darkness couldn't be real.

He immediately woke with his thoughts in a fog—he thought he saw a woman come out of the fog and hold her hands open but when he tried to embrace her she glided back into the fog and disappeared—he'd yet to fully wake. His pupils were so immensely dilated that any person observing him as he woke would mistake his eyes for complete devilish black.

Stumbling over to a deep-red mahogany table stationed steps away; he sat down in a wooden study chair and opened an artist's journal after unwrapping the string that kept the book bound. Anyone who'd examine his journal would notice that there were paper remains on the spine of the book showing many pages having been torn out. His hand was steady while he held the pen firm to the acid paper.

MY BELOVED,

I can think of nothing but you; I ache to see you sipping on your favourite drink: a dangerous Sicilian Kiss with a slice of orange peel.

I know we can never be, men like me never get back the things they've lost. I suspect someone has long ago used a hunting knife to carve out my heart. The fiery passion I have for you burns like the fires of Rome.

I'm reanimated like a lightning bolt that can reanimate a fallen man back to life at the thought of your gaze but then you close your eyes and all hope I have for happiness leads to despair.

CON AFFETTO,

C.

He wasn't happy with the way it came out. He crumbled the paper and smashed it into a wastebasket near his desk. A blank paper held his gaze until he wrote a second time.

I think of nothing more alluring than your perfect hair, each wave looking like a still ocean but thrashing on the sand every time you turn your head towards me.

Your eyes are so beautiful that I can see the universe in them; so deep that once they've caught mine I can do nothing but gaze back like a child's first gaze onto the world.

Your lips are as red as my pumping blood, invoking nothing less than the passion of a man willing to take a life just to feel their warmth against his own.

Your enigmatic neck makes me wonder if whether your body pumps blood or the warm breeze you feel on your face at sea.

I need not say a lot about your body, so beyond the imagination that I have to blink just to remind myself I am not dreaming. Your slim and ravishing legs that go on for days and feet that make me desire to carry you for the rest of our lives so that they would not touch the soiled ground.

You're ineffability is nothing less than an ancient Goddess.

CON AFFETTO,

C.

The second letter was practically illegible due to the passionate scribbling of Clark's bony fingers. After the pen was lifted from the paper a final time, he tore the paper out from the notebook and folded it eight times with the greatest attention to its condition. He slipped it into his right pants pocket. He finally closed and wrapped the journal back with the delicate string that held it together. Then he stopped and looked up to a spot on his ceiling,

I need you to show me something. Show me anything! Show me something I can count on. I need you now. Please prove to me you're really out there. Please. Please....

Never mind, I'll do it all myself you sadistic bast—

He muttered to himself, *You want blind faith but you won't earn it. You won't show me anything that would earn my respect. You want things like some deadbeat who doesn't know what he wants. Damn you, damn you to hell!*

He looked down at the horizon as if someone was sitting across him. Immediately the contradiction presented himself and it irked him; if God was everywhere he was also beside him, in front of him, *under* him, he didn't have to look to the sky. Maybe he did it because the sky reminded him of Her.

He reached for his shelf and pushed two or three bottles of drinks aside before he arrived at the one he wanted: an old bottle of Glenfiddich. He poured himself a glass, and drank it as he opened Oscar Wilde's *Picture of Dorian Gray* and started to read amongst the mist of his newly lit cigar.

III
PARTNERS FOR A CASE... OR TWO

The medical examiner stood over the body of the lovely looking woman lying on the medical slab in the city's morgue. She appeared graceful even in death; dark golden colored hair with each streak in its rightful place; long, thick eyelashes that although now closed, extended out gorgeous hazel eyes; and smooth crimson lips with a perfect supple nose. She examined her body: natural breasts above a slim waist that connected to a perfect set of long legs. Officer Matthews stood over the body in silence until he could no longer bear it,

"She was dead on the streets much longer than she should have. She was a survivor though, held out longer than most, she took breaths even with a hole in her heart; there was water in her lungs. Medically impossible I hear. Tell me Rachel, was she some sort of model?"

The examiner raised her head after examining a wound near the victim's left breast.

"She very well could be with a face and body like that. She had no ID on her. All I can definitively say at this point is that this Jane Doe was surgically stabbed once in the heart... love kills, it had to be personal," Rachel replied solemnly, "You doin' okay? I heard you were there."

Matthews ignored her question, looking intently at a particular part of her skin.

"Her skin was red, a very recent contusion on the left side of her face. Maybe she was abused prior to her death? Hit or slapped there... also another wound here," she pointed to the victim's forearm, "Minutes or hours before her untimely death," Rachel continued.

Is any death timely? Matthews nodded, "Sexual assault?"

"No, only thing we found on her was this," Rachel handed Matthews a designer cell phone charm half-covered in blood. "She was grasping it with all her might... but we didn't find a cell phone."

"Yes," Matthews was visibly distraught, "She looks so familiar to me. Maybe we've met."

"I doubt if you met a girl like this you'd forget *detective*," Rachel smiled, "Oh and there was a ring on her right ring finger, it's in the box over there."

I hate cases like this.

Matthews was not the only one raved by this case. The entire police force and examiner's office appeared overly affected by it. No one could pinpoint the reason. Was it because the victim was an attractive young white woman or was it the location of the murder: one of the wealthiest areas of the nation?

Naturally, the plague of humanity named *confidence* or *pride*, whose symptoms often render each person to justifiably believe himself to be above average, let them to believe that it was others who were affected by this case but not them. Everyone thought they had the quintessential ability to detach themselves from the cases they were working, even if the victim looked or behaved like their son, daughter, niece, or nephew. Observers on the outside noticed that this case was important not only because of the skin color, socio-economic status of the victim, or the neighborhood of the killing, but it seemed to be rather… spiritual. Some things that didn't make sense happened, some things that were rational never came to be. It *was* the circle of life.

Matthews had been recently promoted to detective but often neglected his rank. Most people still addressed him as 'Officer.'

He looked over the files Officer Johnson and Officer Pretuder had sent in following their canvass of the crime scene.

Officer Johnson's suspect was Clark. The second suspect was another man brought to his attention by Office Pretuder. 'Alexander DiCeéver' was a gentleman who was stopped in his car exiting the roadblock placed around the scene after having left a cocktail party at one of the estates in the area. Unfortunately Pretuder had neglected to check the license of the driver and only assumed the driver to be DiCeéver since he was the registered owner of the car. Matthews knew there were quite a few affluent families in that neighborhood who were known to throw parties on any given night. There is no way to ascertain whether Clark, the victim, and DiCeéver were at the same party, and illuminating this small fact to the suspects would give them cause to deny it and render it more difficult to collect evidence should it appear that one of them was the perpetrator. Notwithstanding, Det. Matthews was called into his captain's office for an update on the case. Before he could knock on the door marked 'Captain Gallanté,' he was beckoned by his captain to enter through one of the four small windows on the center of the door.

The captain's office was a modest one with a big desk in the middle of the room and three chairs to accommodate visitors.

There was a chic ottoman placed between the second and third chair. The captain himself was an extension of his office; a humble man of sixty-two or three with thin blonde hair, and small blue eyes that often rested behind a set of prescription aviator glasses.

Precinct lore had a rather comical story about the Gallanté. It was said that although promoted to the rank of detective very young like Matthews, his hairline began receding as soon as he'd taken the post. Other detectives jeered him for being too caught up or too serious. One day, Detective Gallanté was called to the scene of a rather nasty triple murder of a suspected Mafioso, his sister, and his nephew who were ruthlessly assassinated. Another detective laughed over the crime scene photos and roared that Gallanté would finally lose all his hair over this case. Gallanté had quipped, "Grass doesn't grow on a busy street." He didn't give the case much thought after the killer was found dead in his apartment some weeks later. *True* justice is all seeing rather than blind and connected to all things rather than only a perverted system of some obscure Western ideal.

The captain had risen through the ranks having closed numerous high profile cases with solid investigation and interrogation techniques. He was a man more concerned with the truth than his arrest quota. This philosophy often had him skating on thin ice with the higher ups.

Entering visitors couldn't see the third chair in the office from the outside. Matthews entered and saw a man in a tailored black suit leaning back into the chair with his legs crossed and his left index finger resting on his forehead. The captain motioned the detective to sit down. The visitor had yet to acknowledge the entrance of the detective. Immediately the captain rotated his hand with his palm facing up as to introduce the two visitors in his office,

"Detective Matthews. Meet Special Agent Niccoló Durante from Italy."

Why bother with 'special'? If they're all 'Special,' doesn't that mean none of them are? Why not just call themselves 'Agents?' Maybe they enjoy being special. Human hubris.

Matthews occupied the chair farthest from this strange visitor and thereby had to extend his hand fully over the captain's ottoman to meet the agent's hand in return. Durante's handshake was firm and impersonal. It was clear to Matthews that this was a stubborn man.

"Is this about the Jane Doe case in the Prosperous District?" Matthews asked.

The agent chuckled in a subtle Italian accent, "A pretty white girl dies in a rich neighborhood and you think they immediately send government help?"

"No," Matthews fired back.

"Don't worry, I'm not here to step on any toes," the agent slightly bowed his head.

"Agent Durante is here on a different matter," the captain interceded, "He's from the organized crime taskforce. He thinks the Doe case might be connected to the Torrino family."

"I thought you weren't here to step on any toes. We have our own organized crime taskforce," Matthews said cleverly.

"I don't think the two cases are connected such that I'll absorb your case. I've been investigating the family for extortion, murder, and running illegal gambling houses out of their clubs for upwards of five years," Durante pouted his lips in anger for only a second, "Having said that, they live in that area and run some of their rackets there. Rich people love to gamble *and* launder money. It *might* be connected. Even if it is, you have nothing to worry about. I'm not here to take *all* the credit. ... We'll work it together."

"That's what they all say before they stand in front of the cameras and say they caught the guy," Matthews muttered.

"You will give agent Durante whatever he needs detective, I know you prefer to work alone.... So does he," The captain pointed with his eyebrows, "You're partners now. Work both cases together, and if the family is linked to the Doe murder, all the better. One more count of murder for every member of that damned 'family.'"

Both the detective and the agent knew there was no debating the captain's decision. Even though Durante did not take orders from Gallanté, he didn't say anything as a token of respect for the man's authority. After all, what the captain said was true, and Agent Durante did not intend to steal the case away. The point of *all* law enforcement was to catch criminals, so thought the idealistic 'Special' Agent.

IV
QUESTIONS

The newly appointed partners noticed the storm outside as soon as they exited the captain's office. They stepped onto the main area dubbed 'The Pit'. The thunder sounded worse than a man's cries after losing his firstborn. Floods prevailed in various areas of the city including the wealthier districts. Cops and firefighters were thus busy adhering to the wishes of the rich to have to worry about the evil nature of man during this storm. In some sadistic way, it was a blessing; it wasn't man that was evil but Mother Nature. Sometimes only tragedy unites law enforcement: firefighters, paramedics, nurses, doctors, and police officers, who usually do not get along, worked together and aided heaven in the worst storm of the century. Tragedy binds us, love separates us.

"That's something we have in common," *Special* Agent Durante lit a cigar with a long wooden match.

"You can't smoke in here... partner," Matthews thought Durante was a cowboy, that all Italians liked those old Spaghetti Westerns.

"It's a Cohíba!" Durante vowed.

Detective Matthews said nothing and gazed at his partner with an eye that informed him he detests breaking or bending even the slightest protocol.

"Ahh, everything is so different here, so many laws, rules that ought to govern behavior," Durante put out his newly lit cigarillo, "You can't relight a Cohíba, this is garbage now... here," he handed the cigar to a uniform officer who was hurrying by the duo towards the elevators.

"Those are illegal," Matthews was cunning.

"You prefer to work alone, so do I. I'll recon the Torrino family. You work the pretty girl's case. Then we'll meet and discuss progress, etcetera, etcetera," Durante sighed.

Matthews didn't like Durante; aside from the fact that he didn't know what agency he was from, his Italian accent made him sound pretentious and actions and mannerisms made him feel entitled. Matthews envied him. Durante commanded respect without doing much work.

"That's a good tactic," Matthews affirmed, "We can swap notes now. It may not be much but it might help both of us down the road."

Durante nodded and they headed towards Matthews's desk on the far side of the floor. Thunder rang in their ears; a window popped open and some rain wet the desk under it before the officer at the desk hastened to close it. Exiting 'The Pit,' Matthews saw Durante waving and nodding to officers on the floor. He wondered how this visitor was so comfortable in an area he hadn't visited before. Durante's name had already been typed on a piece of paper and folded to look like a nametag. Their desks were across from each other. Matthews pulled out his notebook when they sat down. The pages cracked from having recently been wet. Durante on the other hand, reached into his pocket and extracted a digital tablet and began swiping his fingers as to locate the necessary documents.

"Don't worry, above top-secret encryption," a shark smile showed Durante's pearly white teeth.

Matthews looked at him, and after a moment of silence, finally said, "You first."

Durante grinned back, "Trust issues? That's okay. The Torrino family: responsible for most of the organized crime in the city—although don't let that fool you. They're international. In *this city*, from extortion of small businesses, illegal gambling halls, murders—they have the most loyal, ruthless assassins I've ever come across. Led by Don Torrino himself, who has two children: a son and a daughter, about the same age. He hasn't bestowed upon either of them the name of Torrino yet," he turned the screen towards his partner to show him some grainy surveillance photos of the suspects.

"I don't understand," Matthews probed with an officious frown.

"Don Torrino feels that his name is his legacy. He holds his name sacred. His kids have different surnames than him; that's why it's so hard to distinguish between his family, and his 'family.' When he feels that his children are worthy of his name and legacy, he gives them the name of Torrino."

Matthews shuddered, "Cold," then shuffled his notes, "I have two suspects for the murder of Jane Doe. One was a guy who was stopped as he attempted to drive away from the scene. The other was a flâneur: a man stopped strolling in the streets," he shuffled the pages in his hand.

"In this storm?" the surprised agent of the world liked the drifter, what idiot enjoys the rain?

"Yes, I'm going to bring him in. Something about him doesn't sit right with me."

Agent Durante got up and nodded, "Trust that police instinct. I've got to set up the surveillance."

He looked back at Matthews for a second, "Try looking him up. Go to his apartment and catch him off guard one morning, it might build trust if you go see him on his home turf. If you're still unsatisfied, then bring him in."

Why is this guy giving me advice? Matthews thought. He also knew that personal judgments shouldn't get in the way of truth. He might just follow this advice.

As Durante walked away, Matthews reread his notes and marked the addresses of both Alexander DiCeéver and Clark Kóróna. He promptly left the station, turned the ignition switch on his classic 1972 Cadillac sedan Deville, maintained and restored as if the year was '72 and headed for the latter's house.

The drive should've been peaceful, but no drive was peaceful for Matthews, not since…

* * *

Hospital equipment beeped steadily as eleven-year-old Matthews slowly entered. Seeing his mother barely able to turn her head from the months of chemotherapy and greet her son is a burden no child should carry.

"Charles," she was the only one who called him Charles, everyone else called him Matthews, Charlie, or Chuck, he preferred it this way.

He approached her slower than she wanted.

"It's okay, come closer. I want to see you," her voice was so weak he could hardly hear her.

Matthews's hand turned ice cold when he gripped his mother's palm as hard as he could.

"It's okay my son. It's only cold at first, then it'll get nice and warm."

Charles raised his eyebrows in both fear and shock.

"I think of you Charles, of you and your father. It's okay, it's okay," her voice fell to a whisper, "It's okay, as long as you have people to love."

The hospital equipment suddenly stopped its steady beeping at the same time Deborah Matthews closed her eyes. Instead it emitted a long singular beeeeeep. Charles gagged with tears. He hugged his mother's legs at the foot of the bed. A nurse came in and yelled, "Code blue! Get the doctor, you have to get out son!"

Charles hesitantly walked out as waves of nurses flooded his mother's room. His father, Eric, sat on one of the benches tear-ridden as he turned to face his son. He wiped his tears and lifted his son onto his lap.

V
CONSTRUCT II

The weather calmed down after three heinous days, even angels and demons need their rest. Unfortunately another tempest loomed in the distance while the city was busy in dealing with the usual backlash a storm causes: looters, thieves, broken and vandalized property, etc. Media outlets were also busy calling white people survivors and fighters, and non-whites looters and criminals; everyone is equal in the West.

Among the numerous men and women who immediately leave the house to spend some time outside after such a squall, lest the next one destroy the world, Clark was spotted in an elegant and small bistro in midtown. A woman saturated with divine charm and angelic beauty sat across from him and commanded the attention of everyone around them. Her long blonde hair and chiseled jaw was like a Michelangelo sculpture. Her eyes were so deep they appeared to be floating in a sea of diamonds. Clark's rare smile was accompanied by his leaning towards her, who by this time was scarcely free of a single pair of ogling eyes; even the uniform officer ordering a coffee and éclair espied her in the corner of his peripheral.

Silence reigned between them for some minutes but it wasn't awkward. It was curious. They were staring into each other's eyes longer than the onlookers liked before she finally burst out laughing. The sound of her laughter eased Clark's migraine.

"No no no! That one doesn't count," she said in between fits of laughter then reached for her drink: a Sicilian Kiss with a slice of orange peel, "We're doing it again. Rematch," her thin lips touched a smatter of the drink.

"You lost babe, get over it," Clark whispered.

"No! Ready? 3, 2, 1, go!" she immediately restructured her expression to match Clark's stoic gaze. They continued staring at each other for only seconds this time before she began laughing again.

"Unbelievable. You have to blink sometime. I *will* catch you, bet on it," she said slyly.

"You won't," Clark shook his head.

"Why not?" she inquired.

"I never want to miss a single second when I'm with you. My senses: sight, smell, hearing, taste and touch are all attuned to your presence. To your voice, your touch, your gaze."

Like a super, hyper-sensation... my superpower is hyper-sensation? Good one Clark, any lamer and you'd win an award.

He felt uncomfortable expressing himself and bearing his thoughts and any onlooker would mistake this awkwardness for an inability to entertain a lady of his date's stature, but he'd never been a man to merit attention to what kibitzers thought of him or his actions. The lady however, was so deep in thought at the sound of his velvety voice that her female instinct for sensing male discomfort failed to perceive this. Finally, he leaned back in and whispered, "There *is* something I'd like to talk to you about, but I don't know what consequences it would bring."

"You know you can tell me anything," she licked the residual liquid from her lips.

"I..." Clark's cultured voice struggled to enunciate this elusive phrase from the depths of his morbid soul. When he closed his eyes to compose himself and opened them firmly towards her eyes, where she would've caught him in a blink, he looked at nothing. She'd disappeared. He wouldn't show it but he panicked as he searched around for his mate but instead observed all the people positioned around him staring. There eyes extending outwards and becoming black holes. The aching pain in the left part of his back acted up. Placing his hand there to ease the pain, his hand came back with blood. The thunder resembled laughter. Within seconds it began raining the familiar icicles as the battle of the heavens resumed.

No, you can't do this to me. This makes no sense. It's unscientific. It's impossible. It was lucid... 'I' was lucid, you can't!

One by one, the people disappeared until darkness consumed the entire room and took the remaining objects with it. Clark was now back in the darkness of the construct he'd started to call home. He bled from where he'd been stabbed last time, he wanted to fall to his knees and weep but he was taught that weeping is a sure sign of weakness. There were things he had to do, to say; it was hardly the time for a trivial thing like death.

He collected the required energy to move forward. Like before, a path appeared before him as he took each step. It was obvious to him that the knife had to be removed from his back before he could go further into the abyss. The pain was unbearable; he had trouble balancing himself and didn't want to know how deep the void around the path ran. He lit a Monte Cristo as a mental distracter and with his right hand removed the knife from the left side of his back in one fluid stroke, covering the flowing blood with his right hand. Barely having taken three steps, a similar sharp pain in the lower *right* part of his back.

The old familiar places, he turned around to once again, be facing himself.

"What do you want from me?" he screamed at himself.

The doppelganger's grin had yet to give way to seriousness; it was as if they were two sides of two different coins. He just stared with force and determination. After about a minute of this, he finally said, "The inevitable," and disappeared before a reply could be made.

Clark turned around and noticed that the path had disappeared and instead all he could hear was an intercom sound of some sort. This was in all probability still a dream, and he attempted to wake.

Reality is a haze when you're waking up, what you saw as real and rational in a dream abruptly makes no sense. There are no supernatural escapes and no paradise to look forward to.

Bzzzzzz, the intercom rang in his ears. He moved to the intercom still in the fringe of his brain and not fully awake.

"Yes?"

VI
THUNDER AND LIGHTNING

It was rude to entertain a guest who'd shown up unannounced but Clark let it slide.

"Who's there?" the tips of his fingers pressed firmly against the cold button of the inanimate buzzer. The ice ran through his fingers and into his chest.

"It's Detective Matthews Mr. Kóróna; I have some questions about that night three weeks ago, uh," Clark heard papers shuffle through the intercom, "The night of November 21st."

Matthews stared into the black horizontal lines of the intercom in the lobby. Clark confirmed Matthews as his guest and he signed in at the concierge desk. The intercom buzzed the doors to the lobby open. Matthews pushed the button to the top floor.

The penthouse? The elevator ascended towards the sky. The building was in an affluent neighborhood, just wealthy enough to merit respect when its name fell upon someone's ears. All tenants were either administrators high up in the government, scientists working at the university on groundbreaking technology, or unemployed privileged entrepreneurs who had inherited so much wealth that their small-minded existence could not comprehend how to spend it. Clark was neither a scientist, an administrator, nor heir to a corporate empire. The questions regarding his wealth were already boiling in the detective's head. The elevator doors dinged open. The penthouse only housed two apartments. One boasted a large black door made of oak with metal bars on the outside serving as an outside security barrier to unwanted visitors. From the dust gathered on the metal bar, the detective surmised that this door hadn't been opened in a few weeks; no doubt this penthouse belonged to one of the entrepreneurs who was away on a trip to Vegas, losing money he didn't deserve. The other door was a large mahogany door that was in fact two doors, opening from the center like the pearly gates guarded by St. Peter. As Matthews approached it, he noticed that this door did not have a doorbell and looked at it bewilderingly for a while before noticing an antique doorknocker. The detective drew back the metal frame that hung by a hinge but the doors opened from the center before the frame could strike the plate fitted to the door.

"Afternoon detective," a voice said on the other side of the door before the detective could see the mouth that spoke it.

"Mr. Kóróna, I have more questions regarding the crime you were witness to on the night of November 21st," the detective entered before the doors were fully open.

Matthews was at best average looking. A rounded jaw housing a well-kept beard in front of small lips, light brown eyes and thick eyebrows above a thin lapel dark navy suit and a matching cotton shirt with a light blue four-in-the-hand faux-silk tie, a leather belt with a detachable buckle and causal leather oxford saddle shoes.

"Please... do come in," Clark didn't care if the officer was insulted. He wasn't an idiot, he knew he was a suspect but for some reason this simple act of bureaucracy—the police procedure for eliminating suspects—irked him to the point of hostility.

"I'm sorry Mr. Kóróna, I don't mean disrespect. This is an important case and we're losing valuable time, and with this storm—"

"I understand. Most capital crimes are solved in the ensuing three days," Clark closed the door and the sound of its turning latch sent a chill up Matthews's back. "But you say 'the crime I was witness to.' I made myself perfectly clear to Officer Johnson, I did not witness anything. I was out on an evening stroll following a dinner with an acquaintance."

The missing bell from Clark's door rang inside the detective's head.

He remembers the name of the uniform officer that questioned him?

Detective Matthews entered the inner sanctum of Clark's apartment and realized that this was no haven, one of the walls in the colossal den housed a window covered by two large black silk curtains such that no light would enter. In fact, the place was so dimly lit that he ran into Clark's table and required the assistance of his bookshelf to maintain balance. The bookshelf shook for a second and it was so full that many books exploded out and flew to the ground. Using the residual echo in his ear, he tried to anticipate where he thought the books landed. He couldn't see in this darkness and reached by instinct for the books and tried to pick some of them up. From the other side of the room Clark hit a switch that took the room from Cimmerian to fully lit. Twenty lights embedded into the ceiling fostered a light so bright they seemed to exude the luminosity of the sun at high noon. Matthews looked down at the books as he stood back up. He noticed books of all disciplines, from Aristotle's philosophy, to Einstein's physics, to various ethical disciplines and their opinions on the nature of good and evil.

"Be careful detective," Clark took the books from Matthews's hands.

Matthews noticed a mannequin head on top of the bookcase wearing a white homburg with a black strap, "Nice hat," he whispered to himself before turning back to Clark, "I apologize. What do you do Mr. Kóróna? If you don't mind me asking."

Clark's stoicism didn't betray a single expression. He turned to the detective as he placed the books back in the bookshelf and reached up to fix the crooked hat. Matthews could see that everything had its place. The books were alphabetized by title, the small table was empty except for an artist's journal and a pen, and a bar housed three very fine bottles of scotch and an exotic bottle of champagne. On a coffee table across from the fireplace was a chessboard elevated on a small rotatable wooden pole of some sort.

"Let's not forget why you're here, is this case getting any extra attention?" Clark's voice was polite enough not to insult Matthews. He valued respect and Matthews hadn't done anything *yet* to diminish the bare respect Clark paid all humans.

"Any death... no, *all* death is tragic, and requires extra attention from the land of the living," the detective roamed the apartment, "Maybe someday we'll know what lies on the other end of the lake."

Clark almost smiled, "That's funny detective, I read once that a rather... philosophical samurai ran into Zen Master Hakuin, who was an enlightened man. The samurai, in a moment of curiosity, approached Hakuin and asked where he would go after he died. The master smirked back 'How am I supposed to know?' 'How do you *not* know? You're a Zen master!' the samurai harshly blurted out. Hakuin drew a deep breath, and calmly replied 'Yes… but not a dead one.'"

Matthews glanced back at one of the fallen books, a basic off-white cover with a hand-drawn circle in the middle. Near the edge of the cover in small font were the words: *Writings of Zen Masters*.

He looked back and realized this *kōan*—a word he knew from somewhere but couldn't remember where—required more thought before he could converse with a man of Clark's intelligence. He hardly seemed like a usual suspect anyway.

The problem for Matthews's investigative technique was that Clark wasn't behaving like a suspect. Was this voluntary behavior meant to deter suspicion? He had also just learned that Clark was smarter than he seemed so he neglected to put anything past him, and least of all didn't want to seem like an idiot, even if he knew he was by comparison. Perception is reality.

He approached the scotch and wine table and fixed his eyes on the odd bottle of champagne, almost hidden behind some bottles of scotch.

"I'm something of a grape expert," Matthews pushed the bottles of scotch to the side of the table, "You don't strike me as the type of man who'd sit here, (he pointed to the large leather arm chair Clark had sat down on) and nurse a bottle of chardonnay."

"I'm not," Clark's intensity increased with each passing second, "It's champagne."

"Oh, that's very nice, what kind?"

"It's a 1928 Krug," Clark mentioned in passing, to allude that such details are trivial.

In a cartoon, a construction crane would have been used to forklift Detective Matthews's jaw off Clark's Persian rug.

"I'm sorry, it sounded like you said a 1928 Krug," The detective finally said after having regained his composure.

"That's exactly what I said."

Clark wasn't bragging nor did he hold in esteem his own tastes and ideals, it merely seemed that he was a perfectionist, (and the detective picked up on this) a man who abhorred mistakes and wanted everything in its proper place. Matthews only had to look around the apartment to confirm this. *Devil's in the details*, Matthews deduced.

"The same 1928 Krug series that recently auctioned in Hong Kong for $21,000?"

Even though he didn't show it, Clark seemed impressed at the detective's actual self-proclaimed knowledge of wines and grapes, all people consider themselves overflowing with expert wisdom, even though it is as rare to witness as an Amur Leopard in the middle of the cold Russian winter, "I certainly hope so. It could be fake; I've yet to taste it myself."

"Yet to taste it? Nothing that big to celebrate yet?" The detective seemed taken in by Clark's modesty.

"Yes," the enigmatic man sincerely replied, "It was a gift for a celebration. I couldn't bring myself to uncork it without the person I received it from."

Matthews understood Clark wasn't what he seemed. He was more than the sum of his charm and intelligence. Clark nodded as if to beckon Matthews to one of the two big leather armchairs stationed by the fireplace in the corner of the den past two small steps. He pointed to the empty chair, stood up, and sat back down as his guest placed himself in the chair. This rare act of politeness, practically nonexistent in the modern world, won the heart and mind of the detective.

The fireplace crackled, attempting to burn away the sorrow Matthews felt at having to ask the incoming questions to a man of Clark's caliber, a man he was beginning to respect and admire. *It couldn't be him*, he thought at length.

A wooden table that matched the chairs' décor was in between the two men. Matthews placed some photographs, a small folder, an evidence bag with the victim's cell phone charm inside, and his notebook on it. Matthews placed his items down carefully on the table and thereby failed to notice Clark burning a hole through the evidence bag with his eyes.

As he sat down, Clark realized the detective's discomfort at the proceeding interrogation and quipped, "I do philosophy in these," slamming his hands jokingly on the leather hand-rest.

Matthews smiled amidst the smell of the Italian leather. Being educated in the fields of political science, history, and criminology, he understood the reference.

"You know Clark, talk is a lot like thunder, it's all a bunch of empty noise unless there's lighting to back it up. You're that kind of guy,"

"The thunder or the lightning?" he jested.

"I'm going to be straight with you, you're a suspect in this investigation. I have to ask these questions, please do not be insulted, the farthest of my intentions is to insult a man of your stature in his own home," the detective claimed.

Clark put his hand in the air with his palm facing the detective, "Don't worry detective, I understand that you're doing your job. I would be insulted if you didn't come and see me regarding this case. Murder... is a despicable crime and must be punished to the *full* extent possible," he emphasized the word 'full.'

Did this mean something? Matthews's thoughts were all over the place. He didn't know what to think of his suspect.

"... And I am not a man of any particular stature, do not let my apartment or the champagne fool you."

The detective searched his right jacket pocket for a different notebook than the one sitting on Clark's table and flipped its pages hastily to purposely avoid the suspect's gaze. After a few moments, he lifted his eyes to Clark's, who had now lit and was smoking a cigarillo not dissimilar to Durante's back at the station. Clark caught Matthews's eye and recognized the look of contempt embedded within it.

"I wish you'd told me cigar smoke bothers you, I wouldn't have lit it, and I'm unable to put it out now. It's a personal rule of mine."

"Please sir. No. This is your house," after a few seconds, "But curiosity has bested me, what is your rule?"

"Once I lit a cigar, I am inclined to finish it. It is a waste to relight them. It alters the taste and mood. A cigar's life is meant to be lived in one sequence, not multiple sequential events which are arbitrarily ended," Clark's answer probably had an underlying meaning Matthews failed to see.

"You and my new partner would get along," Matthews could barely see Clark behind the cigar smoke. The interaction seemed too real, moving through mist not being able to see too far ahead. Like life, mist must be conquered and pushed aside in order to get at the truth.

"That isn't strange Mr. Kóróna," Matthews crossed his legs, "Do you mind if we get started?"

"Fire away detective."

Matthews had trouble gazing directly into Clark's still eyes. He learned at the academy that if this should happen, he should stare at the suspect's forehead since it gives the impression that you're staring through their skull and reading their mind. He followed this advice.

"Okay," he consulted his notes between words to appear more informative, "You said… to the officer that you were out for a walk on the night of the murder, which was, for the record, November 21st of this year."

"Yes detective, and although it appears peculiar to you for me to be dressed in such a way in such horrendous weather conditions… I assure you I was returning from meeting with an acquaintance, and I can of course provide you with their information."

"I'm a detective Mr. Króna, everything is peculiar to me," he joked, but the photo Matthews turned over on the desk instantly eroded the laid-back nature of the conversation. The photo was of the Jane Doe, who'd paid her fare to Charon on the river Styx on that stygian night. Matthews presented the photo to the suspect to fish for a reaction. Clark took the photo with his left hand with the cigar laying dormant on his lip. To a trained observer and only for a millionth of a second, Clark's stoic gaze betrayed him and guilt and sorrow absorbed his face. It was not merely the speed of his emotive betrayal that rendered it unperceivable to the detective, but also inexperience. Having been just promoted to the rank of detective, and this case being his first high-profile case, his inexperience in maintaining visual contact with the suspect had him looking more at his things on the desk and the notebook than at his suspect. Moreover, Clark's gaze was not like a suspect's—this caused the same circular thought he had earlier. It was understandable that the detective failed to notice Clark's distressed state of mind as he laid his eyes on this photograph. He'd rather die than admit it but luck was indeed on his side.

"Any life lost is a tragedy," Clark bowed his head solemnly while his eyes continued to study the photograph, "And I am distraught to say I do not know this princess," he grasped his abdomen in a fit of pain.

"Do you believe we make our own choices Mr. Króna, or do we each have a foretold tale?"

"We have to believe in choices detective, we have no other choice."

Their encounters had been too few for the former to get an accurate reading on Clark's mental state. Never had Matthews seen Clark surrender a gaze or alter his expression of neutrality. He was not behaving like a suspect, but he wasn't exactly *Roger 'Verbal' Kint* either. He seemed irascible but nothing seemed to faze him. This made it difficult to tell whether Clark was being truthful.

As Clark handed the photo back to Matthews, the latter rose and headed for the door.

Clark rose with him and eventually said, "First case detective?"

"I'm sorry?" Matthews thought for a second that Clark was reading *his* mind.

"You forgot to ask for my alibi," the detective's cheeks turned the color of nearly all Ferraris.

Clark walked over to his table and carefully took a blank card out of one of the drawers. Matthews walked over and touched the table,

"Nice. IKEA?"

"No, I made this table," Clark uncapped his fountain pen.

"You, *made* this table?" Matthews repeated, mirroring Clark's slow conversational tempo.

"Is that so hard to believe? It's pieces of wood screwed together, not Hegelian abstractions," Clark was insulted at Matthews's surprise.

Matthews noticed that Clark's card was not a personal business card but a blank card that he was writing his alibi's information on. He *did* notice Clark writing a bit of information with his left hand, fixing the cigar on his mouth, switching hands, and finishing the information with his right hand.

Was he ambidextrous? Matthews thought.

After Clark walked over and handed him the card, he could see no discernible difference between what Clark wrote with his left hand, and his right hand.

The Jane Doe case was Matthews's first big murder case as lead detective, he felt as if no detail was insignificant and nothing was without meaning. After exchanging their adieus, Matthews left for the elevator and Clark burned his lip with his cigar. He sat in his 'philosophy' chair and contemplated the exchange that had just occurred. He thought about choices, the void and the photograph the detective handed to him. Photographs were a special plight to him. Truth seemed grim: angels died, scumbags lived. He thought about howling for help upwards, downwards, and ahead. It wouldn't matter, *He*... never helped anyway. He thought about going to Her, seeking *true* justice, the abstraction of his ideas, and as he began to realize how impossible this seemed, how... *idealistic,* he thought about killing himself—it's the only 'philosophical' question that mattered anyway—he was merely one man, a single man can only do so much with one brain, two hands and two legs.

* * *

The sun was setting with an adept braggadocio as nightfall devoured the heavens in the distant horizon, afflicted with the kind of literary foreshadow you'd read about in a Dostoyevsky novel. Clark never walked into places he didn't know how to walk out of but this time he had no choice. She'd invited him to her friend's place and he could never bring himself to turn down her invitations, no matter how isolated and alone he felt.

They wanted to vet him, tick all the right boxes. He was the circus clown riding a motorcycle through rings of fire, or a tiger meant to abide by the torture of a tamer sticking his flimsy head into the tiger's gaping jaw only to show that the tiger wouldn't bite. Clark would never bite *her* but he couldn't say the same about her friend.

A beast stirred under his chest.

The arctic pavement turned into a whirlwind of viscous blood. The fiery shadows on the metropolitan walls blitzed him, avenging overachievers starved for vengeance. The abyss consumed him. His migraine made his head feel heavier than it was. Thoughts of her were coals for the old train engine inside his head.

He could see the building at the end of the dark road. Flickering streetlights illuminated adorable little snowflakes gliding through the mist like party favors over the arrival of the Four Horsemen. He walked in like a '60s actor playing the lone outlaw: Lee Van Cleef after a mysterious treasure or a fabled bounty hunter after some obscure ideal of justice.

"They're expecting me in the penthouse apartment."

The concierge looked like he hadn't slept in centuries and pointed to the touch screen in front of him.

Clark had to search the name. It looked like the thing from *Die Hard*; his luck was as bad as McClane's so he was ready for anything. The looming migraine he'd repressed hitherto tore out like a Roman lion at the Colosseum.

Ding. "Where are you going young man?" the elevator attendant was in better shape than the concierge.

"The Penthouse."

Beep. It took five years to get to the top. His mind was on fire and he'd forgotten to dial 911 and by now it was too late to put it out.

Ding. The doors opened. The attendant acted as a tour guide as he led Clark through the gloomy hallway narrowing as he walked deeper. Another five years to walk down the hallway and get to this goon's apartment. He felt like he aged ten years in the last three minutes, turning as thin as the Grim Reaper.

The door to the apartment was across a skylight connecting to a glass wall. Everyone ran for shelter like it was the end of the Mayan calendar. An Arctic wind forced the snowflakes to dance in a spiral outside the window.

No doorbell. *Focus Clark*. His vision zeroed in on the antique door-knock, it looked similar like the one he had on his own door but there were subtle differences. His was not some hipster knockoff sold at Pottery Barn.

He pulled back the sleeve of his jacket and glanced at his vintage watch tick away the seconds in a conventional way, even though he knew better than anyone that time… was anything but conventional.

6:59, he'd miscalculated the elevator ride and arrived a minute early. He grasped the hinge on the door-knock. He separated it from the plate—

"No. Trust me, he's always right on time, watch," the door swung open faster than an Apple Store's on an iPhone release day.

He hadn't seen the sun for weeks, stuck on a permanent anchor watch deep within his head, waiting for a sunrise that never came until that moment.

She opened the door. Her lips were radiating passion resting on her ivory skin; they called to him.

"What'd I say?" she called into the recesses of the room.

"No way! Did you open it before he knocked though?" a man's voice shrieked like a drowning fish.

Clark handed her the purple lilies he'd picked out. The *genius* florist tried to sell him roses but its thorns triggered an existential reflection of his life. *Life is like licking honey off a thistle*. Lilies represent purity, innocence, and beauty. Purple symbolizes royalty.

I'd made the right choice for once in my life.

"Right on time! I like that!" the man's voice was a high-pitched crescendo.

Easy Clark, it might be this piercing headache that follows you around like a psychotic ex-girlfriend.

Clark shook his hand.

"OWWWWW! Easy tiger," he'd already irked Clark and he hadn't said more than twenty words.

"I'm Colby," he winked and shot one of those silly air bullets with his thumb and index finger.

Clark nearly really shot him.

"What do you drink?" a shark smile showed his teeth in a feeble show of dominance. It was a mental attempt to win the fight before either heavyweight had gotten into the ring.

He was a tall eastern European about the same age as Clark. He appeared smart enough to be stupid and fashionable enough to be boorish, dressed like a tragic anti-hero from an 80's Sci-Fi novel. A white Kung-Fu hipster shirt with big gold buttons and yellow and black stripes down the sides matched with loose gangsta jeans with a huge logo on the left back pocket hanging much lower than his waist. Clark instinctively pulled up *his* pants and wondered how their placement effected his gait, whether or not... *Colby was it?* had to eternally keep his mind on walking just so he wouldn't trip and make himself look like a *complete* fool.

They stared at each other as he waited for Clark to answer.

A Discovery Channel moment, a white man with a British accent echoed in my mind.

'When predators meet. Today, witness the battle between the Great White Shark and the Bengal tiger.'

"Scotch," she answered for him.

She took Clark's hand and they sat down on the cherry leather corner couch overlooking the city through the glass wall.

What's with this building and glass walls? I guess you can look at the insects under your feet and bask in insignificant vanity.

Colby handed him the glass, "I like your taste," Clark put the glass on the long wooden coffee table in front of him without taking a sip.

"Sicilian Kiss. Thin slice of orange peel," Clark noticed she didn't have a drink and didn't like that. He thought about when she took his hand, the feeling of ascension no elevator could equate.

"That's soooooo cute," he extended the Os more than he should have. He should have kept his mouth shut but people never do what they should.

"You guys know each other's drinks. 'This is the beginning of a beautiful relationship,'" every word pulsated Clark's cerebral cortex. His head was a time bomb ticking away at the sound of each word that left Colby's mouth.

The Casablanca reference disengaged him from reality. He thought he knew why he was there but as time progressed he realized he had no idea.

He'd taken the role of the reluctant mercenary stumbling upon some scattered form of truth: Eastwood knowing the name on the grave while Wallach knew the name of the cemetery; two halves of one secret requiring lethargic cooperation and trust. He was supposed to find the answer and follow a straight path of breadcrumbs to a trove, even if this truth led him to the wrong end of a coffin like Van Cleef.

"You're not much of a talker," his voice was almost as annoying as Alexander's.

Clark stared back in silence; some people simply aren't worth it. Their stupidity is only rivaled by their ignorance. She laughed and her voice was like the second act of an opera, drowning out the sound of Colby's exasperating voice.

Clark understood the necessity of participating in social farces like this, "What do you do?"

Colby looked at her and laughed. It was a serious question. The reason why he didn't talk to certain people sliced his chest like the loser in a samurai duel.

Nothing personal, you're just a bunch of useless half-wits.

"Don't answer. It must've been a rhetorical question... I guess."

She jittered with nervous laughter because she knew Clark wasn't the joking type.

What was so damn funny?

"Not much of a laugher either?" he was condescending, "Wait, don't answer, it's a... how'd you put it... rhetorical question," he mocked Clark's slow tempo. It was becoming a pattern with people Clark conversed with and he noticed this pattern and tried to adapt.

They were two boxes he wouldn't tick off. They were *his* boxes, "You are punctual though," a third box was ticked off and he rasberried a sneaking strand of bleached hair that'd found its way in front of his eyes.

"One out of three, if I knew there was be a test I would have studied," Clark pitied the small-minded.

The shark smile formed on his lips again, "Always expect tests. Life is one big test."

He thought he was a prophet freely feeding the sheep truths out of the goodness of his heart.

"Those who roar the loudest often have the smallest teeth."

Sounds like something I'd say. Pat yourself on the back Clark. Antagonize her good friend. Hand the test back in blank to prove a point. Like the misguided and terribly dimwitted student, you'll only get a zero.

Finite minds wouldn't recognize the possibility that an action might be deeper than it seemed, that someone was trying to take a stand and make a point.

"Don't worry, it's pass or fail," he thought he was as smooth as a baby's ass, but he was only as untrustworthy.

'The great white mistakenly thinks it has an advantage.'

Pass or fail? That's deprecating to the woman Clark viewed like an angel, and if he did view her as an angel, he also knew that angels deserve saints and he was nowhere near one, but if Colby talked about her like that again they were going to have a problem. He didn't care how long they'd known each other. He didn't care how swag his contender post-modern bullshit apartment was, the only currency he recognized was respect.

Did he actually think he had a say in whether I was worthy of her affections? Had she succumbed to humanity's nurtured conditioning to seek the approval from your friends when the decision is a singular course of action that only ripples through your own life?

Clark had been humoring him, Joe Pesci asking De Niro if he could come to Vegas and work for the Casinos. It was done out of respect for their friendship, for Her. De Niro thought Pesci was really asking permission.

'A tiger's hearing is unmatched, but the Great White thinks sight is the only sense and moves in for the kill from behind.'

"You think you're better than everyone don't you?" now Colby was being directly antagonistic, wanting to see if it was all an act. The *predator* circled his prey.

"Only those I'm better than," Clark had finally made him break his gaze.

'The tiger evades the razor teeth of the shark and lunges forward, its claws tearing the tender flesh of the Great White.'

She delicately shook her head at him as she squeezed Clark's hand. She knew Clark wasn't the actor; which meant Colby was as scared as a 4-year-old of the boogeyman.

Clark thought he was the one being tortured but he was wrong, it was her. She didn't know what to think or expect. She couldn't anticipate how the night would play out. Clark couldn't imagine how she felt. The thought sparked a masochist flashback of being tortured and liking it, deserved punishment for the pain he'd inflicted on others, on her in the past.

He closed his eyes and she caught him in a blink and squeezed his hand as he stroked the back of her hand with his finger. His hand thumped, her heart raced faster than a zombie for the new Apple iTrash.

Colby went to get something, probably to check the list and tick the remaining boxes.

I wasn't listening. I hope I didn't scare him.

This feeling you seem to be embracing is against your code. A stoic sage leaves no room for trivial emotions.

Clark put his other arm around her and pecked her above her cheek, near her temple. Her skin felt smooth against his polar lips. She sank into his chest. Before he knew it she'd fallen asleep. Her breathing and pulse calmed down. She was prettier than a sunset over a secluded lake.

Now *his* heart galloped faster than a racehorse. His eyelids weighed heavier than an asteroid on a collision course with our wretched world. He hadn't slept in centuries, something in common with the concierge. If he was ever going to sleep, it might as well be here and finally his eyelids met like two star-crossed lovers over a smoky bar.

'The tiger sleeps safely with his tigress, the corpse of the shark serves as a warning for those seeking to enter the tiger's inner sanctum.'

I dare not question Clark's misanthropy. He detested humanity because he didn't like what they'd evolved to, what they'd become, and perhaps in his warped fantasy of where they *could be,* she would serve as the light to illuminate his cavernous heart. It was beautiful to see him wondering whether it was okay to live again. And how beautiful it would be when his soul shatters.

VII
CHARMED

The detective had barely gotten into his car when his phone notified him of a text message from Durante,

Give me a call. want to update u. :) -Durante.

Detective Matthews dialed the number. Durante told Matthews that his surveillance was set up. He was noting the people coming and going and had even set up audio so he could hear the conversations given that they were close enough to the microphones he'd placed in the light switch fixtures. Matthews asked him which judge had signed off the warrant. Durante dodged the question and made a snappy remark about 'rules.' Matthews told Durante that he believes the 'flâneur' is not the killer and further, that before he interviewed the second suspect, he was going to the uptown district to follow up with the cell phone charm lead. Matthews believed that an expensive designer cell phone charm, like the one found in the victim's hand, would have some sort of traceable measure. Both Durante and his captain agreed with his deduction. He hung up as he came off the on-ramp of the highway and made his way to the uptown district. As he entered the 'Prosperous District,' (that was what the poorer districts in town called that region) he noticed that the people seemed unaffected by the blizzard. They were marching about the streets in their expensive raincoats and parkas with their little dogs in hand or in purses, unaware of the doom befalling their fellow man in other parts of the city. Their only cares was not missing their dog's hair appointment or their Botox injections.

From the part of the logo not covered in Jane Doe's blood, the detective inferred which of the many designer brands in the area the charm belonged to and made his way towards the store. He was familiar with this neighborhood and its social etiquettes. He tried blending and making small talk with the strangers on the street but he couldn't quite get the hang of it, not like his partner.

A door attendant stood in front of one of the stores, wet from the falling drizzle, but nonetheless opening and closing doors for shoppers without any particular affect. Apathy is common in a metropolitan city. Cities make a barren wasteland look like a rapture.

The lonely detective entered the store and marched towards the employee dressed in a suit almost twice the price of his own, and who happened to be helping another customer. He flashed his badge and a manager appeared and guided the detective to an office in the corner of the store. It was bad for business to have the police in such a store.

"I own this store. How may I help you officer?" the manager was attractive but impatient.

For some reason, suddenly rank mattered, "Detective. Matthews."

"How may I help you *detective?*" the manager scoffed while rolling her eyes. It didn't matter to her.

He extracted a cell phone charm from an evidence bag and handed it to her. She reluctantly took it from the detective's hands and looked at it. She noticed the blood on the charm and could barely make out the design. Fortunately, the thick string that connected the charm to the phone to made it easy to identify the brand of the charm. That particular store was the only store in the city who used multiple color strings to connect the charm to the phone, half the string was blue, the other half red.

"Is that blood?" shock flustered the fearful owner.

"Do you sell that here?" a determined Detective Matthews queried.

"Uhh... yes, we do, would you like me to pull up the records? We keep records of all our sales and transactions."

Her obedience was sudden, rattled at the sight of the blood on the charm. Such things were unseen in this part of the city. Present realities ran unknown for the wealthy; their tragedies were falling stock prices and ending wars.

She couldn't even touch the charm, instead asking the detective to turn the piece of string to the side and look on the upper right corner of the bloodstained object to give her the embossed three-digit serial number. Luckily for the detective, that half of the charm was the half not covered in blood, and he recited the numbers "eight, zero, four" as she waited for the store computer to load the file. Her trembling hand punched the numbers into the computer, making several mistakes for only three simple keystrokes. Finally she turned the screen to the detective. Looking at the screen, he was shocked to see the charm priced over $400.

No wonder she held onto it with her life.

His eyes glanced over the screen, "What's this GS here?" he pointed to the bottom of the bill where a signature layered over a mail stamp ran over the letters "GS."

"It's our store designator for Gift Sent," she pointed to the signature, "I signed this one myself. We offer to deliver the product to the person free of charge if they tell us it is a gift. We can even wrap it and include a message that you write yourself!" she'd finally calmed down a little.

"$400 and I have to write the message too?" Matthews was getting aggravated.

"It makes it more personal, we can—" she tried saying before the detective interrupted her.

"Show me the message," he'd become rude and obnoxious. Matthews detested this lifestyle: lavish spending and over-the-top luxury. After a few more strokes, a scanned picture of a small card popped up. He squinted in an attempt to read it but couldn't make out any of the writing.

"Is that English?"

She chuckled, "We think so, he often makes purchases from us and sends it to *this* address," she showed him the address, "We poke fun at the person who receives them. She probably can't read his writing," she hopped up and down in admiration of the mystery consumer.

"Can you give me his name or a description? Did he pay by a credit card?"

"No… he always paid cash. His name is…" and after a few more strokes, "He wrote 'The Viking,' that's odd, we usually write down first and last names along with a phone number."

"I guess you can break any rule you want with cash. The description please?" the detective took out his best friend: his notebook.

"I couldn't really say," she got defensive, "I guess he's an average looking guy, average height, decent jawline, big eyes, nice hair," she paused for a moment, "Oh but what's unique about him is his voice. Everything he says just sounds… smart. I was smitten by his voice the first time he came in, it's like he's—"

"—An enigma?" the detective's thoughts roamed to Clark's ravenous curly hair.

"Yes!"

"Thank you," he only then noticed the plaque over her desk, "Deborah… what a pretty name," he rubbed his beard and blushed.

"You're welcome detective. I hope to see you again in different circumstances."

Matthews left the store a little pale. In his hand he held a printout of the address all the items were shipped to, 'The Viking' had spent over $5,000 in goods delivered there, the charm was only one of the purchases. The printout also included the gift notes this mysterious donor had left. Was this mysterious 'Viking' the same man whose apartment he'd just left? Detectives should never believe in coincidence. He couldn't help but think how many people have elegant and soothing voices. Justifying and rationalizing how it couldn't be Clark, the odds were on his side and more research was required before an adequate theory of the crime could be formed. Matthews compared Clark's writing on the card he'd handed him for his alibi and saw that the organized and neat hands that wrote that card could not be same sloppy Viking who wrote the gift notes. He tried reading the note sent with the charm again and could just make out some of the words. He simply guessed the ones he couldn't. It read like a bad poem.

I've got many things to say
like the sun to the moon each morning day.

I can't ever find the words
Since they fly away like a migrating set of birds.

How much longer must we be in pain?
Passengers on this familiar train.

Darkness remains my only friend
Even though I know these tracks hit a dead end.

Everything dies, and even my die
Always come up snake eyes.

It was childishly simple. Someone clearly untrained in expressing emotions they couldn't understand. Its sophomoric feel brought light to Matthews's thoughts; he envied the passion in the words. How close it was to the love Lord Byron had for his mistress.

The Viking could not be Clark. Clark was not white, blonde, tall, and vicious, whereas Vikings were descendants of Nordic warriors. Unless of course, the name was ironic.

He crawled back into his classic car and listened to the sound of her purring engine as pedestrians glared at him. *That* car didn't belong in that particular part of town. Matthews convinced himself that the second suspect: Alexander DiCeéver was the more likely culprit than Clark. Everyone at the precinct knew about him. He was a mafia clown who'd watched *The Godfather* once too many times. The son of the don who also happened to look nothing like him. Light-brown eyelashes in front of a pair of small aqua eyes that never housed any depth. DiCeéver's style was far from elegant and more like a gangster-rapper from some third-rate-bottom-of-the-charts music video on BET. A white or black ribbed tank top always matched with an Adidas or Nike tracksuit with basketball sneakers couldn't make him taller than he really was. DiCeéver was 5'10 and a half of pure spoiled brat with spikey-gelled hair looking like a rooster or a cock.

Matthews's pocket vibrated.

Meet at the corner of espace & hamill, i'm in the black Caravan surveilling the house. c ya soon. :| -Durante

VIII
VERY *AMERICAN* POLICE WORK

Matthews knew the Torrino family ran that area from his days on patrol. He noticed the car and entered the passenger side. The van had been fitted with the latest surveillance equipment, not government issue. It looked state-of-the-art. He began to wonder exactly what agency Durante worked for, if any before noticing that they were so close to the house he could see the stubble on one of the security guard's face in front of the gate of the estate.

"Aren't we a little too close?"

Durante held a headphone earmuff to his right ear towards Matthews,

"Shhh! They're bringing them in. And no, we're not too close. They'd never suspect us to be this close, probably think this car belongs to one of the houses who just happened to park on the street because there's no more room on their driveway."

"Okay, who they bringing in?" Matthews inquired.

"Everyone, there's a party at a club tonight. FACE they're calling it. It's the grand opening. Special invite only. All the new names, and some of the old are attending. Perfect opportunity to install video surveillance at the house and do some searching."

"Warrant?"

"What are you, a philosopher? Always asking questions. Don't worry, everything is on the up and up. I want that family *gone*. To make amends with our maker, or in jail, just *gone*," Durante's eyes filled with rage.

Was it personal for him or is this how Italians get things done and solve crimes? Matthews thought of Clark's neutrality when he showed him the photo of Jane Doe, no emotion, not even disgust.

Perhaps there *was* something personal about the Torrino family and Durante that he hadn't mentioned.

"We're partners now, I trust you," Matthews took care to use this specific phrase.

Durante didn't acknowledge or reply to this expression. The other end of his headphones merited his full attention. Matthews retreated and opened the passenger door as to exit. Durante tapped his tablet and murmured, "Fox and The Viking," by this time Matthews was out of the car but he heard just enough to freeze in his tracks like a dead body in the cold of night,

"What did you just say? The Fox and the what?"

"Viking," Durante quizzically raised an eyebrow.

"Where, who…" Matthews reentered the car.

"You mean you don't know the Fox and the Viking? Wait… why the sudden curiosity philosopher?"

"The Viking is a suspect in my murder," Matthews was sincere about trusting Durante.

"Okay," Durante started his noir-seeming fairy tale, "The Fox and The Viking, 'FV' I call them. They're among the world's greatest assassins. Normally these hired guns will work for the highest bidders but for some reason these two work exclusively for… drum roll please… you guessed it, the Torrino family. Anyone they want to 'whack,' gets taken out, witnesses in federal custody, judges, lawyers, you name it, they've done it. I think they're hitting triple digits soon, just of the ones we know of and can confirm. Legend has it they're supernatural. The Viking is even more ruthless than his partner. His targets are rarely innocent, they're either mobsters in witness protection or corrupt judges, cops, and so on."

"What? What do you mean?" the ever-curious Matthews couldn't help but wonder about the horror movies he'd watched in his youth. Avenging angels of justice or immortal harbingers of death resetting balance to the universe.

"They say they can get to anyone. People with state-of-the-art security systems? Boom. Dead. One guy was so scared he stayed in his private jet for months. Like in the air… dead when he landed to refuel. A guy with 13 bodyguards in a closed elevator? Dead. Just him, not his bodyguards. They say they're the devil himself dwelling in two souls."

"Ooooh, eerie," Matthews attempted to appear unimpressed and uninterested but wanted to hear more.

"Their names are whispers on the lips of the dead. If your number's up you won't know until you know the hard way," Durante continued.

"What do they look like?"

"Here, let me show you a picture," Durante shuffled his pockets he came out empty-handed, "Are you an idiot? Yes I know exactly what they look like and I'm sitting in this van telling spooky stories to a philosopher. But one of the guys keeps saying 'I'm sly like a fox' and keeps referring to himself as 'foxy,' I'll get a video print of him. Fox puns? Not so smart. He'll be at the party tonight. Young guy. Stupid, but if he is the fox, we'll get him."

Matthews exited the car,

"It seems our cases do relate. We'll work it together and solve the murder and arrest these 'devils.' We'll bring down the Torrino family."

"All in a day?" Durante scoffed.

Matthews slowly sat back down in the car and stared at Durante's forehead, "You know, when I was young I wanted to clean up the streets and take out the trash like some rogue action star... the usual rookie bullshit when they give you the badge. Too many movies. One day when I was still in uniform, my partner and I get this call about a jumper on some rooftop uptown. Beautiful 27-year-old brunette. I don't know why I still remember she was a brunette. It doesn't matter. Anyway, she'd been pregnant and lost the baby," he looked out the window towards the house they were surveilling. "We get the call... and she's on this roof right? All the other cops are standing around watching from the concrete like a bunch of extras in a primetime police-procedural, and my partner..." he exhaled, "My partner was an old guy who'd inhaled too many éclairs, lagging too far behind me as I sprinted up these stairs to try and stop her with adrenaline and pain running through me. It was exciting and frightful at the same time. The thought of a damsel-in-distress... like I said, too many movies.

I shoulder down the door and... stumble onto the rooftop of this greedy office building and she looks at me from the edge...

this pretty, young girl the same age as myself. She screams at me not to come any closer and I tell her I just want to talk.

Just want to talk. Who was I kidding?

A couple of tears run down her eyes as she tells me about the baby. I understand; I sympathize; I tell her not to worry; I tell her that she's young, that she can have another baby. But as the words leave my mouth, right as they float through the air towards her, indescribable terror washes over me. I don't know why. It's as if I knew I shouldn't have said what I said. Her sobs worsen and she can barely look up at me when she tells me that the father is mortal. Cancer. She can't have another baby. I freeze for a second, and in that exact second, she looks up and asks me why she should live."

"What did you tell her?" the emotion in Durante's voice was real.

"Huh? What could I say? At the academy they teach you a thousand things to say but I stuttered trying to come up with a reason. Her big brown eyes, innocent, sensitive, full-of-life; they dulled over. I saw the exact moment her will drained from them."

"What happened?"

Matthews's gaze followed someone walking towards the house, "She held out her arms and dove onto the pavement.

I was gonna quit that day. I couldn't, no, *didn't,* want to see that part of the world no matter how real or how... necessary, death is, I want nothing to do with it. I mean, what kind of sick, twisted *thing* makes death necessary to a young, beautiful being like that? What kind of... *God*... would give her life, *hope*, and then take it away?"

"But you didn't... you're still here... quit I mean."

"No, and that's what I'm trying to tell you... Rome wasn't built in a day."

"You're smarter than you look," Durante quipped.

"Better than looking smarter than you are."

Rapport built on a solid foundation meant that these investigators now actually had a shot at solving this case. Matthews updated Durante on his visit to the store that sold the charm and told him the address he thought belonged to the victim. He told Durante he was going to do some research on the assassins, speak to his second suspect, and eventually visit the victim's house.

Normally the victim's house would be the first place to visit since Matthews's lead was solid. However this recent exchange led him to believe that the Viking *was* in fact the killer and he'd be at the club. This also meant that the lead was time-sensitive; there was no time to search the victim's house just yet.

Such a visit would prove to be a waste of time, an assassin of the Viking's caliber would never leave evidence to aid in his own capture. He'd started twisting the facts to suit his theory instead of twisting his theory to suit the facts. He had long ways to go before he'd become *Sherlock*. He asked Durante to secure invites to the club opening with a subpoena or to lean on the nightclub owner for a minor violation as leverage. Durante chuckled that he will do so promptly after taking tea with the Queen of England.

IX
ARTIFICIAL INTELLIGENCE

It was the sort of sunset an outlaw would ride off into with the love of his life. The storm had died down and the fog was satisfying while the rain had turned into a mist. The area that housed 'FACE' boasted an oaky scent mixed with freshly wet grass from nearby trees and an aura of flowing stream water meshing with the smell of petrichor.

As the eccentric and excited crowd awaited the ribbon-cutting ceremony and the opening of its large wooden doors made from the same oak trees the forest housed, high-ranking members of the Torrino family, excluding the don, were spotted exiting their vehicles and arriving promptly for the party of the year. Shockingly, the nightclub was located in the center of the woods, surrounded by palisades on the outskirts of the 'Prosperous District', and not in the downtown club district as expected. The metropolitan smell of sewage, smog and garbage wasn't anything the people missed anyway. The family did not attempt to hide the fact that this club would be exclusive, and the long distance from downtown to the club would not hurt business in the slightest. The people who'd attend this club would be the young children of highly ranked members of society and would therefore be expected to have chauffeurs or no problem paying private taxi fares. Rightful skeptics knew that this club was nothing more than a front to launder money.

* * *

Durante mingled with the crowd while other less important guests got out of their subtle Lamborghinis, Rolls Royces and

Bentleys. He was a natural, and donning a tailored Italian tuxedo did not hurt his cause. Niccoló's keen observation skills aided him in noticing that each pass had a 'plus one' clause. In other words, one pass admitted two people to the club. His mission was to find a sucker who'd be willing to perform this service. After a few moments of roaming the perimeter of the crowd like a shark who's seen its prey, he saw a lonely woman in line fidgeting with a small piece of paper. He walked up behind her and could make out "Why is there such baseness in thy heart?" on the paper in rather impressive penmanship.

Having studied Dante from childhood, he began talking and complimenting the woman on her looks and charm. She made no mention of her plus one and he realized that he might've stood her up. She told him that she was to meet her friends inside. The conversation was riddled with innuendos and obscure sexual references, no doubt thanks to the agent's unique southern Italian accent. They were so deep in words that they failed to notice the ribbon cutting ceremony, the camera flashes, and the line having moved forward ten feet. Their conversation continued as they approached the door and Niccoló cleverly shuffled his pockets pretending to locate his invite as they neared the bouncer. The bouncer received the lady's invite as Niccoló toned down his search and opened the velvet rope for them both to enter, having thought that the agent was in fact the lady's date. Upon entry Niccoló cast an eye around the newly opened club and pretended to nod and wave to a group at the end of the bar,

"There are my friends," his Tuscan accent made everything sound smooth. "I'll catch up with you later?"

"Absolutely," the girl replied, "Come say bye if you leave before me."

Niccoló nodded and moved in the direction of his feigned wave. The highest quality tables and chairs were conveniently located around the club, in the middle of which was a DJ station and a dance floor no doubt for when the real party would begin.

Agent Durante noticed all the lovely women at this VIP party, each one could've been employed as a model, and some of them probably were.

The men were easy to tell apart. Those in the employ of the family partied and enjoyed themselves while those who had inherited their wealth were themselves split into two groups. The first group knew full well what kind of party they had attended and mostly kept to themselves lest they anger those in the mob's employ. The second group was less adamant about their environment, loud mouth undeserving mama's boys who were more worried about their hair and six-packs than whose ears the words out of their big mouths fell upon.

One group above the main platform, past the crowd of people caught the agent's eye. It looked like a VIP room. *Meta VIPs,* he thought: *the* VIPs of this VIP party or *The Chairmen of the Board.*

He approached the curtain that separated this room from the club floor as a bouncer in a black suit stopped him from entering and pointed to the main area.

Only the Rat Pack is allowed in, there ought to be a sign. The agent's thoughts fumed. Had he seen the don or his top enforcer in that room, he'd have broken a glass by the bar and lunged in an attempt to arrange a meeting with their makers.

He turned and walked away, hitting shoulders with a man entering this room and almost lost his balance from the raw strength of this stranger. The bodyguard moved to the side, bowed his head and pulled the curtain to the left. The man entered. Niccoló peaked inside as the curtain closed and glimpsed three well-dressed men and around five women drinking and exchanging pleasantries. He made his way to the bar.

* * *

Inside this VIP room was a vastly different party than the one on the dance floor. There were no strobe lights and the music was barely audible. Three men and five women were dispersed around the room conversing about various issues regarding their personal or public lives. The entitled brazen man who'd bumped into the agent as he entered this private room was none other than Clark. He was sitting far enough away on a couch not to bother himself with the insincere intelligence of those around him but close enough to hear their garbage. The end of a conversation snapped him out of his reverie,

"… And I told him to back off before I brought down his jaw."

The unknown man high-fived one of the women in the little circle. Clark's attention turned from his own contemplation to the man who had just said this. He stood up and approached him with a look that said *you disturbed me.*

"You're Otto Van Couperville, the famous painter aren't you?"

The man, still laughing at his own story turned his attention to Clark,

"Yes, you're a fan?" he faked wiping a tear from his face.

"Your work… it's certainly something," the undertone in Clark's voice growled like a monster.

"Thank you," Otto's arrogance was only second to his ignorance.

"It wasn't a compliment; I said it was *something*," Clark said serenely.

"What? Who is this guy?" Otto pointed to Clark and turned to the other man in the room.

The other man recognized the escalating situation and stepped in front of Otto as Clark lit a cigar. A fight was tempting, and Clark could resist anything but temptation. He was Wilde in such matters.

"You can't smoke in here!" Otto screamed, trying to hide his fear the way a bison attempts to seem unaffected by the sharp fang of a puma.

Clark puffed smoke in Otto's face, "You're one those fake, post-modernist garbage collectors that calls himself an artist—a painter—aren't you?"

Otto stepped by the man who was holding him back and got closer than he'd liked, "I said," he paused and tried to look more threatening than he was, "You can't smoke in here!"

Clark had yet to break the self-proclaimed painter's gaze, "Step back son, before I turn your face into an abstract Kandinsky."

The third man immediately pulled Otto all the way back and threw him on one of the seats and pointed to him.

Sit down little doggie. Humans are apes, nothing more.

He turned back to Clark, who was calmly smoking his cigar,

"Come on brotha, don't be a buzzkill."

"I'll be outside. Keep a leash on your pet."

Clark made his way to the exit with the cigar on his lip, during which time a partygoer saw his cigar and attempted to light his own on the dance floor. A bouncer immediately noticed and told him he can't smoke indoors. Niccoló liked the cigar's aroma and wished to ask its brand but he was staring at the man's back and couldn't see too well in the dark.

One of the girls in the VIP room had to hold back her laughter at the embarrassment Clark had paid to the next-Picasso. She exited the room and moved towards the double-doors. Leaving the club, she inquired about the man smoking the cigar to a roaming bouncer, who pointed up the stairs towards the roof, the door of which was locked. After a second inquiry, the bouncer unlocked the door for her and she went up to find Clark standing on the edge of the roof smoking. She burst out laughing as she approached him,

"Get down from there. You're being silly," she said in an emphatic tone.

As she neared him, Clark looked down the roof of the club, the wind resting on his shoulders. He whispered,

"Do I love her? Do I have a choice?"

Love is pain. The past is a void, you can try to run from it, but the faster you run, the faster its dark matter consumes you, its sharp claws devouring your achilles.

"You always have a choice in love," the lady approached with the poise fabled in stories of yore, "That's why it's beautiful."

Clark turned his gaze from the cold, dark pavement to the deep, light-set eyes of the woman behind him and hopped down from the edge. It was a fair bet that any man who laid eyes on Electra had just gazed at the most beautiful woman he would ever see in his short insignificant life. She had the face of an angel, the body of an athlete, the mind of a physicist, and the grace of a princess, and she was just as ruthless.

"You seem different from the wannabe tough guys that hit on me at these things."

Clark thought for a moment, "Things are not what they seem, nor are they otherwise."

"That sounds like Zen Buddhism or something," Electra replied in her silvery voice.

The rumors were true; she was as smart as she was attractive, "You must be incredibly lonely."

"Why do you say that?" the softness in her voice added yet another thing to love about her.

"Intelligence for such a beautiful woman. It must make you lonely. Men don't want their women smarter than them... and the crowd downstairs," he paused, "They're faker than my ex-girlfriend's personality."

"Sometimes," she grew nearer to his body.

The cigar he'd been smoking burned his lip and dropped but he caught it with the tip of his shoe so it wouldn't land on Electra's long black dress.

"Why don't you walk away from this? From all of it?" she put her hand on his chest and slowly began to run it down.

Clark took her hand away without breaking her soulful glance, "Life isn't a movie where I can walk into the sunset with a pretty girl like you. I don't get to walk away. The genre of my life doesn't permit happy endings."

She was on the verge of tears when she leaned closer and pressed her lips against his. Kissing her, Clark thought of Newton's cruel Third Law of Motion.

Careful Clarky, she can be a regular femme fatale if you give her the chance.

Hovering over the edge, a cartoon moment where time waits for the Puddy Cat to realize he's never going to get Tweety Bird before he's hit with the huge broom by the omniscient owner.

X
NOTHING BUT TIME

The time felt right as much as time can feel. Clark glanced at his watch, where the black hand neared the crossed-and-two-single roman numerals. "11:54, I'm going for a walk if you'd like to join me," the habits of his life were as much a part of him as his convoluted sense of morality.

The butterflies in Electra's stomach wouldn't relent in the presence of respect and charm from a *modern* man. She felt like she was in high school again and knew her own body, knew an ensuing pash for Clark was unavoidable. He was too good to be true.

"Of course, it would… be an honor," she was attempting to mimic his slow tempo and sonorous voice when she extended her hand to meet his.

"The honor… is all mine," he kissed her hand before taking it, descending the stairs and guiding her out of the club area. They walked past people still waiting to get inside.

Such degeneracy ought to be unfathomable.

He held her hand tightly as they made their way into the surrounding woods. There was some sort of trail left behind by some hikers. Clark ignored it and tried to walk through the woods.

"Clark, there's a trail right *there*," her long finger pointed to the footprints on the path.

Do not go where the path may lead, go instead where there is no path and leave a trail. He'd read that somewhere once and liked it. "I prefer to make my own path."

They wandered deeper into the woods before coming to a fallen tree in the midst of the forest. Electra sat down on the log. Clark took her hand, made her stand, took off his dark navy jacket and placed it under her.

"It's designer," she shockingly pointed to its flapping label.

"It's only an object," he sat beside her.

She progressively put her head on his shoulder as time passed. They gazed at the moonlight in the horizon, conveniently placed above a small lake. Clark felt the breeze land on his face. The beast rattled the cage. He watched the wind bend the strong, full tree back and forth in the distance wondering about the dead tree they were sitting on. It was also a strong blossoming tree once and now it had fallen and become useless. A convenient tool for others to use, it'd died like things do, eventually and with no purpose or meaning. Close to the horizon in the greater distance, he thought he saw something that seemed almost impossible: the trees were dancing back and forth as a result of the wind but it was strangely different, the tips of the two trees seemed to meet every couple of seconds as if the wind was blowing in two different directions—towards and into them from behind. They kissed for a second when their tips delicately touched before being viciously separated by a huge distance only to reunite again as the breeze came in. They lived for the breeze.

Electra was practically asleep on his shoulder while his thoughts roamed the great abyss.

*   *   *

He was drinking alone in a booth at his favorite restaurant. The waitress came over, "How's the drink?" she asked.

"Excellent. Thank you."

As the waitress departed, he saw someone familiar in the distance. It was Her. The one. His *dream* girl.

The problem with dream girls is that they eventually become too real to handle.

He was getting restless of dreaming of her. She saw him and gifted him a slight, ever subtle smile. He smirked back.

Her food was a rice dish of some sort. The coaster on her table twirled like a ballerina before the waiter put her drink on it. She glanced over, immediately playing with the toothpick that held the olives in her drink. She ate one seductively. Lucky olive. She lifted the goblet, *salud.*

Indeed my love. He sipped his drink, it was smoother than usual.

She beckoned him over. It was what he secretly wanted anyway but when he tried to walk over to her but couldn't move. It felt like he was glued to the chair. He looked down at his hands; tree bark and vines had meshed the skin of his forearms completely to the chair. He was bound and couldn't get up. He tried to signal her but couldn't. She tilted her head and looked at him with bewildering guile, *she's getting aggravated.* The vines dug deeper into his hands. The pain was excruciating but wouldn't compare to the sort of chronic distress he'd feel because of his inability to reunite with his heart. Even the beast couldn't break free.

She paid without having touched her food and paced out.

You've offended her. Get up Clark. Get... up.

He mustered all his energy and attempted to force his hands free. Eventually his left hand broke the tree bark and he used it to tear the vines from his right hand, and then raw strength tore the rest of the vines off. It wasn't just strength, the tree had loosened its grip as if it was conspiring to keep him away.

He threw money down on the table and got up in an attempt to give chase to where She'd gone but the waitress stopped him,

"Sir, you're bleeding!"

He looked down. His arm was covered in blood, scarred where the vines had dug into his veins.

"I'm okay. The girl that was just there," he pointed to her table, "Does she come here often?"

"She's trouble!" the waitress proclaimed.

"I'm sorry?" he asked.

"We're in trouble," she said.

"You're not making any sense," now Clark was getting aggravated.

Her face slowly transfused into Electra's. He was back in the forest.

"Clark, we're in trouble... wake up!"

He immediately opened his eyes, "Are you okay love?"

His pupils constricted to the size of a pen point. He heard rustling in the leaves. Some young kids had wandered from the club.

"Probably drunk kids," he said to Electra.

He knew better. He knew about the big bad world. Still, he had to reassure her. Faith must be rewarded more than truth. Truth is pain.

Her breathing intensified but this caused the opposite reaction in Clark. He showed equanimity and seemed more like himself in the face of perilous adversity.

Three people came through the woods from behind them. He stood up with his chest puffed and positioned himself in front of Electra almost as if to hide her behind him.

"Stay behind me. On my signal, run," he whispered through the howling breeze.

"Okay. Wait, what's the signal?" she asked in a trembling voice.

Clark looked back at her and smiled. His smile frightened her.

The man on the right approached Clark, who said nothing and held his gaze, watching all three men simultaneously.

They're big mouthed, hair-gelling mama's boys. I'll take them all on if I have to, so he thought.

"Hey brother, we're lost. Where's this club?"

Clark maintained his suspicious war-like discipline in case this was some sort of ruse to vamp him to drop his guard. He was more than a simple pessimist.

He pointed in the direction of the trail, their right, his left, "Just follow it back."

"Thanks man. You're a life saver, saved our night," one of the other men was more thankful than he should've been.

They walked away towards the path and Clark heard one of the other guys say,

"Guy's like Tarzan, what's he doing in the woods at this hour? Sun's going to come up soon."

He looked through Electra with a fixed gaze at the lake behind them. She started laughing.

"I guess you can laugh at it," he said.

"You're so suspicious of everyone and everything. You can let go you know. Relax a little."

"The difference between life and death is but a single second in time. Focus must be eternal."

Thunder cackled and startled Electra. She fell into his arms.

How cliché.

"Whoa, that scared me," she felt safe in his arms. The wind continued to howl and she wondered if after all this time, she could really fall for this tortured soul.

"We have 8 minutes until the storm. I'll take you home," he took her hand and put his jacket on her shoulders.

"8 minutes? Who are you?" she asked.

Who am I? Who are any of us? Does anyone know who they are except maybe the late Schopenhauer?

It took roughly seven minutes for them to exit the woods. They got into one of the cars outside of the club, and it began hailing as soon as the driver turned the key on the ignition. She gawked at him, putting her hands on the window of the car and watched the sleet slam against the glass. Clark turned her chin and kissed her.

They arrived at Electra's place in less than an hour. He got out and opened her door.

When he tried to walk away, she said,

"Such a gentleman," and took his arm and guided him up to her place.

He would never describe the details of his intimate encounter with her, relive the experience in fifty shades of garbage.

XI
CONSTRUCT III

Trapped in a gliding cage, Clark appeared as a deity or a spirit of some sort and hastily flew around the city without any control. The cage steered him through the streets and narrowly avoided death by colliding with the hundreds of skyscrapers in its path before finally opening its doors in front of an old building. All the other buildings disappeared into the darkness when he stepped into the building. The various walls and decorations of the building took their shapes as he looked around.

He tilted his head and looked through his nose like an arrogant politician. Holding onto the railing as he ascended the stairs in the left corner of the room, the building appeared vaguely familiar to him. He mounted the last step and a hallway formed before him, not dissimilar to the path he'd seen before.

It didn't feel like a dream, his senses were heightened and he could feel himself breathe. It appeared as a vision. He didn't know what to think or what it entailed but he'd come too far to turn back, he put the tip of his loafer on the newly formed hallway to test its integrity. He didn't want to fall into the screaming abyss under it, no matter what his instincts whispered in the depths of his mind.

Tap tap tip. It *felt* safe. He took a step. Six doors appeared in the hallway, five of which were barred by the same metal security deterrent he'd seen across his penthouse. He approached the only unbarred door, labeled '13-9-12.' He turned the knob; it rotated but wouldn't open. A keypad lock appeared on the knob. Skeptical surprise formed on his face when he punched in "1-2-9-5" and the knob clicked. He inhaled deeply as he entered what was no doubt a world of sentiment for a man proclaimed not to have any.

Inside Clark noticed a man who looked identical to him in every way: mannerisms, facial and body structure, voice patterns. It was but the youthful arrogance, the thicker hair, and the wilder eyes of the man sitting in the desk that separated them.

A cosmetic surgeon might have hypothesized that they were the same man save for ten or eleven years. A woman of the same age sat across him in a big leather chair. Her hazel eyes intently scanned the words of a book titled *The Morality of Values.* Her tantalizing hands struggled to hold up the approximately 700-page textbook vertical on the table. The young Clark's eyes attempted to pierce the cover the book to meet her irises but *morality* intervened.

The older Clark had yet to move from the doorway, he held back the river of sorrowful tears as he recognized this memory from his past, having yet to learn of the cruel, consuming world that had would be plagued upon them.

Afraid to disturb the scene, the older Clark tearfully mouthed the words the couple exchanged.

"You're staring… I'm trying to study," the woman's voice sounded like a Chopin Nocturne, "… And you should be doing the same."

"I am," the young man's eyes glanced up, focusing on the small streak of dark blonde hair he could see sneaking out from the top of the textbook, then down towards her body through the glass desk, before moving back up at the title of the book; presumably where he thought her eyes were placed.

"What could you possibly be studying staring at me?" she said in an undertone.

"The art of perfection," a slight smirk formed on his lips, that natural confidence that renders all young men Don Juan.

The young girl rolled her eyes and sighed, "I can't study here."

The noise of her packing up her things generated a migraine in the young man but he repressed it as best he could. She was still packing up her stuff when he quipped,

"What'd I say?"

As the woman took a step towards the door—where present-Clark was standing, watching this exchange with feeble eyes—darkness crept from the side of the room and ate the young man.

The old familiar feelings.

The door was about eleven steps from the table. The woman aged a year for each step she took towards the door. Everything else disappeared with each step: past-Clark's journal placed on the desk, the sliding door, the office itself, and eventually the doorway the present Clark was standing in. Everything was melting away into space. The woman stopped as she neared present time and Clark backed away from the doorway to let her through.

The smell of strawberries sent his mind to Dante's *Paradiso.*

She stepped through the doorway and turned towards the direction of the office; now both present figures were facing the same direction.

All Clark could see was darkness but when he leaned down a little towards her eye level, he saw through her eyes the same scenario before everything had melted away. She was sneaking a peek through the sliding office door to the young Clark marking something in his notebook. She abruptly turned around blushed forward while present-Clark struggled to back up quick enough as to not make contact with this memory for fear of losing it. He tried following her but she began to fade away until he could no longer bear the pain. He finally recognized his long lost love and reached out to touch her. He was in 'spirit' form and his hand went straight through her heart.

She gasped, as if she'd noticed the touch.

* * *

Her eyes were a glimmer when she rolled out of bed and moved towards a small desk. It wobbled as she sat down. She assembled a piece of paper and a pen:

CLARK,

I can bear to dream of you no longer. I see your face everywhere. Everything reminds me of you.

The smell of a cigar, orange peels, scotch, talk of love or passion. Talk of philosophy or paradoxes. All talk in general. Not a day goes by where I don't wish I could take back my deception.

I want to see your face, feel your lips against mine, hold your hand tightly, and feel the heat of your body against my own. I know this is not possible, and I often wonder what sort of God—

you probably just scoffed at sight of the word—would endure his subjects the pain inflicted upon you.

I remember that we had a conversation about dreams once. You told me you dreamt for years and I mocked you. I understand now how it's possible. I understand because I've dreamt a thousand dreams of you, and within one, dreamt more dreams of you, dreams which I've dreamt a thousand times before. I'll never forget what you did for me.

I physically tremble at the thought of seeing you again and I ache for it.

ETERNALLY YOURS,

L.

XII
GENERATIONS OF FLASHING A USELESS TIN

It was no surprise to anyone working in the precinct that First Grade Detective Charles Matthews was tense when it came to rules. His father, Eric Matthews, had been a detective in the same precinct and had an almost perfect arrest record on top of being a great man to hang out with.

On a particular triple homicide, Eric Matthews made an arrest that was later revealed to be bogus. The man arrested and charged with the crime was in fact innocent and was framed by Eric Matthews and his partner Andrew Buffont. After 8 years of incarceration, the supposed 'killer' was released from prison after his attorney proved that he couldn't have been the killer. The case had been appealed all the way to the Supreme Court.

Charles Matthews didn't quite understand what was happening to his father, why were his peers, newspaper articles, and his mom criticizing him with relentless cruelty?

At the academy, some young punk made a crack towards his father being an "on the take bent-copper," and Charles made quick work of the recruit's face. When he'd calmed down and looked up his father's cases, he saw 27 years of solid detective work and a single case that ruined his father's reputation. 156 solved robberies and homicides and *one* case made all the rest worth nothing.

Charles Matthews realized that the whole sum of all your reputation and core as a human being rested upon your worst case. With this logic, he understood that if your worst case was by the book: fundamentally solid police work, no damage could be done to you or your family. He had an obsession to play the odds; he never took risks and never acted on impulse. He believed whatever he was expected to believe.

Rookie Charles Matthews was lucky to get a traffic and roam beat in the uptown district after graduating the academy. There's rarely trouble in this part of town. His first partner was Joseph Crow, an experienced uniform officer who was training Charles to be an honorable cop, "A good cop. Nothing like your father," he always said to Charlie.

The quips about his father no longer bothered him because he'd learned to hide his anger and detach himself from the poisonous rage at the mention of his father's 157th case. How quickly other cops, cops who proclaimed to be smarter and more vigilant than average civilians and have better instincts and memory, forgot about his father's 156 *other* cases.

* * *

Eric Matthews was a grape connoisseur. He could smell a bottle of chardonnay, champagne, or wine and immediately know the vineyard that made it. Charles remembered his childhood through waking up late at night to the smell of luxurious wine. His father would spend half his paycheck on a good bottle and share it with his wife, Deborah Matthews. His mother came from wealth so financial security was never a question for them.

Charles would sneak downstairs and peer through the kitchen door rubbing his eyes with his knuckles and find his parents sharing a bottle of wine.

It smells fantastic, he'd think to himself.

His dad would lift him up and place him on his lap and tell his young impressionable child about the vineyard that this particular bottle had adventured from to reach their kitchen table.

"This came from the mountains of France, deep within the castle of Pétrus. It was bottled and sent to the local specialty wine shop, where I bought it and carried it with me on my day as a detective. Then I clocked out and brought it home."

Charles couldn't remember the exact words his dad used anymore; the details in his memories had faded but not the fact that the bottle had seen half the world and traveled that far to be consumed by his mother and father.

Charles didn't quite appreciate what he had: expensive bottles of wine and a father whose knowledge matched his nose for exquisite tastes. He never took a sip. His fondest memories are the moments when he sat on his lap, smelling the fantastic wine as his father talked grapes for hours and he listened attentively like his mom.

* * *

Matthews and Crow roamed the streets for what seemed like years with minor things to report like *suicide* and traffic violations. Charles was thankful, he liked the fact that they weren't needed, his beat was at ease. Charles's first epiphany came on one day where they stopped in front of a bistro, Joseph had sent Charles in for coffee and doughnuts. In this part of the city though, coffee and doughnuts meant a *venti* dark roasted Colombian nut with a toasted Danish dessert for the affordable price of $16.28. Charles walked into the bistro and approached the counter, training himself to mind his surroundings. He looked at the numerous faces in the bistro. Three people sat by themselves and ate sandwiches, a couple sat and stared at each other silently until the woman burst out laughing and they whispered words, and a woman read a book: *Eyeless in Gaza*. It seemed like the world he grew up in. People were content, happy, at peace. He wasn't as affluent as these people, and yet he felt connected to them. He realized the balance of the universe was always in place, an ubiquitous connection to all things even if people were unaware of it.

* * *

His first big case as a uniform officer came on his second month. It was a robbery at one of the banks in the uptown district. Joseph and Charles were first at the scene; the robbers cleaned out one safety deposit box and stole bearer bonds, immobilized all five security guards and had the bank under their control within seconds. A man had been made an example of, pistol-whipped in the face resulting in six or seven fractures near his chin. Robbery-Homicide had been called in. Other detectives arrived dressed to kill and an attitude to match. Matthews was not only reminded of the respect his father commanded when he was a detective but of his own ambition in showing these short-sighted officers that the Matthews name was a badge of honor, not of shame.

Investigators thought this was the work of a new and rising crew at the beginning of their crime-spree. Matthews however, deduced this to be false. He noted that the employee who'd been pistol-whipped had been hit while he was alone near the vault. It couldn't have been for an example to the others and thus had to be personal. They raided only one safety deposit box and took the bonds and cash lying freely in the vault. The safety deposit box was their objective. Everything else was simple coincidence. Matthews checked the registration. The place read like a mob bank, better than state-of-the-art security with most of the guards holding ties to organized crime. Even the clientele read like the characters out of a Scorsese film. Matthews was sure that almost all the safety deposit boxes were registered to people who either had ties to the mob or were members of its inner sanctum. Someone was making power plays.

He informed the detectives of these leads and upon further investigation, they found that the injured employee was in fact the inside man at the bank and tracked the robbers down through him. An apartment rented in their name in the building where the employee had lived and an email sent from his work address to one of the robbers. It was amateur hour... even for the mob. The case was closed within hours of the robbery.

The thieves were charged and remanded to the custody of the city's correctional facility. Unfortunately, and outside Matthews's control, two were killed on transit to prison and the third somehow escaped, circumstances that made Houdini look like any number of those abundant fools doing ridiculously stupid internet dances. The case remains open, and even though it's not his case, Matthews considers it the only case he's yet to close. He fears that this is the inevitable case that would bring down his reputation if he ever screwed up, the ammo to the villain's loaded gun.

His fear is misplaced.

The detectives acted honorably and did not take all the credit for the case and praised Matthews for his sharp police instinct. He received a commendation. Gallanté captain immediately fast-tracked Mathews for a detective slot within his homicide unit. He told Matthews that officers with a detective instinct and an ethical police mind are rare and must be nurtured. Knowing full well the details of Matthews's father's past and knowing that Matthews would not want to be affiliated with his father, he told Matthews that one mistake does not erase the hundred-and-fifty-something excellent decisions his father made during his career. His father was a good cop that lost his way in the end and despised the cruel world that he had to put up with.

A lot of that going around.

Days after his promotion, Matthews got a call for a suspected assault and robbery on a Jane Doe at one of the intersections in the 'Prosperous District.' The victim, a beautiful 28 or 29-year-old woman died on the wet pavement trying to hold onto hope on this decadent planet and it was only his first case as a detective; he still had about 155 cases to go. He'd seen dead bodies before but this was different, he vowed to himself that he'd get the guy even if he went down with him. He understood how his father felt.

XIII
THE ART OF WAR

Jonathon Ventoni lived on the 27th floor of the Hilton Hotel. He was a methodical man in his thirties. His disciplined behavior and posture made his military service rather obvious to anyone with half a brain, but these days, that may very well be asking too much. Like all soldiers who put their lives on the line for corporate profits, his eyes always sparked anger and volatility. His buzz cut matched his light blue dress shirt and black army pants, which were always tucked tightly into a pair of thick military boots.

He stared at a chessboard with the piercing glare of a man possessed, slowly unbuttoning the top three buttons of his shirt. The opponent across from him watched his inevitable loss in agony.

"Rook to Bishop 8, I believe that's mate friend," Ventoni was always proud to crush his enemies and he viewed nearly everyone as an enemy.

"What is that? 28 in a row?" he continued, "Don't worry, you can only get better."

"Why are you even talking smack John, you're some sort of chess prodigy, you have to be. It isn't possible!"

A third man was cleaning and maintaining weapons across the room, he cleaned a pistol, the barrel slid back... click.

"Ladies, let's go. Review the game plan again."

The winner stood up from the chessboard amongst an air of self-assurance, "Jax, you worry too much, let me help you clean that."

Wiping the guns with a cloth, Jax sneered in John's direction, "You know I'm the only one who touches the weapons, why always insist?"

"The easiest players to beat are those who never change. It's the same moves over and over again. Predictability exposes your patterns and adversaries are beatable when their patterns are exposed. You can limit their movements and strike at the opportune moment."

Jax chuckled throatily,

"Coming from a man nicknamed *Rook*... take away that piece and you can't win."

"It's not just a piece. The rook is a vital symbol. It stands for inevitability."

Ivan, who'd just lost to John *The Rook* Ventoni, picked up the fatal rook and moved towards him, "Whaaaa?" he rotated the piece bafflingly.

"The rook is about the end-game. The last piece. The fatal dagger. The foreshadowed straight line taken right into the belly of the beast. The enemy's castle. He can support, defend, attack or all of the above in a split second."

"Deep," Ivan squeezed the piece in his palm until it left a mark.

"Enough ladies," Jax polished the last weapon and placed it on the table across the room, "Show me the plan again."

Ivan walked over with a cold cup of coffee as Jax and John made their way towards a common area in their apartment. The trio approached a whiteboard with markings of a floor plan. John flipped the whiteboard to reveal another whiteboard, which had the following message,

Jax: Bishop—Weapons and support, from the 2nd floor down onto the main floor room.

Ivan: Knight—Roamer, watch your left, stay on the main floor and pay attention to everything. No detail is too small.

John: Safe-man—I will be at the safe. You will secure the people, and when I have the safe open, I will switch with the 'Knight' role as Jax fills the bags. When this happens, Ivan will switch to the 'Bishop' position and watch everyone from the top.

John read the message and pointed as he explained the plan to his seated partners.

"Sounds simple enough," Ivan said.

"Everything is simple in theory friend," John replied. "Two things are vital here. One, Jax, you stay on the top floor no matter what, you're the guard of the castle looking down. This is psychologically and tactically important if something should happen. Two, Ivan, stay in Jax's line of sight at all times, he can cover from all positions, if you're moving away from his eye-sight, communicate. Tell him so he can gain a better vantage point. Three, you," he points to Ivan, "Like Jax, stay on your floor… the main floor, we can't be caught out of position on this, there are only three of us."

"You said two... that was three," Ivan chuckled.

"Four, remember that some people watch too many Clint Eastwood movies. They think they're heroes so you have to watch them. If someone makes a move, pistol-whip them in the nose or jaw, blood will squirt everywhere and stain their clothes. The noise alone will horrify everyone. No one will say anything afterwards. Five, we do not fire bullets unless necessary. The noise might be loud and be heard outside, we do not kill, this is important," he looked right at Jax, "Kill someone, fire bullets and we'll have more heat on us than Mercury. This mission is contingent on stealth. We do it properly with precision and accuracy as I have outlined here."

He flipped the whiteboard over, revealing the floor plan with names such as "Knight" and "Bishop" with arrows pointing in different directions in various timestamps,

"... And we come out rich and alive. I want to come out both rich *and* alive gentlemen, not rich but dead or poor but alive. Keep this in mind if you get any fresh ideas and want to call an audible during the game. Don't forget—I am the quarterback here."

Jax crossed his arms and looked at Ivan, then at John, "I'm good to go with the equipment. When do we hit?"

"We need another drive-by, check out the security shift. There's two on the main floor, probably three hidden in the back or in plainclothes, I have them circled here," he handed them some pictures.

"Same guys in the bank everyday, but none of it will be a problem if we do it according to plan. This plan supports neutralization of up to 12 guys with just us 3. Security isn't going to risk their own life, they're getting paid minimum wage while rich piranhas with delusions of humanity come in to deposit and withdraw their ill-gotten gains."

Ivan looked at John, "I'll do the last check. I have to pick up some stuff anyway."

"Okay, we'll be here when you get back, it's almost show time. Ivan, you've still got our escape covered right?" John was skeptical about Ivan. It was the first job they'd ever done together but he came highly recommended.

"Of course," Ivan grabbed the keys near the table and headed towards the exit, John and Jax both sat down across the board and stared at it with still eyes, memorizing and studying it. Eventually John lit a cigarette and began smoking it. He offered one to Jax, who took it.

They exchanged small talk about their conquests of women, their lives, and their favorite sports, the usual meaningless conversations men have with each other but somehow form irrevocable bonds by the end despite having said nothing worthwhile.

Hours passed and they started drinking. Their conversation never withered. Finally, Jax turned to John and said, "You know, you're alright Johnny."

"Everything is alright with enough whiskey."

"And so clever," Jax slurred.

These two slowly but surely became good friends. Ivan finally walked through the door with a brown paper bag, no doubt full of groceries and a small blue notebook. He handed the book to John, who studied its contents attentively.

"What about the plainclothes?" Jax asked.

"They're not *officially* on the payroll, and since there's metal detectors, it means they'll be unarmed. We just have to stay on our toes."

Ivan put down a gallon of vodka on the table.

John's eyes darted to the board and Ivan's blue notebook and back, until finally,

"We hit at 2:25 two days from now."

XIV
VENTED FRUSTRATION

Ventoni had always slept like a baby: tossing, turning, whimpering, and wailing. He has always been prone to nightmares. There are few things in this universe worse than reoccurring nightmares.

His IQ was tested at 159 at the age of five. He had taught himself ancient Latin, Greek and Italian by the age of seven. He was suspected of having an eidetic memory because he never seemed to forget anything. He mastered chess at eight and took an extreme liking to it. This was rare for him. He'd mastered numerous instruments, sports, philosophies, and religions. He fancied himself an Adonis, a Greek demigod amongst weak insects.

He stuck with one other thing other than chess, football. He played competitively at a young age all the way through university, which also happened to be where he met Clark.

From the moment he met Clark he didn't like him. Clark played fútbol, which is called soccer in *one* part of the world. Despite not playing the same sport, Clark was in a lower division than John. John despised him regardless. Where John seemed to enjoy bragging to 'insects' (his word) about the higher intellectual capacity and acute sense of athletics bestowed upon him, Clark viewed them as curses.

Clark was the only other person who could both intellectually and athletically challenge him. John was a natural athlete and could play fútbol fairly well and Clark could play football fairly well. John saw Clark as an *opponent* and always sought to be his better. He was always envious of the ease that Clark seemed to demand everyone's attention. Clark was suave yet brooding, the complete opposite of John, who was affable, light-hearted and *appeared* kind. But John himself knew he was duplicitous, he hated that Clark was honest with himself and others. Clark knew who he was, what his principles (or lack thereof) were, and he hated how Clark applied these practically to his life. He hated Clark's confidence. He abhorred Clark as the strong silent type to his talkative buffoonery, especially after he realized Clark was as smart if not smarter than he was. Clark didn't feel the need to show off his intellect, to challenge others. John did. He saw Clark as the other side of his coin.

Practically every night, John would lay his head on the pillow and lie in the dimmed illumination of his nightlight (he was afraid of the dark ever since an enemy combatant in Somalia had snuck into their camp), unable to sleep for fear of night terrors.

John knew who he was and what his nature was but he betrayed it every day. Every man strives to be the opposite of what he is. It is not that he fails to actualize his best self. It's because his best potential self includes ideas about who he is and what he ought to accomplish, and these ideas always tend to be the opposite of his nature. Clark knew that any man who understands himself understands his limits and his frailties and weaknesses; this is the most powerful man. John did not.

* * *

To add fuel to a raging flame, John and Clark bumped into each other at the stadium in between training sessions six or seven times a week. Clark would always get there early and train first as the sun rose whereas John would sleep in a little longer and arrive at eight or nine in the morning. He'd always see Clark leaving just as he entered. He hated that Clark never smiled. Everyone smiles; it lets people know you're not a threat. Clark didn't care what others thought of him. He possessed an unwavering fearlessness that frightened those dared stare into his wild irises. Perhaps this was what John hated.

Further goading their silent competition, John progressively became rapt, his hyper-competitive nature immersed in a tradition that eventually became a competition itself: *who'd get to the stadium first?*

It was stupid to train before the sun rose so eventually both men arrived every day at dawn and trained together. John failed to realize that this was what Clark did anyway, that if this were in fact a competition, he'd have lost. He liked to think of it as a stalemate.

Clark taught John the philosophy of his fútbol, to forget the individual and share the ball to assure victory, and John taught Clark how to quarterback a play properly and call successful audibles in the blink of an eye.

John detested Clark's honesty in his ideas. He never attempted to hide the few beliefs he had.

Some thoughts are dangerous and mustn't be shared, so John thought.

As time progressed, John labeled Clark a 'practical utilitarian.'

Clark would disagree with labels but gladly admit that pedophiles and murderers ought to be killed to save thousands of taxpayer dollars since they rotted in prison anyway.

"Sanctity of human life is a human invention, what's sacrosanct about a pedophile or someone who takes another's life?" he asked once.

John agreed but hid behind a fake compassion for human life. Where Clark was a strange idealist, John was a fierce materialist. The latter hated the former for thinking the way he did, arriving at ideas *his* way. It was an original, invented form of 'passionate logic.' It wasn't as disconnected from the world as logic nor was it the blind emotion of love but rather a perfect harmony of both.

John feared that Clark was the type of man with the strength to take infinite lives to save those he loved and wouldn't even mind suffering afterwards as a result of his decision. He didn't understand this selflessness; he knew he would never be that strong. This thought made him angrier than usual and this anger transferred to those around him.

Clark seemed not to care what John thought of him even when they found themselves in clear intellectual and athletic competition. This only provoked John's hatred and Clark enjoyed seeing him try in vain to best him.

During a training session, John told Clark over sandwiches that he had his eye on a girl who came to every one of his games, not because of him but for the spirit of the team. He asked Clark what he thought about lying to impress a woman, 'padding the resume,' he called it.

Clark loathed deception but understood its necessity. This particular case had no necessity for it. He told John that engaging in deceit to win the affections of this woman would mean they could no longer be friends.

Clark quipped that he didn't understand *why* John would even have reason to lie; he was a star football player and a very smart man. Lying would be simply stupid.

Stupid? I am not stupid! John was sensitive to the use of this word.

Lying to her meant losing Clark's respect. John felt the tide change; he'd always disillusioned himself as the superior man but this interaction made him feel inferior. He wanted to show that he was smarter than Clark and quoted Walter Scott,

"What a tangled web we weave when at first we practice to deceive."

Clark wasn't as dumb as he looked and replied,

"And come he slow or come he fast, it is but death who comes at last," from the same poem.

"We're honest in death so we must be honest to those we wish to die for. This lady might be such a person for you so you mustn't lie," his eyes, it was the look in his eyes when he said it that made John take it seriously.

At least he still had chess, Jon thought, although he'd never play Clark, he wouldn't risk losing and shattering the boasted image he'd cultivated of himself, that one time didn't *really* count; he was tired; the sun was in his eyes, *and* he was distracted...

He told Clark they'd play even odds. Since both men were much smarter than the average Joe, their only solace was random games of chance like flipping a coin or guessing the results of a random number generator (even though both knew no true random number generator existed), and offered to flip a coin. Tails they do it his way, heads they do it Clark's way.

Clark famously told him,

"We flip that coin enough times, it might land on its edge, what then?"

For some strange reason this question echoed in John's mind more than he liked. In his nightmares, he asks himself what the next choice in his life ought to be, simple things such as: go to *this* school or *that* school; rob *this* bank or *that* bank; ask *this* girl out or not? His superior intellect made cost-benefit risk analyses benign and boring. He *needed* random games of chance. When he flips the coin in his nightmares, it lands on its edge and forces John to make the decision himself and go through the boring dull risk assessment. He hated making decisions this way since he was unable to ascertain the ripple effect the decision would have on his life. His pedantic, logical mind couldn't comprehend the need to make decisions. It didn't matter to him either way; it was all the same. He associated the results of his random games of chance with fate. What he was *meant* to do as shown to him via a coin or the random selection of a letter from a multitude of choices each assigned to said letters. A coin landed heads, fate wanted heads. Fate cannot be altered. He believed a man could not change his fate. This idea swam in the oceans of his mind like a shark, devouring any new or conflicting ideas.

How did it all end? Even hatred has a limit and John's reached his when Clark fell in love after they'd known each other for a year. He could see it in Clark's eyes. Love oozed from every fiber of his body and John was envious. He thought if he ever fell in love like that he would hide it. People like himself would use that love to try to hurt him. It was information best kept in a treasure trove hidden deep in the recesses of your emotions. Clark did not believe such things.

He tried probing but Clark rarely spoke of her. All he would tell him is where she was from or what she thought of various ideologies and philosophies. He told Clark that his eyes told him everything he wanted to know and did in fact warn Clark as a friend that he should hide his love.

"Bury those feelings deep within a box and show them to no one, people would use it against you. Your passion for her would be your downfall."

Clark didn't understand this at the time.

* * *

They hadn't seen each other in years but for some reason John thought of him the night before the robbery. He closed his eyes and entered the dream world.

He asked a two-tailed coin whether he was a better man than Clark, tails if he was, heads if he wasn't. It was a laughable attempt to cheat me. What humans don't realize is you can't, no matter how much you try, run contrary to your nature.

Fling. The coin spun in the air with John's grin nearly tearing his cheeks off. The coin bounced on the marble floor of the bank and landed on the edge. Clark appeared from behind the bank counter,

"You're stupid John. Stupid. A fool. An idiot. An *insect*," and he laughed at him.

The mighty Rook sobbed in his sleep.

XV
OVERMORROW

Jax and Ivan were outside the bank at 2:00 P.M. sharp. John had been sitting in his car watching the bank since 10:20 in the morning, periodically moving pieces around on the mobile chess set he kept on the dash of his Ford sedan. In addition to the three separate cars each thief arrived in, a fourth getaway car was parked in front of the bank with a filled meter from the night before, thanks to Ivan.

John moved some of the knights around in an effort to relax himself before the job at hand.

Jax took multiple deep breaths and considered self-reflexive questions: a wife, kids, a house with a lawn, what he thought a family would look like. Ivan drank vodka from a brown paper bag.

2:24. Like a synchronized Olympic swimming team, each man got out of his car at the same time with matching steps. They were organized and professional as they approached the bank. Jax held the door open for an entering patron. *What a gentleman.*

They entered: Ivan, John, the patron, then Jax. Ivan put a mask on and walked over to the security guard,

"Don't be stupid," he said coolly.

His 357 Magnum greeted the security guard's nose. The guard's choices diminished to a singular one and he disarmed himself. More guards flooded the main floor but the others had their masks on by now and disarmed them with relative ease.

Jax took his position on the upper floor while John grabbed the manager. Ivan eagerly roamed the main floor just like the arrows on the diagram.

"Four minutes," John whispered over the headset.

Jax's watch beeped their counter to a start.

John had no trouble getting the keys to the vault room from the manager. He handcuffed the employee to one of the tables near the vault and began cracking the safe door. He was glad that the manager and unlucky patrons silently understood that the government insured their money. No one would lose a cent.

Ivan was doing exactly as he was told on the main floor. There was no trouble until a roaming Jax spotted an uncooperative 'hero'. Before the manager got to the main area to rejoin the rest of the hostages, he seemed to want to approach Ivan more aggressively than Jax liked. He told Ivan and the latter quickly followed the instructions he was given. Blood sprayed everywhere as the man sank to the ground. No one made a sound or moved after that. A few minutes later everyone heard a howl coming from the direction of the vault. Seconds later, John appeared,

"Knight, switch to the upper with Bishop. Bish, I need you."

Jax descended the stairs as Ivan ascended them, he could see everything from the upper floor. John was right. It *was* like a king reigning over a kingdom, a psychological and tactical advantage. Ivan liked the feeling. Who doesn't enjoy power and striking fear into the hearts of their fellow man?

John and Jax made their way to the safe,

"I nearly died from the voltage, it's higher than standard!?"

Jax smiled, "Private owned, I thought you knew."

"I do now," John replied.

"I trust it was no problem. Not for the mighty *Rook*," Jax's condescending leer was only directed at John's arrogance.

John smirked as the vault door hissed out the compressed air and opened.

Open Sesame.

Inside the vault were stacks of money and bonds as far as the eyes could see, millions worth, ending with a wall of safety deposit boxes.

John took out a key and walked towards box number 857A. He took out an air suppressor from his bag, put one key in the left lock, presumably the one he got from the manager, and put the suppressor in the right keyhole.

BANG!

"Everything crispy?" Ivan's voice rang into John's headset.

Rook takes King.

"As KFC's chicken," John emptied the contents of the safety deposit box.

Jax had in the meantime filled the three big black duffel bags with the money and bonds lying freely in the vault, beckoning him to be taken. The three men calmly walked out of the bank and took off their masks as soon the front door closed behind them. Ivan let a smoke grenade roll out of his hand and street was filled with smoke in a matter of seconds. Police arrived just as the men got into the getaway car on the side and drove away. The police set up the roadblock *behind* them. Jax's watch starting beeping.

With eighteen seconds to spare.

John looked back at the police cars in proximity of the bank.

* * *

Back at the apartment was a night of celebration: drinking, partying, talking, and laughing about the mission.

Ivan's phone beeped, he hastily tapped it in between three or four mouthfuls of vodka and turned his attention back to the others.

"Girlfriend?" Jax didn't see Ivan as the commitment type.

"No, it's the manager of the bank. He's updating me on the police's investigation."

"Tell me you're *joking*," John's pent up anger nearly gouged Ivan's eyeballs out of their sockets.

"No… why?" Ivan's reluctance to answer was superseded by the ire in John's eyes.

"The first suspect in all bank robberies is the manager. They're going to find us. We have to leave."

"I know *that*. Besides, the email isn't registered to me, and he's using an unidentifiable proxy email."

"I hope you're…"

The door exploded open,

"Wrong," the words hadn't left John's mouth as waves of SWAT officers led by then-uniformed Matthews stormed the apartment.

XVI
33%

"Your honor, case number M8907, accused are: John Ventoni, Jax Siegfried and Ivan Toorman," a man in a suit stood in front of a judge in a court of *law*.

"Pleas?" the judge sighed. It'd been a long day. An older gentleman with a record of assault had courted his promiscuous daughter. Any compassion present in this man's darkened heart was lacking on that day.

"Not guilty,"

"Not guilty,"

"Not guilty," the nocent replied in succession.

The judge looked back at the prosecutor. He stood up again,

"Your honor, all three men have records: robbery, violence, and or assault. There are multiple gun charges. Jax Siegfried is wanted in three countries with ties to seven murders and he is suspected of being tied to the Torrino family. Racketeering charges might—."

"Stop there," the judge opened his mouth and everyone fell silent, "All three will remain in custody. Remanded."

Down came the gavel of justice.

The judge, *God* for all people concerned in the room had spoken.

Human authority. How apishly amusing.

A corrections officer guided the prisoners back to their cells. They were to be transported separately to each prison until their respective trial dates. Their guilt set in stone like Excalibur. They were probably to be sentenced as guilty. The evidence was overwhelming. The link between Ivan and the bank manager was too prominent for any attorney to weasel out of, notwithstanding the stacks of money Matthews and company found at the apartment.

The three men sat in separate cells inside of the county police station until an officer approached. "Evan... Tarman."

Ivan stood up and walked to the bars, *stupid pig,*

"It's Ivan Toorman, you know I was going to be a cop but I wasn't dumb enough," he grinned through the jail bars. Two officers exchanged a humorous glance at one another. One of them guided Ivan to a bus parked on the roof of the building.

As Ivan exited the station, he heard another officer through the window call Jax and John. It was time for each of them to travel the long and tedious road to the desert.

A prison cell is nothing but four small walls that close in during moments of contemplation. You can't breathe, think, or move. Worst of all, you're alone and in bad company. All your thoughts and conversations circle back to your miserable core, thinking about that *what if* world where you made a different decision and became a different person and led a different life. Escape is the only solitude. The best chance of escape was before arriving in that room. The best chance was during the transport.

Ivan thought the people that hired them would surely come to their rescue. They needed what John had stolen from the safety deposit box, which was hidden at *Leon* train station locker number 416 immediately after the robbery. Only John knew the password: *utopia.*

Each man went through their head count as they entered their respective buses separated by hour and a half intervals. Each bus individually pulled out of the police station and minutes later was on the highway to hell.

* * *

All prison buses are the same, they smell of sweat and vomit, the chairs are torn, the guards are abusive, and you never know who's who. This guy could be with that gang, that guy is enemies with this guy, look at a guy the wrong way and you're going to die. Don't look at a guy and you're going to die. Pretty much, you might die. It's a heightened form of life, the thrill of inevitability with The Grim Reaper potentially waiting at every corner.

We're all dying, some sooner than others, Ivan thought when he craved some *Stolichnaya Elit* vodka (not to be confused with the more popular *Stoli*). Hell, he'd have settled for *Smirnoff* at that moment.

The guard behind the gate standing beside the driver finally sat down to take a breather; he pulled a lunch box from under his chair. Out came a fresh pear.

Mmmm. A pear, I could enjoy a pear for days. It was the shape of a planet held by a small stem rooted in the universe, a perfect sphere resting in space. It was plum, fresh, the smell carried through the bus when he cut it with his knife.

"Arghhh, owwwwwwwwwwieee!"

The guard howled when the bus mounted a bump. He'd cut his finger with his pocketknife. The bus slowed down,

"What are you doing?" he asked the driver without looking up.

Ivan turned his head towards the aisle so he could see. A woman's car had broken down in the center of the road. She was wearing a headscarf covering her short blonde hair, big sunglasses and tight jeans, her figure was far from ladylike but this was probably the last woman he was going to see for a long time if his employers didn't come to his rescue. Beggars mustn't be choosers. This was his chance to escape.

"We have to help her," the driver turned to his companion, who was busy sucking the blood out of his finger like an overgrown baby.

"Protocol says we don't stop for anything."

"Protocol can kiss my ass, look at her," he opened the door.

The woman entered, "Thank you," she said in a man's voice as she slipped her hand from her back and shot the driver in the head. The second guard fumbled for his weapon but he was too slow, a second bullet pierced his olive cheekbone as he fell down. The sliced pear rolled off his lap.

Ivan was ready to go, giggling and bouncing up and down on his seat like a 10-year old pony-tailed schoolgirl on Christmas morning. The assassin took the keys out of the guard's pocket and opened the gate separating the prisoners from the guards. They laughed gratefully, thinking he was a man to grant them their much-coveted freedom. Their cheers stopped when he made a beeline towards Ivan and fired a single bullet into his brain. Ivan greeted his maker. The assassin walked out of the bus and got into a parked car stationed on the side of the road hidden through the wooden area.

She took off her fake hair and big sunglasses. Alexander's stupid grin formed on his face. He took out a phone and dialed three digits, feigning a woman's voice,

"Oh my God oh my God, I just heard shots. There's a bus here, a prison bus, send help, send everyone send everything. What's that? My name, my name is…" Click. He threw the phone on the trail and peeled out. *Sly like a fox*. He chuckled at his own skill.

* * *

The guards in Jax's bus were on immediate alert. The report had gone out about two guards murdered on a bus (no love lost in a convict being killed, street justice is the closest thing to *True Justice*). Some officers believed it was an organized escape attempt. They drove down the highway for hours. There was only about forty-five minutes of road time left. The guards felt more relaxed, no one ever tried anything this close to the prison, back-up was too close.

* * *

Clark was gazing through the rearview mirror of his exotic motorcycle idling on the side of the road. He gazed into that mirror and saw his own eyes through his helmet. *Who's staring at who*, he dozed off into thought.

* * *

He entered an apartment amongst the smell of fresh ground coffee and strawberry mousse cheesecake filling his nostrils. He was holding a small box of some sort. He approached a woman standing over an oven.

"Hey," he kissed her on the cheek and ran his hands down her shoulder blades.

"God you're beautiful... like a sunrise over a secluded lake somewhere in Europe," he massaged her neck.

"I'm beautiful? Or are you talking to God again?" she reached behind her and felt his rugged stubble.

God and I aren't on speaking terms, he thought.

"I'm talking to you love," he said.

As she backed up into him, he'd have sworn he felt the wings of an angel on his chest.

"I have to freshen up." Clark followed her with his gaze until she disappeared into one of the rooms of the apartment. As much as he despised seeing her walk away from him, he enjoyed eyeing her leave. He set the gift-wrapped box down on the moderately sized wooden kitchen table and sat down on one of the chairs. The table wobbled. He wobbled it and looked at its legs. One of them was shorter than the others.

Even the Mona Lisa isn't perfect.

The table's imperfection bothered him more than it should have. He thought she was perfect, he thought everything about her was perfect. A migraine hovered over his brain like a dark cloud. He grabbed a mug from the cabinet and filled it with water. He set it down on the counter when he saw her coffee machine. He cleaned its filter and hit the ON button. He never drank coffee, other than the occasional espresso, but she did, so he showed the machine the respect it deserved. He knew how she liked her coffee: three milks and two sugars.

Sugar? You're already sweet enough, he said to her the first time he heard her order coffee.

He put his back to the counter and reached for his cup. He lifted the cup to his mouth. Before the brim touched his lips, he heard a voice emanating from one of the other rooms,

"DAMN IT! GOD DAMN *EVERYTHING* TO HELL!"

He almost dropped the cup. It sounded like a child, and whoever he was, they'd get along just fine. He moved towards the sound. The door was half-open. He entered donning his usual attire: a black suit, white dress shirt with a slightly grey collar, and a black Hermes tie.

"Hello? Anyone there?" he knocked thrice and entered.

Inside was a blonde boy no older than twelve years old situated comfortably on a big leather armchair not dissimilar to his own back at the penthouse. The smooth maroon colored walls were empty except for a beige poster labeled "Life" housing quotes about life by various philosophers, artists, painters and poets. The wall mount holding the TV hosted an interesting painting near the ceiling and Clark was taken back by its genius, a small boy with a big mind.

It was a landscape painting of two families enjoying breakfast split down the middle of the canvas. The left side of the painting housed a black woman dressed in a janitor's uniform in an urban apartment serving cereal to a white, browned-hair child dressed in a school blazer, baby blue polo and dark navy dress pants. There was graffiti on the adjacent apartment building through a small window behind the boy's head. The tone on this side of the painting was dark, as if the sun hadn't come up yet. It looked like a run-down urban environment, not the place you want to stumble upon after a night of heavy drinking. The right side of the painting seemed to be the opposite. A woman (of Latin or Middle-Eastern origin) dressed as a maid was placing a bowl of fruit and a mug of coffee in front of an older white man dressed in a suit with prescription glasses. He was reading the newspaper. Opposite the man was a small black boy with shorts, a thinning T-shirt picking fruit from the bowl with his fingers. A streak of light reflected from the breakfast fork near the boy's hand. The sun was in full swing behind him through the huge window and the sky was crisp blue. The light from the sun reflecting off the marble island nearly blinded the viewer.

The child probably stared at this painting morning, noon, and night. Physically he seemed small for his age, and had small thin fingers; he gripped the game controller as hard as he could, his hands seemed too small for it. The screen read "GAME OVER," in huge bloodstained letters.

'RETRY' and 'QUIT' were the flashing highlighted choices. The boy buried his hands in his face for a second as the controller rolled down to his thighs.

"What game is that?" Clark was intrigued.

"Prince of Persia Warrior Within, have you heard of it?" the boy jerked his head back to meet Clark's gaze. He held Clark's gaze longer than most adults did.

Impressive.

"Prince of Persia? When I was little, it's about a prince who saves a princess right? From an evil Vizier?"

"Woooooooowwwwwww," he emphasized the 'ow,' "That one's so old, you're old."

Clark let this go. He *was* old relative to the boy. Relativity is everything.

"Well, what's the new one about?"

"This one is soooo cool, it's about this guy called The Prince. He tries to change his destiny by altering time using this dagger but that's in the first game right? But it's impossible to change your destiny so he has to travel to the island of time in order to change the universal timeline and change his fate," the boy said in a single breath. He talked so fast an average person wouldn't have been able to keep up.

"Time is linked to destiny?" Clark was far from average.

"I suppose so."

"And The Princess?" Clark liked the idea of a prince and a princess. It seemed germane.

"There is no princess!"

Yet, there's no princess yet, every prince has a princess. Clark thought.

"You're stupid," the boy smacked his lips.

Clark let this one go as well. He *was* stupid.

"You're probably right, so... are you going to retry?"

"I can't, I'm stuck, I've been trying for hours. Wait, you try," he handed Clark the controller, "Prove to me you're not stupid, or old."

I like this kid. Clark took the controller. "If I beat the area, you tell me your name."

"Deal," the boy laughed.

"Tell me the controls then," Clark said as he pressed START on the controller, RETRY flashed twice and faded out.

"Figure it out smart guy," the boy smirked.

I love this kid. He smiled.

Clark couldn't help but see himself in this little boy. A rebel who marched to his own tune and didn't care about anything. A hedonist... he'll grow wiser as he ages. Clark contemplated the possibility that he'd grown dumber as he aged and really hedonism was the correct answer to life's problems—the game's loading screen flashed 'complete.'

"I take it the game's philosophy is that no man can change his destiny?" Clark enjoyed symbolic metaphors. They added a necessary oomph to complex concepts.

"Like everyone's philosophy," the boy returned.

Wise for a ten-year old.

The Prince was a tall man with a light olive complexion, long streaky hair, dark set eyes, athletic and often made quips about absurd nonsense. Wondering about his choices, why he's there, why he's being chased. How to change his destiny. The similarities in thought put aside the almost identical physical appearance Clark had to The Prince, except that Clark's hair was curly and he didn't have a soul patch.

Clark used the right analog stick on the joystick to control the camera, he moved it and eyed the scenery. It took him a couple of seconds to become comfortable with the controls.

The Prince took a few steps forward, the wall beside him was smashed open by a creature about fifteen feet in height, it was a black being, just pure black smoke… like,

"There he is," something trembled the boy's mind, "The *Dahaka*. The darkness."

Darkness? *You've got to be joking.* The creature personified darkness. Its long ram horns twisted like mirror images of each other to form the infinity symbol. Its fierce golden eyes burned with a powerful inner light even though everything around it melted into a perpetual shade the creature carried with it. The Darkness had no hands, but black shadows shaped like swords.

Yes, it was darkness, is this what the beast looks like? The darkness in all of us?

"I take it I run away from the big piece of darkness."

"Duhhh," the boy returned.

The Prince rapidly turned corners left and right trying to outrun the darkness; *the parallel was almost amusing.* Swinging across poles, running across walls; nothing seemed to work. He couldn't get away from it.

This game is… interesting.

"Can't we turn around and fight it?" Clark was a warrior, it was the only thing he knew how to do with relative ease.

"No, the Dahaka is the guardian of the universal timeline. He restores balance to the universe. Your destiny was to die. You lived... balance must be restored."

"My death results in balance?"

"Yes. Because your destiny was to die," the boy scoffed.

"So I'm running away from my destiny," Clark had The Prince slip down a pole and use a sword to rip apart a flag while sliding vertically down a wall.

"Yes," the boy returned anxiously, watching Clark barely survive every second.

My destiny is the void? Death? Those who fight hardest against the Reaper are those most tempted by its salvation. Perhaps this game is onto something. Why am I—I don't need a game to tell me what my destiny is.

Clark began projecting himself onto The Prince, their similarities were too much to be coincidental.

The world is getting too small for comfort. Too many 'random' coincidences. Perhaps some beliefs must be altered, others abandoned. A Descartian cleanse. Solipsism appears false since things exist outside of me: this boy, the painting, Her. Some things are unbelievable and yet true whereas others are rational but false. Random things are connected by the slightest weaves like a sewing thread holding up an anchor.

"Here, this is the part I always get stuck, right there, I run up, but he's waiting for me at the other end."

"The most obvious path is seldom the best... you run *up?*" Clark had The Prince march down instead of up the stairs ahead of him,

"The stairs going down are broken smart-guy," the boy patronized Clark as The Prince fell down into a bottomless pit. He was dead.

"Wait!" the boy was in a hurry to say something, "Quick! Hold the left trigger! It'll rewind time!"

Rewind time? Clark held the button, the game moved backward; *time* moved backward and The Prince was back on the ledge. *I wish life were this simple.*

The beast whispered, "No one escapes the Dahaka," in the middle of this time jump. No one can escape death, the balance, fate. This was both unbelievable and rational. It *had* to be true. Clark ran down the stairs again a second time.

"You're going back down? You die there! Didn't you learn your lesson?" the boy hissed.

"We haven't tried jumping... a leap of faith," Clark jumped across the gap, The Prince grasped a tiny, almost imperceptible ledge, then climbed up and kept running.

Footsteps approached, the door swung open, it was Her,

"By the way, I'm babysitting my *nephew*, his name is—"

"Shhhh," the boy yelled at his *aunt*, he'd never been this far before.

"Ooooo, sorry, didn't realize there was something so *important* happening here," she dried her hair with the towel in her hand, she'd just gotten out of the shower. The smell of her shampoo danced in Clark's nose. He inhaled deeply.

Flowers: jasmine and lilies. His feelings for her were as subtle as a knife wound piercing his beating heart. He nearly dropped the joystick. He'd closed his eyes to relish the moment.

"You're playing with your eyes closed? I like your friend aunt—," the boy interrupted himself and turned back to Clark.

He watched the television less and progressively watched Clark more.

The Prince turned down a hallway and walked through a waterfall. The room was safe. A cut scene began that showed the disappearance of the Dahaka. The Prince made a quip about water being the Dahaka's weakness. Water cleans things, stands for purity, it's transparent, it doesn't hide anything, doesn't hide what it is. It made sense that darkness would be afraid of it.

"You slayed that beast," the boy extended his hand when Clark handed him the controller.

"If only all beasts were so easily slain," Clark returned the joystick as he rubbed the kid's head, "Now I held up my part of the deal, your name?"

"Vero," the now smiling boy was a man of his word.

"Vero? That has to be Latin for something."

"Truth," he returned.

This boy was far smarter than Clark gave him credit for.

How fitting, Clark thought. "That's awesome," he said.

"Well… are you going to tell me *your* name?" the boy asked with an arching eyebrow. Clark had seen that eyebrow somewhere before.

"Clark."

"WHOA! You're named after Superman. That's awesome-r!"

Is that a word? the boy thought.

"Superman's fictional my boy."

"So is truth nowadays," the boy looked down at his feet.

I knew I liked this kid. He turned his attention to his fair lady,

"Boys will be boys Elly."

"You call her Elly? That's not her name, her name is —" the boy interrupted himself again, "Ewwwww, I hate pet names."

"What should I call her then O Wise One?" Clark bowed with his hands cynically.

"Elle, it's sexier."

"Vero!" she gasped.

"How old are you?" Clark's curiosity had bested him. He caught a glimpse of what Matthews would feel like when asking of his cigarillo rule without even being aware of it.

"Old enough. It's French for *she,* or *her*, it's much more enigmatic.

"You're a smart boy," Clark recognized an above-average intellect.

"You have no idea," Vero replied cleverly.

Had I stepped into a portal into the past? Held the button too long? Was I here to alter the timeline and have a conversation with myself as a child?

His thoughts unexpectedly took a different turn,

What if he is me? A kind of me? What if... is this... my child?
The thought nearly consumed him. Vero was her sister's son, that's what she told him anyway, he calls her Aunt *Elle. It can't be... it's not.* His absurd ideas were his weakness.

"Okay, come on boys, enough banter," Elle said.

Clark and Elle headed for the door,

"Wait!" Vero screamed.

He paused the game, ran up and hugged Clark, "Thanks," his head was barely above Clark's abdomen. Clark rubbed his head. "Sorry I called you old and stupid."

"You did what?" Elle inquired.

"You're welcome buddy, don't worry about it. Don't let anyone change what you want. Focus on your passion and follow it. No matter what people say, the Dahaka only covers the most obvious route. Look for secret passages and shortcuts," he kissed the boy on the head and walked out of the room, the boy's hair was so short that Clark felt his scalp when he ran his hands through it. "Nice haircut, like an Air Force pilot; disciplined. Maybe you'll soar through the skies as an eagle one day."

Vero's eyes widened, he liked the idea, "She cuts my hair," he pointed towards the main room, "Doesn't like it long, too painful for her or something. She's not too pleasant when its long, so I respect her decision."

"Hmmmm," Clark thought this was rather peculiar but he was never going to question her. He forced a smile at Vero and slowly walked out of the room, his eyes inadvertently catching the painting as he shut the door behind him.

Elle was waiting in the doorway with a steaming cup of coffee.

"Not the advice I'd give to a twelve year old," she shut the door, Vero's gaze still fixed on Clark as the door latched.

Clark could hear the ambient noise from the game through the door.

"Kids mustn't be nurtured. They have to learn to feed their nature. You can't fight your nature," he told her. "You have to embrace it, the sooner you understand it, the better."

"He never shows affection, never hugs or kisses anybody. Not even me. You might be the first," Elle teased, "Know anyone else like that?" she arched her eyebrow.

There it was.

They walked over to the kitchen table, Elle's eyes fixed on the gift-wrapped box like a surgical laser.

Clark noticed where she was looking, "Oh, now you've gone and ruined the surprise. Go ahead, it's yours."

"What is it?"

"Are you joking? I'm not going to tell you."

She picked up the box and shook it, lest she could deduce what it was without actually opening it. Something he never understood, why do people insist on doing that? Just open it. Is figuring out what it is 3 seconds before you rip apart the packaging going to make the gift suddenly more preferable? She tore the wrapping, his thoughts zoomed back to reality and he couldn't look at anything but her flawless hands opening the box. A piece of her tongue sticking out of the right side of her upper lip, something she did when trying to focus.

She opened it and her eyes lit up,

"The Divine Comedy, hardcover Longfellow first edition? Where did you find this?" she was breathless.

"It doesn't matter, although I hear the more modern Pinsky isn't too bad either."

She looked at him with an ineffable affection. He looked up to the ceiling and felt like he was outside with the storm wetting his rough complexion and the breeze idling on his cheekbones.

"What are you doing?" she smiled.

"Thinking… something I do before I talk… sometimes."

"You should meet my dad… you two would get along."

I would love to, it'd be an honor, he thought.

"I would love to, it'd be an honor," *a harmony between mind and heart? Between logic and passion? What's wrong with you Clark, what's happening to you? You're in danger of becoming a noble man. In danger of falling in love.*

She smiled again.

That gaze, the art of perfection, he chuckled inside.

"Here," she said, "Take the *Inferno*, so you have an excuse to come back," she took out Dante's *Inferno*, jotted something inside the front-page with a roller pen and extended her hand to him.

"But… I don't need an excu—"

"Take it. I know how you are Clark. Bring it back when you're done,"

127

He kissed the hand holding the book, starting from her forearm until he got to her long slender fingers. He finally took the book and her hand. The note she wrote made it heavier than its weight.

The pen's cap rolled off the uneven table and bounced on the parquet floor, the dark cloud over his head thundered harshly.

* * *

The sound of a bus engine roared Clark back to reality. These are the moments he thinks of every second he can. He lived and died in them. Becoming reborn as his identity fluctuated with the ideas, as deafening as heavy metal on maximum volume on a surround sound system. The past is like a shattered mirror. You try to put it back together but cut yourself on the glass. The blood reshapes you, changes your principles, and you try to make sense of it all.

The bus approached and passed him, he revved the engine and peeled out in pursuit.

He pulled alongside the bus a few seconds later,

"Look at this fool," the driver chuckled to the guard beside him.

"Should I call backup?

"Nah, he's on a bike, what can he do?"

"Wellsworth Penitentiary, Wellsworth, Wells-worth, these people are worthless? To be isolated at the bottom of a well? How… appropriate," Clark read the words on the side of the bus. He pulled a rock out of his leather jacket and hit the window…

"No," he tried it again, this time hitting a different window.

"No…" and he threw another third piece at a window that was open at the top.

"Perfect," he pulled out a hand grenade.

"He's got a grenade!" an inmate screamed from inside the bus. The guard rushed to get his rifle but Clark reduced speed and the guard couldn't fire. Eventually he sped up quickly and lobbed the grenade inside the bus.

"Stop the bus!" another inmate yelped. The grenade popped. Smoke gently filled the bus, the driver looked back with eyes as wide as the sea. He slammed the brakes, Clark followed slowly behind on his bike.

No rush.

The bus came to a stop on the side of the road and lightly crashed into a tree. Clark parked behind the bus. He broke the glass on the bus door and entered. All the people inside were unconscious. Clark walked over to Jax.

He forced Jax to eat a cyanide pill. He shook and convulsed on the floor of the bus until he became as still as a meditating Zen Master. Clark walked over to the driver and took his radio controller.

"Mayday mayday! We're crashed at the side of the road about 2 clicks from your location, send help. Over and out."

"Repeat! Alpha Tango 5030. Repeat transmission," the radio hollered back.

Clark lit a cigar and rode away in the opposite direction. The only thing missing was his babe and a sunset over a secluded lake.

XVII
THE GREAT ESCAPE

The third bus arrived at the prison on schedule.

"Ven-ton-ee? Where's Ventoni?" a guard with the clipboard glanced back at the guard stationed beside the driver. The latter shrugged his shoulders.

A prisoner has gone missing? An armed robber? A murderer? He was just in custody. Surely our justice system is more careful than that. Surely we have deluded ourselves into a false sense of security.

No matter, the government will protect us from the big bad terrorists who seek to rip apart our freedoms from the other end of the world. What could one armed robber do? It's the terrorists we should be worried about.

"Ventoni! Up front," the second guard screamed at the empty bus, "Sometimes they try to hide in weird places," he checked under each seat.

As empty as a politician's heart.

* * *

The three men were in their respective cells back at the station. Except of course, for John *The Rook* Ventoni. After a bout of interrogation with Matthews, John asked to phone his attorney. Matthews and the detective left the room since they could not listen to the conversation due to attorney-client privilege.

The Rook had other ideas. As soon as the detective stepped into The Pit, John called the police station. He could see the officer by the cells answer the phone. He posed as a bail bondsman who had allegedly posed the bail for a *John Ventoni*.

Ergo, John was released moments later while being escorted back to his cell. As soon as he collected his items and got out of the police station he walked to the nearest ATM machine and withdrew $500 from his account. Payable to the first homeless man who reenters the police station and turns himself in (he'd call in and revoke his own bond by saying the check bounced) as *John Ventoni* and gets on the bus. John knew that this bail scam would be discovered eventually unless he turned himself back in. Of course it really couldn't be *him* but some other poor sucker looking to make a few bucks. This way would render ample time to escape and hide somewhere until his trial date, where the officers would arrive to testify and recognize that the man is not John. This plan called for luck. Unfortunately for John, luck was elsewhere when the call was placed, and Matthews looked inside the cell John was kept in as he was going to lunch and noticed the homeless man inside. He'd met Ventoni and knew the man in the cell wasn't him, he didn't bother checking the name. Some homeless merely aggravate an officer just so they have a 'safe' place to sleep for a few hours. He opened the cell and freed the man.

One ounce of luck that John drew was the lazy corrections officer who merely did a head count, and didn't cross off each inmate's name as they entered the bus, and because John's name would've only appeared on the master list since he was technically still being questioned; the officer couldn't have noticed that a prisoner was simply gone.

It took the prison system and the police fourteen hours to deduce this scheme. During which time, Ventoni kept busy.

* * *

"Next stop, Leon. Next stop is Leon," a voice over an intercom rang in The Rook's ear as he came to aboard a train. The train screeched to a halt and John stood up using the pole in front of him. He brushed past the people and squeezed past the two women talking on his way to the door. The train station was packed but it didn't matter, John knew where he was headed. He looked for an arrow pointing towards a hallway to his left with the words "LOCKERS" above him. He looked like a zombie. The sleepless nights had taken their toll on his complexion. Evading police and his nightmares was exhausting. He staggered down the hallway. Rows of lockers greeted his droopy eyes at the end of the hall. He looked for the sign, 'Lockers 400-550', and headed in the direction of the arrow. He approached number 416. He tapped the screen, "PASSWORD" the screen inquired.

Open sesame, U-t-o-p-i-A, each press of the screen emitted a beep that sounded like sweet music to his ears. The items inside this locker were his salvation. It sprang open. Inside was a gun, a black old monotone-screened cell phone and two folders. John looked around. The coast was as clear as the Australian reef. He stashed the gun inside his jacket and emptied everything else in the small leather briefcase he kept in there. He boarded the next train and headed to a different city.

* * *

He stared into the cocktail wrapped around his fingers at a local dive. There are rarely any self-respecting dignified men taking up bar stools at 3:00 P.M..

It was just the usual everyday, alcoholic losers. He wasn't one of them. He opened the folder bearing the seal of the bank. He was curious to see what was of such vital importance that would merit his employer's betrayal. They hadn't failed the assignment; they were hired for the contents of the safety deposit box, which was retrieved, but somehow, for some reason unknown to him, they were still targets.

The folder cracked open, John took a sip of his drink, inside were professionally crafted reconnaissance files on every member of the Torrino family, including outside contractors. Under the seal of the bank, on the first page of the main folder, was the seal of the Calvanos, a rival family. This was collateral in case of war. The Machiavellian in him appreciated the foresight.

He looked through every file carefully. They had files on everyone from the don on down. The list even profiled the victims. It included things they indulged in and the writer even drafted inductions on what each indulgence meant in his/her professional opinion.

Alexander's file for example, included his like for rap music and one-night-stands. The person who wrote it thought his self-destructive and misogynistic behavior was a sign of Alex's hatred for his father; a form of rebellion towards the affections rooted in his father's nature. Alexander merely wanted to feel loved by his father. He thought his father loved his sister more and this enraged him further. There was even a file on Jax and himself but he didn't bother looking, what could some psychiatrist working for the mob tell him that John's superior intellect wouldn't have told himself already?

He flipped the pages aloofly until one caught his eye. He'd recognize his silent enemy anywhere. Giddiness consumed him, the square cheekbones, the big Roman nose, ravenous curly hair. It was Clark. He sipped his drink and ecstatically opened the file. *The Art of War* wasn't wasted on him. *Knowledge of the enemy's dispositions can only be obtained by other men.* He said a prayer to the Calvano man who'd put this file together.

Fate connects all things to me.

He rubbed his palms together and giggled silently like a child.

There were hundreds of pictures of Clark, only his file was this large.

Why? John wondered. Were they afraid of the things he knew because he was an outsider? Not one of *them* but one of himself. The Henry Hill of these *Goodfellas* and therefore the easiest to recruit as a possible spy? He flipped through the hundreds of photographs, keenly studying each one.

Know thy enemy. Ventoni's reverie of crushing Clark beneath his feet was only temporary when his dilated pupils met with Clark's in each of the photographs.

Only four of the three-hundred-something photographs interested him. It was surveillance photos of Clark with a woman. A tall Caucasian with gorgeous, unique hazel-aqua eyes, long wavy blonde hair that flowed like a river down her right side. The elegance of her back arched sublimely to a set of long legs. They were the perfect place to house angel wings. She looked like a flower, thorns and all. Clark's weakness perhaps? It was a safe bet. She looked oddly familiar to Ventoni.

Rook takes Knight.

The first photo was Clark sitting across the laughing woman at a small bistro during one of the many storms. A uniform officer behind them in the background no doubt ordering doughnuts at the counter. The second was a photo of the woman coming out of a building holding a big book. This was followed by the third photograph, Clark outside the same building, the timestamp had them minutes apart. The last photo was Clark in a residential neighborhood with the woman in the rain. She was barefoot holding her red high heels in her hand. It looked as if Clark was offering to hold them for her, his hand extended towards the direction of her shoes with her left eyebrow quizzically slanted upwards. He recognized the look on Clark's face. Some men never have that look their entire lives. That look can't be feigned. John recognized it, the undying passion of a man who'd do anything for the target of his passion.

He flipped through the pages. Clark's phone number and address were there. He dialed the number but did not place the call. He looked up at the two other people at the bar and shook his glass at the bartender, who obeyed John's drink order. John thought it through.

Let's see how his Zen tapes help him now. If I have nothing, why must others have something so sacred? I am not loved.

This thought boiled in his head like a lobster at a high-end restaurant.

No one loves me, ME! The genius, the prodigy, but someone can love Clark? That hypocritical, idealistic prick?

His inner voice echoed his failures and relived his nightmares. His bigotry leaked through the mask he'd been wearing all his life.

He placed the call in anger. It rang. There was no answer.

Voicemail? No.

The bartender came over with John's new drink. John nodded and handed the bartender a large bill.

"I'll be back with your change," the bartender smirked.

John waved his hand, "It's not necessary, that's for you."

The bartender thanked him and walked back behind the bar. John sipped his drink slowly, contemplating what he was condemning another man to. The thought excited him further. The inner voice egged him on.

Minutes passed in contemplation, what if Clark came after him? Was it worth the risk? Good thing he didn't pick up, *another drink barkeep, this time give me the good stuff.* The liquid courage warmed his body enough to make him feel like John Wayne.

Redial. It rang twice... click. Someone was on the other line, John first heard a woman's voice in the distance, "When who said?" then Clark's slow tempo and low timbre, "Go for Kóróna."

"Clark, my oldest friend... don't talk, just listen. I hold here a folder. This folder has everything about everyone. If I go down, everyone goes down. Out of respect for you; and I know respect is the only thing *you* respect, I won't release any of it just yet. I'm leaving, don't ask me where. But," he said slyly, "I noticed a lady... *your* lady in a few pictures, at an office, at a bistro, walking through the rain like a scene out of some chick flick, you're still with her? I'm going to watch you for sake of amusement," he sipped his drink, "And if you go near her again, I'll kill her, and only her, not you. Why not you you're probably wondering. Simple, you aren't afraid of death. Besides, this punishment will be worse than any death my limited imagination can conjure. You can still meet other women just not her. Our world offers quite a healthy selection of beautiful women," John took a deep breath.

"I'm going to make copies of all the files and have them sent to you. Just so you know I'm not bluffing. I know how much you love proof. There'll be a package waiting for you when you get home. Remember, you contact her, see her or even think of her... and I come straight for her. The grief of this will serve as your atonement for the betrayal of your friends, and we are old friends after all. Unlike you, I don't betray my friends. Understand?"

"I'll get it done. Have you told Alex?" Clark's calmly returned.

Rook checkmates Knight.

"No. No one will know, only you. I will give the files only to you and you can do with them what you please. We are after all... old friends," he took a liking to this phrase purposefully, deliberately, attempting to guilt Clark into a reaction. His attempts were feeble. He thought Clark hated it, which meant he loved it.

He started mimicking Clark's voice and tempo of speech. "Take everyone down. I don't care but I'm going away. Don't try to find me, and leave that woman alone. You don't deserve her."

He's right. I don't deserve her, Clark thought.

"Wherever you are... I hope you aren't alone right now, because if you're alone you might catch your own reflection and we know that kryptonite isn't good for old Superman don't we?"

Click. John took a deep breath, his stomach turned. He sprinted to the bathroom to throw up. The bartender and the laborer sitting at the bar exchanged a look and laughed, *what a lightweight.*

John made his way to a copy store and copied all the files then couriered them to Clark's apartment. He'd kept his word. He boarded the train to a far away land with great pride. He did not intend to follow Clark or the woman to make sure Clark abided by his word but he was familiar with the look in Clark's eye in the photograph. He'd seen it during their only chess match. Clark would never risk it, even though he's an impulsive tactician. He would never risk her life.

* * *

Clark arrived at his apartment. He entered the glass doors. His concierge, a man of about fifty-five or fifty-six, handed him a folder.

"Clark, a courier dropped this off for you. I'm holding onto it."

"Thanks Mick," Clark took the folder.

He entered the elevator in deep thought. He hadn't noticed that he'd reached his floor. The doors closed again when someone called the elevator back down and they opened to the lobby. He had to ride the elevator up a second time. He exited at his floor. The dark wooden door stared back at him, the folder clutched in his left hand. The key rattled in his lock. He entered the apartment and locked the door behind him. He slid the folder down on his island and it stopped at the edge, he'd almost pushed it off, used more force than he needed to. Something sparked his synapses. He walked over to the sink, brewed tea and lit a cigar. He opened the file. Rook wasn't kidding. This file had everything, pictures of him and his heart, of every member of the family, complete with photographs, descriptions, comments, and *profiles?* Who took these? It definitely wasn't the cops, if it were, they'd all be arrested by now.

It didn't matter who took them. It mattered that they existed and he figured out this could potentially be to his benefit, he'd use this as a safety valve. If anything ever went wrong, he'd hand it over to the cops. He owned no loyalty to thugs and killers with no professional code, thugs and killers that forced him away from his passion and nature.

His profile read him as, "A man without any code, rules, or principles. The silent type with only one weakness, the woman in the enclosed photographs."

Close enough.

He removed his rug and counted three tiles, smacking the fourth and forcing it open. He placed all the files except his own inside it. He looked at the same four photographs John was looking at in the bar. Rubbing her face in the photo, his head throbbed, a little alien wanted out. He stumbled and descended the few stairs from his den, nearing his armchairs. He lit the fireplace and stood over the blaze, looking at the orange and red inside the fire, the small blue flame near the wood, it was the hottest part, it looked like the sea; he wanted to swim in that blue flame. He looked up at the ceiling, the smoke from the fireplace and his cigar watered his eyes enough to make him flicker them. That's what he told himself. He knew it wasn't the cigar smoke or the fireplace that was making his eyes tear. He threw his file into the fire. Gazing at her raised eyebrow in the photograph slowly disintegrate in the flame, he was filled with a burning rage. He punched the fireplace wall. It was pure concrete. He broke three knuckles but felt nothing.

The beast approached the cage, it was locked but its bars had become fragile, it bent the bars and roared out. He began throwing everything at arm's length in a fit of fury, no longer did stoicism appeal to his core, no longer did nothing shake his indifference, no longer did the thought of *her* eased his headaches, the possibility of feeling her warm, plush lips against his own in some distant horizon was all but possible. The beast was in control. He shook the bookshelf and most of the books fell out and he whipped what remained across the room. A couple went in the area of the kitchen and hit one of his bottles of scotch. It hobbled violently and nearly fell. He prayed for it to fall and shatter, his rarely heard prayers were answered as it rolled off the small table. He didn't care. He didn't care about anything anymore.

If you don't care about anything or anyone, are you really alive?

He lifted his armchair over his head, a feat that reminded him of Vero calling him Superman, and this thought made him angrier. He threw it on his coffee table, the wood exploded and a book flew up and hit him in the chest. It knocked him back. He hit his head on the back of the fireplace wall, his calves burned from the fire. The book landed at his feet face down.

He looked at the book, barely drawing breath, *Dante Alighieri was...*

It can't be. It isn't. It is.

He took the book and turned it to its cover, *Dante's Inferno.* Clark let out a roar that resonated throughout the building, Mick stood up to investigate, lest it be an intruder harming a tenant.

He fell to his knees, the beast walked back through the bent bars into his cage and rolled to its side like a man who has accepted his fate before the executioner and walks to his death willingly. Clark had to harden the bars.

He looked around his apartment with everything broken and out of place and *Dante's Inferno* in his hand, it still weighed a ton. He opened the cover and read in her perfect penmanship,

'You *can* escape the Inferno. Dante didn't live there. He was guided through it and eventually went to Paradise, you're only reading the first one.'

He hated the universe, hated everything in it but her. He saw no way out of this, no way to see her again. He couldn't risk being with her and having a momentary lapse of judgment, losing focus for a second and causing her death. He could barely live with himself as it were, let alone if he were the cause of pain to Her. His gun tempted him, if his purpose was to care for Her, to love Her, to recognize that happiness was a life with Her, why was he so tortured? So miserable? A lion without a pride and no interest in forming one. Only one choice remained. A tear cringed off his cheek and stained her writing on the paper. He didn't wipe it. Men must be honest and transparent; they should never wipe their tears.

XVIII
DURANTE

Niccoló Durante never wanted to be a police officer. His mother, Allegra Durante nurtured his analytical mind. Niccoló's father was a famous tailor in a small town in the province of Sicily. They lived in the town of Gela, on *Via Achille Grandi*. There were multiple streets in his neighborhood but all were dead ends. There was only one way in and one way out. It was a tight-knit community, the epitome of a small town mentality. Everyone knew each other, knew who did what and who was who, it wasn't a bad life.

Niccoló didn't understand why many people would come and order suits or dress pants from his father in a town that rarely hosted weddings or other formal black-tie events, at least not until he was older.

Around his house, Niccoló cherished the memory of poems and quotes, printed on an old family typewriter and framed up on the walls. His mother enjoyed American literature: Edgar Allen Poe, Ralph Waldo Emerson, and Robert Frost. There were two poems in particular that caught the young man's eye. The first was above his father's workshop, it was an anonymous quote,

We were given:

Two hands to hold. Two legs to walk. Two eyes to see. Two ears to listen. But why only one heart? Because the other was given to someone else. For us to find.

The second was in his bedroom, vertically placed across his large window, the frame equaling the length of the long side of the window. It was Edgar Allen Poe, a long poem titled *The Raven*. Niccoló memorized a passage that always caught his eye, not for philosophical reasons. When he laid in bed, the moonlight would pierce through his window and illuminate this passage,

Presently my soul grew stronger; hesitating then no longer,
`Sir,' said I, `or Madam, truly your forgiveness I implore;
But the fact is I was napping, and so gently you came rapping,
And so faintly you came tapping, tapping at my chamber door,
That I scarce was sure I heard you' — here I opened wide the
door; —
Darkness there, and nothing more.

He'd started believing in immortal souls, each waking moment was spent trying to strengthen it, he wanted to become a better man. To never hesitate, to breathe an honest emotional response, to use his two eyes, two ears and two legs to find his other heart.

* * *

He admired his father's trade, the elegant trimming, the fitted cutting, the laser-precise measurements. Like all children, his father became his hero. His father showed a piece of cloth patience, dedication, and commitment Niccoló hadn't seen anywhere. The thought astounded him more than any philosopher, poet, or writer ever could. He started to believe that his father could alter a man's image, did the clothes make the man or did the man make the clothes? In today's half-wit world, people believe perception is reality. They're so ignorant that they believe it's the clothes that make the man. His father could make a simple carpenter look like a Spanish prince, a criminal like a demigod.

He began training under his father, helping the men who came into the shop and order suits. He watched his father turn pieces of insignificant cloths into a fitted tuxedo; it was a Hegelian transformation, dense and incomprehensible.

This continued well into his teens. Niccoló would come home from school, skip dinner if need be and go straight to his father's workshop and watch him, often glancing at the framed quote placed above the ironing board.

Niccoló's life didn't lack the one element every man's life has in common. There was a little girl in their small city about the same age as Niccoló who often played with him when he wasn't helping his father. They ate lunch together at school, they walked home together (her house was only six houses before his), studied together, laughed together, cried together. They were children living the American Dream in Sicily.

Niccoló began to admire his faithful companion, Beatrice, who was not only beautiful and charming, but was also more intelligent than the materialist bimbos he always came across.

Their relationship flourished steadily until Year Two of the *Scuola secondaria di secondo grado* (10 grades past kindergarten). Niccoló never told Beatrice how he felt and having thought he was uninterested in her, Beatrice began showing interest in other boys. This was understandable behavior for a woman.

Like most schools in this chasm, the population of their school was divided into a vicious hierarchy. Absurdly but from the top down: the low-minded but physically capable athletes were respected the most. Then followed the women who admired them, followed by the less-physically-able but intelligent bookworms, then the recluses or loners, (although some are this way by choice). Lastly are the physically able and intellectually superior to all other groups, the lone outlaws or rebels those who don't care for arbitrarily fabricated rules for governing what others have deemed *normal*.

In rational words all the hierarchies of our world are reversed.

Niccoló belonged to the final group; he was well versed in literature of all kinds, knew enough about all cultures, about all worlds, and excelled at almost every sport he thought was worth his time. It was by choice that he detested the hypocrisy of cliques and disunity. He wanted a world where all students united to learn about the arts, about politics, philosophy, about sports, and all students united to achieve this dream. He wanted the athletes to help the bookworms compete, the bookworms to help the athletes learn and think, the women to have minds of their own—like Beatrice. As time progressed, he realized his world could never be. The world is ugly, barren, and contradictory.

* * *

Beatrice took a shining to a fútbol player who was the same age as Niccoló and naturally belonged to the top of the hierarchy. In Europe, Italy especially, fútbol is very important, a lot of unnecessary importance is placed on the ability to kick a ball into a net, and although Niccoló was a much more capable player, he rarely played.

She spent hours talking to Niccoló about this boy, and naturally, the former grew to resent him. The object of her affections was a bully, pushed weaker people around and always got into fights. He wondered how such a highly capable person (of both mind and body) such as Beatrice could be attracted to him. A silent rivalry began to stir between Niccoló and this boy, Dev. Whenever the conversation granted him permission, he'd quip *'Dev's name is short for Devil,'* and Dev's short red hair and beard did very little to help his case.

An Internet meme would have labeled him as 'friend-zoned,' something some ignorant clown thought up in a dark basement.

Nonetheless, Niccoló respected Beatrice's decision. It was the quixotic thing to do. He wanted her to be happy. Perhaps Dev was intimidated by Niccoló but was deep down a nice guy. He wanted the best for Beatrice and Dev was incredibly wealthy. Financial security is important to all women despite feminists constantly saying otherwise.

As time progressed, Niccoló and Beatrice spent less and less time together physically although they were always in each other's minds. Dev was the only boy in their school with a car so he drove Beatrice home. He played fútbol so Beatrice spent all her time watching him practice, no time for conversations about Ralph Waldo Emerson with Niccoló anymore.

Niccoló's only succor had been Father Antonini, the priest of the local church. He often visited the church if for no other reason than to aggravate the holy man. Niccoló stopped believing in God the moment his beloved walked away to a worse man than he and his only entertainment became questioning the priest's faith or pointing out contradictions in the bible—of which there are too many to keep count. The only spiritual truth that made sense to him was the interconnectedness of the universe. The balance of all things, two people, worlds apart connected to each other via a certain subconscious frequency, feeling their smiles, frowns, and aches in each other's hardened bones.

* * *

Two years passed, Dev and Beatrice remained in Sicily while Niccoló attended the University of Florence for *Philosophy, Art, and Latin*. Beatrice was never far from Niccoló's thoughts until her voice was not far from his ear. He answered a fatefully ringing cell phone.

"Nicky?"—he hated that name.

"Bee?" it's what he called her, a bee makes honey, the sweetest thing there is.

Something was wrong, her voice sounded troubled, almost trembling. "What's wrong?"

"I… uh… screwed up, I need someone to talk to."

She sounded scared. He decided to go back, to see her in person.

"Is it Dev? Are you okay? Where are you, I'm coming back down, are you safe?" he was in a panic.

"Yes, I should be okay… no you don't have to come back, I just need someone to—"

"No, you don't sound like yourself; I'll be there in less than 17 hours."

The University of Florence was 1, 150 kilometers away from his old neighborhood, a place he hadn't returned since he moved to Florence, and required a ferry ride. Sicily was an island province on the coast.

*   *   *

It was back to the familiar *Via Achille Grandi* for Niccoló. His studies were always second to Beatrice. He would've said everything was second to Beatrice but the flowery metaphors and literary devices can only stretch so far and for so many characters.

He arrived in Sicily in 14 hours, three hours earlier than expected.

No one ever locked their doors in the old neighborhood. Everyone knew each other, he simply walked back into his own house and realized he walked out of a time machine set for three years in the past. Nothing had changed. His visit surprised his mother. Niccoló entered the kitchen abruptly. They exchanged greetings,

"Where's papa?" he inquired.

"In his workshop," his mother returned in a soothing Sicilian accent.

Some things never change, Niccoló walked out of the kitchen, noticing a newly framed poem by Robert Frost above the kitchen doorway,

> *Some say the world will end in fire,*
> *Some say in ice.*

From what I've tasted of desire
I hold with those who favor fire.
But if it had to perish twice,
I think I know enough of hate
To say that for destruction ice
Is also great
And would suffice.

Death is certain. I'm not afraid of death. Eventually everyone's number comes due. Why be afraid of something natural, of a universal process: to live and die. This is the order of the universe. It would be irrational to fight it and attempt to reject it.

Not afraid of me? Human hubris amuses me.

He walked towards his father's workshop and opened the door. His father was ironing a tie. The first thing that greeted him was the quote above the smiling shirt collar of his father's back,

We were given:
Two hands to hold. Two legs to walk. Two eyes to see. Two ears to listen. But why only one heart? Because the other was given to someone else. For us to find.

His father slowly turned around to see who it was. Tears of joy filled his eyes. He dropped the hot iron and it began sizzling the carpet floor, Niccoló immediately dove down, picked it up, turned it off and placed it on the board as he rose to meet his father.

"The prodigal son has returned father," Niccoló's Sicilian accent had almost disappeared even though he grew up there.

"You sound Tuscan beloved," his father returned.

Niccoló laughed, "I apologize for having not visited and I'm sorry again, but I have to leave. There's been an emergency."

"With that girl no doubt? She's the only one who can get you to do anything," the father hugged his son.

"Yes father, I fear she is in trouble."

"Go forth my son and save her, but ask for God's guidance first, visit the church, Father Antonini would like a word with you. He asks about you every time your mother and I visit."

Niccoló was pleased to hear this, Father Antonini understood things better than most. He could go to him for advice, to confess, or just to talk about current events, politics, religion, and or philosophy.

He made his way to the church. It was a seven-minute walk. Numerous deep breaths calmed him down. Where was Beatrice and what had become of her? Was she okay? Perhaps Father Antonini will know. He arrived, looked up at the overwhelming black door that led into a small circular window that housed the crucifix at the steeple of the church.

We meet again, old friend. He creaked the door open and stepped inside.

The church was empty, dusty pews had gone unused for a while. Keeping with the tradition invoked by the Father since the first time Niccoló entered the church, he entered the confessional.

Their tradition was far from original, Niccoló would enter the confessional and confess a sin, the father would slide open the veil to reveal his face to the young man's which would lead to an intellectual criticism or discussion on the nature of sin, and whether or not absolution was a necessity. One such conversation for example, regarded the arbitrary nature of all sin: God seems to have bestowed the sins arbitrarily and could have named other sins if *She* pleased, this renders the idea of confession futile. Niccoló brought to the father's attention that rape was not among prohibited actions through the Ten Commandments but taking the lord's name in vain was. He could rape a woman and God would forgive him if the father absolved him through *Our Fathers* and *Hail Marys*, but screaming "God damn it" nested him a cell in Lucifer's iced lake. The father began to realize that he'd been preaching faith as fact and that perhaps some of the other things in religion didn't quite make sense either. The Vatican adores sheeple. Antonini stopped giving sermons that very week. Instead he began discussing the nature of a healthy, serene life with his congregation, with those that remained with him. Not all people are open to growth and intellection.

Niccoló sat down on the small confessional bench. The cold, damp wood pierced his pants and a shiver ran up his calves and paralyzed his legs. It was a fear of things to come. He suddenly realized he was afraid of what this journey may hold. Dev was a dangerous man, he could die. Would he care? Death was natural and if his death saved Beatrice, all the better. His heart pounded, his head and legs swiftly followed.

"Tell me father, I am in love, is that a sin?

The silhouette of a man could be seen through the veil.

"No my son, the sin would have been never to love at all."

The screened veil slid open.

"Niccoló? Have you returned?" the man of the cloth was quite affectionate to this young soul.

"No father, I've come to help a friend."

"Beatrice?"

"You know where she is?"

"She was with that thug Dev. He runs the neighborhood now you know, gets the boys hooked on drugs and pimps out the women."

Rage filled the young man's heart, "You know where they are?"

"He always hangs around the sit-down bar, you know the one."

"Yes, I know the one..." Niccoló's beast violently shook his frame.

They both stood up, exchanged a hug, and Niccoló made his way to Beatrice's house. Her sobbing mother answered the door.

"Mama?" Niccoló thought of Beatrice's parents as his own.

"Niccoló! My beloved Niccoló," and her parents thought of him as their son.

"Where is Bea—?"

Beatrice's mother sobbed hysterically, he couldn't make out what she was saying, it could have been: "He took her," or "I don't know," or "She's missing."

He'd kill Dev. He pecked her mother on each cheek and made his way to the bar. As he approached the corner he could hear the raunchy, crude language and high-pitched laughter of boys deluding themselves that they can pass as men. He turned the corner and saw Dev and his friends hanging around his car, drinking and shattering beer bottles on the street.

"Still a class act Dev," Niccoló stepped towards Dev aggressively. One of Dev's friends stood between them and tried to stop Niccoló. *Bad move.*

Niccoló hit a pressure point on the side of his neck and winded him then used a practiced 'tiger paw' technique on the left side of his face,

"Down monkey. I wasn't talking to you."

"Nicky!" Dev feigned pleasure in seeing an old friend, "The prodigal son has returned. Tell me, how are those Tuscan women? Or men, I don't know what you're into."

"Where is she?" Niccoló's oceanic gaze frightened two of Dev's goons.

"Where is who?" Dev's friends crowded closer at the thought of an inevitable confrontation.

Niccoló stared back,

"Oh, you mean that whore Beatrice... I don't know, probably around here somewhere."

"Talk about her like that again, and we're going to have a problem."

I have to find her. Two legs, two hands, one heart.

"Nicky Nicky Nicky. We've had a problem since the tenth grade, you know this. What you don't know is that things have changed since you left, maybe you haven't heard but I don't take kindly to threats. I want you to look around and see my friends, the bar-owner, that guy across the street, they all work for me. And I," he took a knife from his pocket and moved towards Niccoló, "Would not hesitate in spilling your blood in front of them all, that is the meaning of true power… they are afraid… as you should be. Don't come to me in a fury, trying to prove to yourself that you're more than a man. You don't understand me. I am not one of the sissy poems your mama has framed. Don't come here again… trying to pretend like you understand this life."

Niccoló looked at the knife, then Dev's henchmen, that was what they were after all. There was eight of them, not including the one recovering from the neck wound, that made nine monkeys total, ten including Dev. He didn't like his odds. He backed away, taking care not to turn his back to any of them. They weren't known for their honor.

He chuckled, "That's going to scar, something to remember me by," he pointed to the man holding his face and neck.

He walked backwards, felt the corner wall behind him and turned the corner slowly.

* * *

Niccoló ceased his schoolwork for fourteen months and remained in Gela to look for Beatrice. He attempted to put a stop to the corrupting influence of Dev and his gang. It was never enough, he couldn't become *The Rock* from *Walking Tall*. Unlike what movies perpetuate as myths of opportunity, he was only one man, and one man cannot change anything, even if he believes he can. Nearly all beliefs are illusions fit for distracted and misguided idealists.

Is the belief 'nearly all beliefs are illusions,' itself an illusory belief?

On top of his worsening mental condition, he couldn't find Beatrice. There were absolutely no leads on her whereabouts. His beard grew out, his face wrinkled; his forearms and palms looked like a sixty-year-old man's, he cried himself to sleep every night, living with the feeling of failure is not for all men.

After eighteen long months, her mother came to Niccoló and asked him to stop searching. She said he was destroying himself and he was perhaps the only good young man left in their little town. He should leave and find a new life somewhere else, that Beatrice was in all probability dead. Although merely speaking these words seemed to shatter her essence, it was the most probable outcome. Niccoló knew the odds were against him but since when had he become a man who only played the odds? Since he turned back on that day outside the bar? He eventually realized that everyone played the odds. He had to move away, and he did.

* * *

Eventually so did Dev, although no one quite knew where he went or what became of him. The kind of life he led and the people he did business with, odds were he was in jail or dead. If he wasn't, Niccoló vowed that he'd kill him if the opportunity presented itself. Beatrice made Niccoló feel alive, without her he felt dead and used up, he felt like a useless piece of space in a godforsaken land.

He joined Interpol and slowly created a taskforce to hunt Dev's organized crime ring. Even if he couldn't find Dev himself, he tried to take down all his friends, anyone he did business with and anyone he looked at. If no one would do business with him, he couldn't control anything or anyone.

Six years later, Niccoló got a lead on Dev's crew when he heard about the Fox and the Viking, it had his stench all over it. It seemed like the kind of dishonor Dev loved.

XIX
LOGIC

Clark's ringtone ascended and vibrated his ears as he woke from this nightmare. In a nightmare, every choice is wrong, every path is corrupted, everyone is taken away, a sick joke the dream world plays on its subjects to test their character. He felt dark, broken, and unhinged. As if the *Dahaka* had already consumed his entire essence and he'd become a zombie. Eventually his ringtone became so loud that it caused a migraine when he opened his eyes, he reached for it and missed, dropping both the phone and a bowl of oranges that someone had placed on the nightstand. He heard one of them rolling towards the light, each thump of its roll sounded like a knife repeatedly stabbing his brain.

A ray of light met his eye through the small gap between the curtain and the window. His migraine got worse as the light pierced his pupils, which constricted immediately. He could hardly move. He crawled to the window through the tiny light stream escaping from it, illuminating the room with a thin yellowish line. His head was ready to explode. He could count the seconds by the throbbing of his brain. Some*thing* knocked on his temples from inside him and wanted out. He reached up and completely closed the curtain, the yellow strip of light slowly disappeared. Darkness took over the entire room. He fell down with his back against the wall. He was at home in the darkness.

A light turned on, Clark squinted, his eyes were not used to so much light, the time bomb in his head ticked to a start.

"Hey hey hey, are you all right?" the familiar voice sounded like a silenced gunshot in the dead of night biting his heart from behind. Blood oozed out, there was too much of it inside his chest. He'd stepped into a parallel universe: Noirsinki, the squalling sky was barely a color, a dulling whitish grey that foreshadowed the consuming darkness in a matter of hours.

"Electra, the light. Please," he moaned.

Electra's hotel room was no doubt paid for by her father using extorted money from the little bakeries near Hamill. Thoughts of elitist *justice* and inequality only worsened his headache. She doused the Edisons and came over with a pill, a glass of water, and a pen in her right hand,

"Dream?" she walked across the room.

"I used to have dreams," he exhaled, *'Now they're nightmares,'* he thought.

"Here, take this… another migraine? You should really see a doctor," she placed the pen on the floor beside him and fed him the pill.

"Doctors are walking paradoxes," he gasped, "What's the pen for?"

"For the obvious," she said in a smoky voice.

"A love letter for me I hope," he was faking modesty.

"In your dreams," she said softly.

"You have no… idea," he attempted to rise. The pill scantly did its job. His cell phone rang a second time; Electra picked it up off the floor beside the bed and handed it to him.

"Business, I presume."

"They weren't lying when they said you were smart," Clark clicked and answered his phone.

"When who said?" Electra's perpetual subtle smile turned into an overt one.

Click. "Go for Kóróna," Clark greeted all people who called him the same way.

Electra could only hear one side of the conversation. Clark rarely made a sound, he listened attentively to every word at the other end of the line. After a minute or two, he finally said, "I'll get it done, have you told Alex?"

He hung up and closed his eyes for five seconds; the seconds felt like an eternity to Electra, Einstein's *Special Relativity*.

He reopened his eyes and looked at Electra, he looked as if he wanted to say something but the inner conflict was overwhelming. She smiled at him, the call must have been important.

He made his way to the bathroom and opened the bathroom drawer to reveal his used toothbrush and razor. He opened the mirrored medicine cabinet to take another migraine pill because he was hardly able to keep his eyes open from the pain. He brushed his teeth, put shaving cream on, ate the second pill, shaved, and closed the medicine cabinet. He suddenly noticed his face staring at himself through the mirror with small bits of shaving cream still on his face. He froze.

Who's staring at whom? Am I staring at him, or him at me?

Electra appeared behind him as he considered this thought and threw her arm around him. She kissed him through the bits of shaving cream—a cute scene for a Hollywood romance—and fixed her gaze to his eyes through the mirror, where he'd been staring. Their silent stare went on for too long until she used her index finger to turn his chin towards her eyes, their eyes now locked.

"You're not alone you know," her voice exuded compassion.

"I know," his was still, deep, and cold.

"You seem alone... lonely. You have me, we could go you know, away from all this," she was trying to reassure his nature, tame the beast...

"My love, alone and lonely are two different things."

Before she could respond, he put his hands on her waist and leaned in for a kiss. After a few seconds, he changed his mind and backed away.

"You're... too kind," he was surprised, "I don't deserve you, I don't want to hurt you, or see you hurt. I can't get attached." *Again, I can't afford to be attached to anyone ever again.*

Electra looked at him with her liquid, clear eyes. They were beautiful, *almost* perfect.

"How can you say that?" her soft voice nearly fell to a whisper.

"It doesn't matter," Clark stepped back and wiped the rest of the shaving cream off his face using a towel to his right. "Nothing matters," he whispered.

Electra arched her eyebrow.

It wasn't the same.

"That's a paradox."

"No, it's not," he fired back firmly.

"It is, if the foundation of this philosophy is 'nothing matters,' this includes within it 'everything matters,' because nothing is all-encompassing. Vice versa, if 'everything matters' is the base of your thought, everything includes within it the philosophy of 'nothing matters,' and everything is all encompassing. Ergo, the thesis and antithesis guide us to the conclusion that they are probably both false. Like believing X and not-X at the same time."

Clark's stoic gaze froze in a moment of awe. He looked at her with such admiration and respect that Electra's natural elegance could scarcely hold his stare.

"You're... right, I must alter my ideals," Clark understood his own paradoxes, he knew that the strongest man was the man who knew exactly where his mistake laid.

"You knew that though didn't you? It was too easy... you were... testing me?"

Clark stared back as this question echoed amongst the throbbing in his brain; he moved towards the closet and got dressed, selecting a dark suit from the many he'd brought on his previous encounters.

"I'm sorry, I hate to leave you but I have something rather pressing to attend to, we'll catch you later."

A Freudian slip.

We'll? Am I a different person than the beast? Are there two of us?

Is the beast a complex overture of his own identity and his own self? Or was the beast an independent and solitary character all on its own, complete with thoughts, beliefs, and ideals? He couldn't believe that the beast was singular, independent, that sometimes he was a monster regardless of the existence of this 'beast,' he had to believe they were different people as to disengage himself from the actions which had damned him.

As he walked by the table that Electra had been writing on prior to his awakening, he noticed the following note in Electra's writing,

"What is it then? Why, why do you resist? Why does your heart host so much cowardice?"

He was vexed for a moment, *Clark which edition is that? Shouldn't it be:*

"What is it then? Why, why dost thou delay?
Why is there such baseless bedded in thy heart?"

The note or letter appeared unfinished; Clark recognized this passage from the *Inferno*. He knew it too well. Logic told him he'd forget the past and focus his entire soul on the attentions of the worthy woman he'd grown to admire. Logic was a liar, it was only the Mandelbaum edition anyway. Who the hell uses *that* version?

Still, not liking things to be unfinished, Clark recited the rest of the passage to her as he approached the door, using the *Longfellow* translation,

"Daring and hardihood why hast thou not.
Seeing that three such ladies benedight."

Electra's eyes lit up, she could count on her fingers the amount of people on the planet who'd understand a Dante reference, and the odds of two of them in the same room left her in a moment of astonishment.

"I hope you won't be seeing three ladies though," she quipped as he opened the door.

Three billion ladies couldn't save me from the Inferno, "Three billion ladies won't compare with you," his use of such archaic phrases were vexing to the average person just as using the *Longfellow* edition of the *Divina Commedia* would be in this day and age, but Electra appreciated them. She understood that he was born in the wrong period, in the wrong species of the many 'intelligent' ones in the universe.

It ought to have given him hope for our perversely spiraling and deranged species. It ought to have but it didn't.

Are all *intelligent* creatures in the universe consuming, perverse, and evil? Then perhaps a different adjective ought to be used to describe them.

He left for his apartment. Electra thought she heard a thud outside her door but shrugged it off. Clark was standing near the door with his back to the wall, smashing the back of his head into the wall behind him. It wasn't helping his migraine... but there were things he wanted to forget.

*   *   *

He didn't know what he was thinking. Most bars wouldn't know a triple espresso if one climbed onto their counter and told them how to make one. At least it was better than the ostentatious low-fat soybean vanilla mocha cappuccino the girl in front of him ordered.

The storm was vicious. It nearly tore the glass doors off its hinges, startling the two women in front of him. It looked liked it wanted to talk to him but he wouldn't let it. He and storms weren't on the best of terms.

"*Triple* espresso?" the barista asked, emphasizing the 'triple.' They must not get many people here other than the mindless drones or zombies who order what they'd advertised that week.

"Yes," Clark tried his best not to appear condescending.

Most people conflate stoicism with apathy. She was only doing her job. Reminded him of Her...

Do you care about her? If you've never cared for anything or anyone, have you lived? His thoughts roared, asking millions of questions.

She started making the low fat mocha. The girl who'd ordered it looked attractive enough to hit on and dumb enough to fall for the first guy who complimented her intelligence. Their eyes met and she froze.

Knight takes Pawn. Clark you sound like John.

She's probably used to staring at men and having them gnaw at her toenails. She blushed and her cheeks turned scarlet red.

Knight takes Queen. Stop it Clark.

She flipped her hair in Clark's direction.

Checkmate.

Her hair smelled like fresh strawberries, how he loved the smell, how he hated it.

The barista grounded the Nicaraguan coffee for her latte. The smell inebriated him, that's what She smelled like. It triggered a hundred flashbacks. He felt like The Wolverine to her Jean Grey, fated for pain, an Algerian love knot turned in the pit of his stomach.

His mind howled with ferocity. He traveled the world to get away from her.

Paris: The Louvre only reminded him of her body. A canvas of perfection, an inherent piece of art. He wanted to tear every painting off its easel and replace it with portraits of her.

Milan: her simple elegance, she made a light-coloured t-shirt and dark jeans look like a long black Prada dress.

Venice: The City of Lovers, it was self-explanatory. He could barely spend an hour there.

Perhaps something in Tokyo? There is no hope for some people... her discipline echoed a Zen Master's stillness.

The desert in Dubai will surely help him forget, there's nothing out there but heat and sand. It did for a while, until a stand storm diminished his visibility and the dancing specks of sand reminisced her enigma. He couldn't see ahead with her, couldn't push aside the sand in their hourglass and reveal his true passion.

Where would his thoughts be free of her? Drowning his past in a wine chalice at a remote bar in Juankoski, he realized he'd never be free.

You can't outrun your thoughts. You'll run in circles, fall into an abyss, spend years crawling out only to fall back in, only the hole's grown deeper.

Thoughts are a broken record of memories had, you pick up the pieces in order to reassemble it but cut yourself on its edges. Your identity shifts and changes with each scrape because your memories change. Each shattered fragment tells you the same thing, *"If you've never cared for anything or anyone, have you lived?"*

The scar on his right cheek ached, his rough flesh wouldn't allow for such ideas. It wouldn't stop hurting, he got it years ago, it didn't make any sense. If pain was weakness leaving the body he'd be Superman by now. Maybe he was, and she was his kryptonite.

He wanted to clench her hand in his, let the smooth smell of her lavender body wash fill his nostrils. He wanted her warm lips pressed against his, her perfect body next to his. He wanted to gaze into her eyes; they say the eyes are windows to the soul, but her eyes were like doorways to utopia.

There he sat, in some post-modern bullshit café drowning his thoughts in a tiny espresso cup blocks away from her and realizing they were worlds apart. Maybe the thing moving inside his brain was really a bullet that wasn't there yet.

XX
The Only Currency

Clark's key rotated the little cogs in the lock system, he opened the door to his apartment. *Home sweet home*, the prior night had opened another door in his head. A resonance of his past, a beast blinking its eyes in the pits of his skull, he closed his eyes and the black void consumed the images in his head. He locked the door and moved towards the right corner of his apartment. He rolled up his oriental rug and counted three marble tiles, removing the fourth and running his fingers on the silenced Colt 1911 handgun placed on top stacks of cash of moderate to high denominations. In between the wads of cash were pieces of paper and numerous flash drives. He extracted the gun and the holster from the tile and put it to the side. He closed the tile, placed the holster inside his jacket via a strap, cocked the gun, administered the safety and placed it on the inner left side of his jacket. He placed the rug back on the false tile and headed out. He was waiting at the corner of *Espace* and *Hamill* for the person he was set to meet.

He noticed a suspicious black caravan parked across the street. Durante, monitoring the house took a video print of Clark to run against the database back at the station, oblivious to the fact that Clark was a suspect in Matthews's Jane Doe case. Clark lit a cigar and placed a small set of ear buds in his ear. Durante zoomed in on the cigar,

"Man has good taste."

Durante watched Clark stand like a statue, lost in thought for ten to fifteen minutes before a second man yanked the buds out of his ear and leaned in to listen,

"According to the conditioned traditions of my preceding generations, I am not 'me' right now, as in presently, but rather, I am the me from the past, or rather, the sum of my past identity.

Naturally, this leads to a bad logic jump, my past is identified as more the 'real' me than the present me.

Random memories are selected from a bank of infinite ones and abstracted as vital or significant to the shaping of my identity, making identification with the past easier than governing my present identity."

The man threw the headphones back at Clark, who was so enchanted by his fool's paradise that he'd barely noticed his companion had removed a bud from his ear, let alone threw it back at him.

"Ya don't even listen to music like the rest of us," his friend sneered, "Such an OG."

Clark puffed the last bit of his Monte Cristo Club, dropped it, and stepped on it as he retracted the headphones wire and placed them in his right back pocket,

"It's an obscure Zen tape a friend recommended some years ago. I don't expect you to understand," he looked at his Breitling and at the same time noticed Alexander's brand new Air Jordan basketball hi-tops, "You're three minutes late."

"Ye ye ye, I know, I was with this girl… thanks for da wing…" his sarcasm wasn't funny, "Leaving me like dat at da club… also guy, Otto said he saw you with my sister in the woods?" his enunciation became half-decent as the words left his mouth.

"Otto is a reliable source for gossip. You should always take what he says seriously."

Alex knew Clark was being sarcastic.

They made their way into the house through a side entrance.

The silence was uncomfortable. Clark thrived on silence and relished it. His partner did not.

"Okay Tin Man. Besides, you're my partner, I *should* know everything about you," he finally said to Clark as he unzipped his Reebok windbreaker.

They entered the house to a haze of cigar smoke. There were three men in the main room. Sliding doors on each wall and anti-surveillance tape on each side isolated this room from the rest. This place was safe from Durante. Behind a large wooden desk was the boss, Don Torrino himself. A man of fifty-five to sixty years of age with an ever growing belly from all the underserved indulgences, a thick white beard, and gelled white hair. He had a big nose and a big mouth to match, small ears that nonetheless seemed to hear everything. To his right was his consigliere and sitting on the couch opposite him behind two large empty chairs was his second best enforcer, Draco Laufeia (pronounced laa-fee-ya, his articulation). The don's top enforcer, Devo Niemetti had been missing for a while now. It was like entering a scene from a Coppola film.

The don was talking on the phone, his voice was higher-pitched than anyone would like but he was the don.

"I understand Benetto. Two million here, three million there, pretty soon you're going to be talking real money," his eyes darted up, "I don't know where Ventoni is... I'll call you back."

Did he just say Ventoni?

Click.

The don looked straight at Clark, "The Calvanos seem to think we had something to do with that safety deposit box mess downtown."

Clark slightly tilted his head. Was the don implying something?

The don continued, "No matter. Bullets never lie."

"What's this business with Otto last night?" Laufeia barked, "His father is on retainer. Show him respect."

Clark bowed his head in the direction of the don, not the man behind him. Laufeia didn't like Clark. The feeling was mutual.

"Don Torrino, we have but one currency in this world—"

"Respect." The don interrupted.

The respect shared between these two men was past the point of comprehension for the onlookers. They seemed to understand each other. "You could learn a thing or two from this man Alexander."

Clark's partner had been none other than Alexander DiCeéver. Had the room not been fitted with anti-wireless surveillance tape, or had Durante actually had a warrant for taps on the Torrino house, he'd have heard that the two suspects in Matthews's case were people with ties to the local mob.

The don had finished about half of his cigar; his eyes dashed to Draco, a subtle nod that presumably meant he should offer Clark one.

"I know these are your achilles tendon my son."

Amongst other things.

Clark extracted one of the long cigars from the don's humidor and lit it.

It's only a Don Tomàs, nothing special.

You'd think this guy would have better taste in cigars, but hey, watching Goodfellas half a dozen times doesn't make you an elegant gangster. An elegant gangster, is there such a thing?

The consigliere placed two folders in between Alex and Clark, who now sat down in the chairs across the desk. Clark glanced at the folder on his side of the table for a few seconds, studied it, and put it down.

"As always don. No women. No children."

Draco laughed and said in Italian, "He thinks we care about *his* rules."

"As always. Look at the honor Draco. The honor runs through his whole body," the gilding of his voice cracked for a second, "Your airplane tickets are provided. Weapons will be provided via a hidden cache by one of our guys there. You'll be going to northern Europe. You should love it there V. Besides, I heard the storm has slowed down but I also hear it's always sleeting, snowing, hailing, and I don't know—raining cats and dogs up there. Don't worry, I've assured them to secure you a silenced Colt with a custom printed handle grip."

Clark got up with the cigar on his lip, bowed to the don and exited the dwelling, Alexander followed soon thereafter.

Durante took video and photo snapshots of the house and the people entering and exiting.

"What took you so long princess? Never mind... have them check out that car as well," Clark pointed to Durante's minivan, an action the latter saw on the camera. He knew his cover was blown but this didn't matter to him. He had often heard or seen Alexander boasting and making fox puns on the tapes inside the house, his suspicion that Alexander was The Fox grew from a mere belief to fact and he hence deduced that if Alexander was The Fox, Clark must be The Viking. He drove to the station with this new intel as Clark and Alex made their way to the airport.

XXI
INSTANT REPLAY

Clark and Alexander had an uneventful adventure through security. No doubt airport security was so worried about the non-existent terrorist threat, a gratitude owed to useless, corrupt leeches, *politicians* for short, that they neglected to notice two young gentlemen, one of which with overt ties to the mob, boarding a plane bound for a northern European isle.

The first class cabin was very nice, and although Clark refused the champagne offered to him by the steward and opted for a glass of scotch instead (twelve-year-old Springbank), Alexander had drinks of all kinds and was completely hammered by the time the plane had reached cruising altitude. Dozing in and out of consciousness, he turned to the brooding Clark,

"You know what you should do? Smile more, women love men who smile... they hate thinkers, love doers."

Clark turned to him with a look that could be described as contempt.

I'd rather be hated for who I am than loved for what I am not, he thought.

"I'll keep it in mind."

"You're always thinking (he pronounced it *tinking*), always swimming deeper than—(pronounced *dan*)—your ability as a swimmer merits," Alexander slurred, unable to keep his eyes open, "But I guess that's why my dad likes you more," he sighed.

Clark took out the journal from his inner left jacket pocket. He put the pen to the paper but couldn't write a single word.

* * *

He set his schoolbag down at his favorite café.

"Ahhh, Clark, *so* nice to see *you* again, the usual?" the flirtatious waitress was a petite redhead with adorable little freckles around her nose.

"Not yet Olivia, I'm waiting for someone."

Aren't we all, she thought.

She smiled as Clark pulled out the latest draft of a rather large paper from his bag and made notes on it.

"3:56," he checked his email from his phone. The meeting was set to start at 4:00 sharp.

4:00, 4:05, 4:10, time was passing linearly and Clark was starting to hate this girl before he'd even met her. They'd have to work together for a year? Talk? Share? Engage in social events? This girl could barely make a meeting on time.

Maybe something came up Clark. A gentleman never questions a lady.

4:12, *who is 'that'?* Clark couldn't think. He couldn't breathe. His eyes were set on the most beautiful woman he'd ever seen. She hastily entered the café but managed to look as elegant as a goddess addressing her mortal subjects. Her legs went on for years, her doe eyes dashed around and looked for someone in the café, her transcendental lips pouted to probably catch this lucky low-minded but physically capable athlete.

Whoa. Am I meant to be here? Is she the reason I'm here? I'm sure the silly girl I'm supposed to meet with will email me with a list of excuses on why she couldn't make it. This other girl though, she's something else. Give her your number Clark. You're an idiot. You don't give a girl like that a number, she has enough numbers to last her a lifetime. You give her the world, the sun, the moon, the entire galaxy. You give her your heart, your soul. She'd take good care of it. She's an angel, they're hard to come by... Move Clark.

He got up to approach her and for some gloomy reason found himself wondering if she'd ever cry.

She'd never cry. Angels don't cry.

I know I know, but 'if' an angel cried, what would it look like?

"Excuse me," she said before he could open his mouth.

Oh wow, her voice is slowing your heartbeat. It sounds like an ancient harp—what are those called again?

Shut up, I got this.

"Do you have a second?" she followed up.

It's the delicate plucking of thin strings to create a sort of tranquil resonance and create a stillness deep within you, or I, or the both of us.

Time is anything but linear.

He broke her gaze. *What the hell are you doing Clark? Did you just look away, you look her in the eyes damn it! What's the matter with you? A stoic sage leaves no room for trivial emotions like love, anxiety, fear, or courage. There is nothing but truth.*

HEY! Her eyes are like flames, they burn through to my soul. Can I... let me do this. Shut up for 3 minutes.

"Yes," Clark's extraordinary voice forced her to watch his lips and try to *see* the words leaving his mouth.

The café's entire attention was focused on the couple, her beauty created a harmony with his cultured mannerisms; the noise had died but for their conversation. The woman took *everyone's* breath away.

"I'm looking for a... Clark," she shuffled a small piece of paper. "We're supposed to serve on a committee together... I'm boring you. Do you know him?"

Boring me? You could talk about paint drying and it wouldn't bore me.

HEY. WAKE UP CLARK! The voice in his head screamed.

I think she said your name, did you hear your name? Or are you hearing things, going schizophrenic like Van Gogh?

I'd cut off my ear—my eye, my heart for this woman, he thought. "I'm sorry, did you say Clark?" he couldn't tell whether she'd actually said it or if he imagined it.

"Yes, a Clark..." she searched in her bag, pulled out her phone and scrolled through an email, "Kóróna, Clark Kóróna, please tell me you know him. I hope he's nice."

"I know him yes."

"Do you know him well?" she asked, "What type of guy is he... not very punctual..." she pressed her phone, the screen lit up her face, she was prettier than she looked, "Since he's late."

So are you but you were probably talking to God up there in heaven.

Oh come on Clark. You should order a cheesecake with your espresso. You're a walking cliché.

"Unfortunately not, but I've heard he's very charming, quite handsome, and a little dry in his humor."

"What does he look like? Is he here?"

"Yes," *I can't wait to see where you're going with this.*

"Well... could you point him out or are you going to keep wasting my time?"

Feisty, nice.

Clark extended his hand, "Clark Kóróna, it's a pleasure."

She rolled her eyes, "Of course."

They shook hands, her soft touch tamed the beast. There was no need to keep it caged nor worry about it suddenly breaking free.

He escorted her to his table, slid the chair out and placed his palm up to help her sit down.

"Thank you," she sat down.

Olivia rushed over.

"Hi, what can I get you?"

The princess looked at Clark. There was a faint smile on his part, "Ladies first."

"A coffee please."

"How do you like it?" Olivia seemed to be in a sudden rush, didn't want to keep them waiting.

* * *

"Ladies and gentlemen, this is your captain speaking. Just wanted to let you know that the wind is on our side and we'll be landing twenty to twenty-five minutes earlier than scheduled.

Clark looked down at the inkblot formed on the empty paper from his pen. He intricately folded the paper and put it in his right pants pocket. The pocket bulged from the pieces of paper he had stashed there.

Their flight landed at 2:00 P.M. local time. The storm was worse here than back home. The cursed thing followed him wherever he went. Raindrops as big as a man's fist and as hard as a boxer's jab sloshed across his face. Alexander was wobbling all over the place and hitting on everything with a pulse, and some things without. He was feeling the residual effect of listening to too much *music* where people with backwards snapbacks rhyme about all their women and money. Clark checked them into the hotel drenched, told Alex to rest, they'd take two days off and strike on the third day at 8:30. He set Alex's alarm in case he lost track of time, he wasn't known for his punctuality. No doubt Alex would be sober when it came time to do the deed. This intoxication was nothing new to Clark, it had become a ritual for Alexander, who was forced into these cruel jobs by his father, Don Torrino, in an old-school hope that Alex would 'toughen-up' and be aptly prepared to take over the business one day. Clark almost pitied him… almost. It was natural for someone who was forced to take the life of another man to drink himself to the grave or drown himself in an ocean of meaningless sex and decadent luxury. It was all an attempt of harsh deletion, like a gambler who thinks his system will beat the house or a computer user dragging files to the Recycle Bin. You can never win back the money you lose to the house and you can't just erase your memories.

The past can't be deleted. Nothing is *ever* quite so simple.

Clark entered his hotel room and moved towards the bed. He laid his head on the pillow and felt a bout of insomnia creeping from the remote parts of his mind. He couldn't sleep; his head was filled with thoughts of the past. The past was an action reply he couldn't stop, everything reminded him of it, everything echoed of his love. He'd get mad at himself for letting his thoughts stray there and get mad at everyone for reminding him of it, but it wasn't their fault, it was his. It was all in his head. The past can haunt him, but the haunting isn't real, he was imagining it and it was consuming him. He tried to focus his thoughts on Electra, on the present just like his Zen tapes taught him. Electra *was* beautiful after all but he hated her for making him feel this way. To make him choose. He felt the rise of the old familiar feelings, he hated them, he welcomed them. Before he could gather his thoughts he realized he'd been contemplating this for nearly five hours. He went down to the hotel bar, scotch cures the ails of the past.

*　*　*

Two days later, he studied the folder of the reconnaissance mission the others had set up, the routine, the people, everything about the target. He got up slowly and put his carry-on suitcase on the bed. He opened it to reveal a set of black clothes: dress shirt, dress pants, long pea coat, dress shoes, and a belt, no doubt his attire for the job. The target was a forty-two-year-old man who'd *turned dark side*. *Turned dark side* was a reverse joke the don made about any member of the family that turned state's evidence. He said they all enjoyed the gangster life. He actually took a shot at Alexander's style and pronounced it *gangsta'*. He said they loved the money, the power, and the women but it wasn't enough, so they go to the cops and try to live in peace by betraying the rest of their family. Everything is never enough.

The don said, "Some of us have enough and we don't want our lives trifled with."

The guy was a killer and a rapist, Clark was happy to abide: *street justice is the closest thing to true justice on this greed-filled planet of consumption.* Institutional justice is so perverted and damaged that it's hardly worth commenting on. The rich and powerful abide by their own laws, a secret lawlessness similar to the town of Deadwood, while the masses are forced to abide by a rigorous set of rules and regulations that carry consequences much harsher than the supposed 'crime.'

Clark received a call from the front desk informing him of a package. He rode the elevator down to the lobby and signed for it, it was no doubt the equipment for the job. He tore open the box, inside was his own silenced Colt 1911 and a silenced 22-caliber handgun, the latter belonging to Alex. He made his way to Alex's hotel room.

He opened the door and found Alex dressed in *his* attire for the job: black pants, shirt, and windbreaker jacket. Alex reached for the box Clark was carrying and extracted his 22 and placed it in his windbreaker's pocket. No words were exchanged. Clark strapped his gun to the inner left side of his jacket and they moved to the lobby separately, they didn't want to arouse suspicion. Clark had studied the route from the hotel to the rendezvous on the plane.

It was within walking distance and he was there in minutes. Alex, having no mental awareness for such things in between shots of vodka and gin, got there six minutes late.

"I know I know, two minutes this time though (pronounced *dough*) right? New record?"

"Actually, it was six," Clark thought it was one kind of new record.

They approached a house foreshadowed with a darkness that would've made Bret Ellis wince. From the front of the house, Clark looked in through the window and could see the target sitting on a couch watching TV.

He pointed to his eyes and then to the target, Alexander nodded and made a half-moon shape with his right arm to signal that he'd go in through the back door and surprise the target. As Alex walked away from Clark and made his way around the house, Clark froze knee deep in freshly cut lawn grass. Looking in, he saw a woman come from an area that looked to be the kitchen holding a bowl of popcorn. He was adamant about his rule: no women. He's not a barbarian, he was happy to deliver *true* justice to members of the Calvano family or other murderers walking free, victims' families having hired the help of Don Torrino for true justice. Women were sacred to him. Goddesses trapped amongst monsters and thieves.

"Alex, abort, Alex... abort," his whispers fell on empty air near the direction Alex had disappeared to. He took a step towards Alex's path in an attempt to get to him before he'd entered the house. He knew he was too late when the back door at the far end of the den opened and he saw Alex entering the house. The woman was now cuddling with the target on the couch as they enjoyed a movie. Neither had the slightest inclination of what was about to befall them. People live their lives never quite realizing how close they are to their demise. Alex extracted his gun and quietly cocked it. The horror in Clark's eyes grew with each step Alexander made towards the targets.

Calm as a politician caught with a high-end escort, he made his way to the front door and picked the lock via the tools the don bestowed upon him. He cut the alarm keypad from the inside and neared the living room. Alex was unaware of the approaching Clark behind him. Alex stood above the woman and pointed the gun to her head.

The target should always be the first to be eliminated. Clark wondered if he'd been deceived. Were he and Alexander given different files? He remembered there being two files... and Alex did stay for a few moments after he had left. *Was she the target?*

It seemed like the rain came down harder at this realization, either that or his hearing suddenly improved. He could hear every raindrop land on the window to his left. He tried staring outside. Too many rainy nights, too many misguided campaigns for absolution. Time moved forward, nothing changed.

The fury of the storm echoed the linearity of his life, blasting forward into an eventual bloody climax.

Every story must have a hero and a villain. This is how Clark understood every story he'd ever read and all of them abided by this rule. He knew he wasn't a hero. Did process of elimination render him a villain? His life was *his* story after all. Was he the villain in his own story? Was this how tortured he'd become? How dark? Maybe goodness *was* a myth. There are no heroes, just rivalries between villains, the villains inside us.

A silenced gunshot carries a foreboded omen. Alex pulled the trigger, "death," the bullet whispered to the woman's companion on the couch. A lightning flash blinded Clark. Another fallen woman he'd failed to save. He fell into the void and saw now how deep it'd become.

She was dead. The man jumped out of his seat and pulled a sawed-off shotgun from underneath one of the couch cushions. He aimed it towards the sound of the gunshot in the blink of an eye. Alex dove behind a small counter as the first shell blew half of it away, the debris blinding all three of them. Clark lain on his back with his gun aimed at the man and had yet to fire. The man had another round in the chamber. Clark hadn't moved, lying on the floor of the living room like a jungle cat, half-hidden behind the couch already stained with the stream of the woman's blood. Maybe this was a dream and darkness was about to consume everything and he'd wake up beside his long lost love or beside Electra or alone in his apartment. It wasn't real, it couldn't be. How he wished he were right but he knew he was never that lucky.

"ANYTIME now V," Alex yelled from behind the counter.

The man looked in the direction of the kitchen and could scarcely see Alex crouched behind his island. He had The Fox cornered. He turned his head as he took a step towards Alex and spotted Clark lying on his back just outside the door with a gun pointed at him. The man knew he'd been beaten. Clark shook his head once to signal the man that he'd been bested, that he shouldn't try anything, but his still eyes were conflated with coldness, which made the man think that Clark would fire anyway. He lifted his shotgun towards Clark. Our *villain's* sole choice was to squeeze the trigger, and as soon as the bullet pierced the man's heart, it destroyed the identity of the man who'd pulled the trigger.

The man fell to his knees and into a pool of his own blood, reaching towards the couch where his heart truly laid. Clark fell into a pool of tears he'd shed for this man. All things start as black and white but before you know it, the colors meet and smudge, becoming some unrecognizable shade of grey. He sank into thoughts about the choices he'd made. Were they his choices, or were they merely a predestined linear sequence of events? Was he a hero? A villain? Did he love her? Did he have a choice? The abyss is clever. No matter how long you spend trying to run away from it, you fall back in the second it wants you.

The victim's shotgun would've surely woken the neighbors. The police were probably on their way.

Get up Clark... misanthropic lethargic self-loathing will come soon enough, trust me, but for now, get... up!

* * *

He would've lain there for days had Alex not come hobbling out of the kitchen clutching his shoulder. The widespread shotgun shell had wounded him. He deserved it. He was the kind of guy you love to hate anyway. His pains amused everyone. Clark was hard pressed to help a wounded Alex as they made their way back to the hotel, walking at a normal pace as if not to stir the pot of inevitable suspicion. Although any cop spotting two men; one of which is bleeding from the shoulder dressed in all black, and being carried by a friend, would be stupid not to stop them for a spot-check.

The plan was to drive back to their native land using separate cars and various trains in case someone discovered the body and an investigation placed an alert on airport personnel for departure flights. The neighbors calling the police snatched their head start and they had no choice but to go to Plan B.

Clark hadn't thought about fate two days. Nor had he slept, but he did thank her for this contingency plan even though it was his idea. He had no intention to return to the city *or* to the family. Nor did he want to sit next to a murderous thug for two and a half hours.

He understood their deception. He was an outsider, a loner without any real purpose or goal. It was obvious that his would be the next file placed before Alex. The picture of him and the barefoot angel in the rain suddenly popped into his head. Death was a certainty; the time of our meeting was not. For the first time in a long time, Clark realized he didn't want to be dead. He decided it wasn't his time yet.

It was cute… really.

What if they went after Her? He had to stay alive long enough to bring down this house of cards. What if Ventoni *wasn't* bluffing? What if he *is* watching her? Clark had to risk it, risk his own life for her safety.

The worst-case scenario was that he'd die before killing *any* of them but that wouldn't be too bad either since they'd leave her alone. He wouldn't be so tortured if he were dead. He'd be at peace.

I'm not going to die at the hands of murderers, he thought, neglecting the paradox of his circumstances. Unless he died of natural causes, it would have to be a murderer that'd kill him by definition. Besides, dying of natural causes in his line of work was rarer than a virgin Playmate.

He wanted to give up the life and get away. He wanted to live in solitude with Her. The scorching arched eyebrow melting in his fireplace was all he could think about.

He helped Alex stitch up the wound, not saying a word about the change of plans until the latter broke this silent promise.

"We had to dawg. The witness was the woman. I needed yo help, I know y'all don't do bitches, although I don't know why not," Alex cringed and looked away from the stinging of the wound.

"Don't talk," Clark was colder than usual.

'The *witness?*' he thought. The poor woman wasn't even a criminal, not a murderer or an enforcer for a rival family. She was just somebody someplace at the wrong time.

Sounds like my life story.

He blamed himself. He should have never underestimated the capacity of other people to use his skills to further their own motives. There'd only been one person he didn't mind using his soul. It belonged to her anyway. She was the samurai and he was the sword, she could do with his... *her* soul as she pleased.

An innocent life taken, this was his first time. He wondered how many times he'd been lied to, how many innocents Alex had executed while Clark stood as the token henchmen or punk that's the first to die or get arrested as soon as the heat mirages toward them. He'd become the worst kind of villain: the expendable one. At least the man's death was honorable, he wouldn't have wanted to live anyway, his woman died in front of him, what or who would that man become? *Him?*

That is how I would want to die. That would be a good death.

His thoughts scrambled into incoherence, they should never roam freely. He had to cage the beast. It was becoming harder to control; this was perhaps the last time he could. There were only a few serene moments that could tame it and even now he doubted whether the memories of those moments could keep it caged.

Alex wobbled up and handed Clark the keys. They got in their cars and drove away in perpendicular directions. Alex to his father's house, no doubt to transform into the son he'd wanted all his life: Alexander Torrino, how Kafkaesque.

XXII
TRAINED IN MADNESS

Clark scrapped the plan and drove to a remote city in the Scandinavia, still wondering about the choices he'd made. His depth had become a cliché. His past choices were all he thought about, lost in the void he'd been trying to evade all his life.

There are no choices. You do something because you have to do it. The choice qua choice comes after when you ask what if I did 'this' instead of 'that.' The what-if world, erroneously presumed to be all bliss and no mistakes, exists only in abstract theory.

A friend once told Clark "Everything is perfect in theory."

The paradox was; if you had acted in the *'what if'* scenario, it wouldn't be *you* asking these questions, it'd be a different identity asking a different set of questions.

He loathed himself. He tried to run from his past but he realized the past wasn't about geographical distance. Running from your past is impossible. A man can't run from himself. He can't run from his destiny and deny his nature. His nature has to win. The gravitational pull of the abyss is too strong. He'd spent so much time in the void he'd started to consider it his home.

He stopped at a small town six hours away and parked outside a train station. Staring at the steering wheel of the car in the dark he finally got out and tried to enter the remote station before he heard a voice,

"Excuse me."

Clark couldn't see where it came from, it sounded like a whisper and it grew louder and louder,

"Excuse me..." he finally saw a man silhouetted under a dead light post, exacerbating his already ebbing mental condition. He never had trouble seeing in the dark, all the time he spent in the dark of his apartment and the forest during his ritual night walks had rendered his vision like a cat's. Here however, he could scarcely see the man, wondering if he was a figment of his imagination. His fearless curiosity got the better of him and he approached the character submerged as if nearing him through a mist.

"Yes?"

The man took a step forward to reveal his face under the adjacent lamppost. He was an old man of about seventy to seventy-five wearing a light grey homburg to hide his thinning white hair. He wore a casual shirt under a leather vest and old dress pants. Despite all this, Clark noticed he had perfect teeth and commanding eyes.

For the second time in his life, Clark had trouble holding a gaze and it was he who broke the silence, "Yes old man? Would you like change?"

"That would be fantastic."

Clark reached for his wallet.

"No my son. I didn't mean change as in money. I thought you were asking me generally."

"Like change the world? An aphorism?"

"Yes."

"Clever for a man who sits in darkness waiting for visitors to enter a train station in a town whose population is fifteen hundred," Clark was not in the mood for games.

The man placed his hand where Clark's heart should be. "Better to be cleverer than you look than to look cleverer than you are."

"There's anything there old man," Clark took a step back to negate the touch.

"Hmmm," the man waved his hand in the direction of Clark's heart as if he were still touching it. Clark's heartbeat elevated for the second time in his life, he thought it was impossible.

"Who is the woman you dream of?" he looked up through the brim of his hat, "In the bistro, in an office, at a party?"

Clark took another step back so he was completely out of the man's reach. His augmented 1911 trembled above his belt.

"Excuse me?"

"The woman. Who is she?"

"It doesn't matter," Clark replied.

"Okay, tell me what matters. Tell me *who* matters."

"Nothing."

"Nothing matters? That's a paradox son, nothing matters means everything matters and vice versa.

"Do we know each other?" Clark took a step towards the man.

"Of course not."

"Who are you?" Clark inquired.

"If you never care about anyone or anything, can you say you're alive?" the man ignored Clark's question.

"Who are you?" Clark repeated aggressively. Charlatans irked him almost as much as hipsters.

"Just an unknown... like you," the man smiled.

"I am not bothered by the fact that I am unknown, I am bothered by the fact that I do not know others," Clark returned.

"Confucius. What else you got?" the man was certainly ticking all the boxes and passing all of Clark's intellectual tests.

"You did not fail her son, it's important you know that. I know what you dream and why you yearn for death," the man hovered his hand over Clark's forehead. "Why you think of her. It is not your time, you'll know when it's your time... she's always thought of you... what is her name? Ahhh. Of course. Someone else? *Electra* is not your destiny; no man can change his destiny."

Someone probably hired this guy. How does he know so much about me? Clark thought about the *Dahaka* for less than a second. It'd look like a person if it existed in real life. The depiction in the game wouldn't be literal. That wouldn't make sense. It'd be like saying Bigfoot was after you. He'd doubted his belief system before his skeptic instinct clocked in like an alcoholic in the midst of a mid-life crisis. He mistakenly thought this was some mentalist who had memorized a universal set of questions he'd ask and mastered their linked responses in a form of cold reading. Asking a broad question and waiting for the slightest reaction from your prey by reading their facial reactions or body language and pushing them on the subjects they seem most uncomfortable with. He seemed like a man who hustled young people out of some cash now and again. After all, which young man or woman doesn't think of love, passion, death. These are elements of life youth are only becoming accustomed to and thereby it is only natural that they would think of them as soon as they are presented with their illusionary manifestations.

He mentioned Electra though, how would he know that name? Lucky guess?

Even Clark had to admit the exchange was more enigmatic than he preferred. He offered a cigar to the old man, who refused, and instead pointed to it and said,

"When it's time, look for it."

"Look for what?" Clark looked down to light his cigar but when he looked up, the man was gone. He turned his head left and right in an attempt to try to find him. He could see perfectly through the darkness again. Had the man's presence diminished his vision? Was this exchange real or was he going mad?

Probably the latter.

He didn't smoke the cigar. He just stood there under the cold lamppost in the darkness in deep contemplation until the cigar burned itself out and burned his lip. A new scar on his lower lip. He snapped back to reality and began searching for the man in the nearby alleys and streets, all to no avail.

He wanted to look for a motel as far away as he could. He entered the train station, bought a ticket to the farthest city on the map, population 780, and boarded the train.

XXIII
THOUGHTFUL INSISTENCE

He took the first available seat. The thing inside his temples banged on them, it wanted out. The pain traveled to his chest and the throbbing grew as each moment passed. He felt like one of the nimrods from that *Alien* movie. A beast about to tear out of him and take his life with it. To be reborn as a monster from hell. He tried to focus his thoughts. Think of the sea and its calm still waters. The sky with its crisp blue color. A cloud appeared overhead and the thunder almost tore his eardrum. The still waters suddenly formed waves bigger than a skyscraper. The mental image was too pronounced and nearly blinded him. He closed his eyes for a second and tried to repress the migraine.

"Look at me when I'm talking to you!" A voice bellowed from the end of the train. He opened his eyes and immediately looked in the direction of the voice. The long train car slid into focus.

He felt the blood flowing from his heart to his head, every drop of it. *Why me? Why is it always me? Every time.*

He looked around. There were ten other people there. One of them was a 6 foot-something black guy with shoulders as wide as a *Biggest Loser* contestant. Was he just going to stand there? How about that guy? He's got Chuck Norris's beard and Arnold Schwarzenegger's hair. He's going to watch too? Bastard actually looked like he was enjoying it. Clark looked at the operator to his left.

You don't see that down the car? The man shut the operator's door. Not his problem. *Degenerates. Losers. All of you. Are none of you going to make a move?*

The voice stopped being just a voice. He became a hand moving violently towards his lady's neck. *Get up Clark. Get. Up. That's your cue.*

The warm blood traveled swiftly to his legs. His head and chest became as still as a statue, the throbbing stopped. He exhaled deeply. He did what he did best: save defenseless women. A knight whose only purpose is to save damsels in distress. Feminists would eat him alive.

He stood up and looked back where he'd been sitting. The beautiful girl next to him somehow managed a smile with eyes full of shock and fright. He had to open the cage and free the beast. Her smile meshed with the inevitable freeing of the beast reminded him of one of the cantos in the *Inferno* about beholding a beast while being protected by a famous sage. The canto was argumentative, was the fair lady the beast or the famous sage? Perhaps Dante himself was the beast, who knows?

I'll take it. You are what you are. You are your nature. I can't change that. I accept it.

These thoughts conflicted with his yearning for that normal day 13 years ago, that uneventful, serene, quiet Wednesday. He went to school, listened to a lecture on human nature and Plato's *Euthyphro*, conversed with his friends, played a round of chess, condemned himself to a life of pain and torture, and went home. If only everyday were so simple.

"She'll miss me too!" he barked at her, his grip tightening on her neck.

The black guy was purposely avoiding looking in that direction. Clark was fuelled by rage and thoughts of the Norwegian Sea.

I wished I had Her to miss me. How humanity quickly damns itself from Eden, he has no idea what he possesses, he thought.

She was the one, she could have been, should have been mine.

Could have should have would have. Move Clark. Your nature calls and its calls aren't calls you can ignore.

He vigorously caught Arnold Norris's eye as he strode past. He lifted his right cheek and lip and showed him his teeth, the beast growled at him. He abhorred hipsters almost as much frauds. This bastard was both. He glanced up at the emergency yellow strip Arnold was standing under.

Afraid of a delay you pathetic excuse for a human being? You prick. Her cries of pain aren't worth your time? You're going to be late for your hipster meeting? Where you're going to tell some other hipster—who talks like Clint Eastwood and acts like Don Juan—prick about this over your venti low-fat soy bean chocolate latte?

He nearly threw up at how true that sounded. How likely that was to occur. How every single scumbag on this godforsaken train car would use this girl's pain, real and tangible, as an intangible descriptor, fury filled his fists.

An older Asian man was recording this on his iPhone 5. He must've waited hours for a phone but he couldn't wait on a woman in need. *Whatever*. Clark could probably watch himself on YouTube as soon he stepped outside. He could think back, reflect and wonder what he could have, or should have done differently.

He continued towards the Hand. It took an eternity to get to him. He didn't seem this far away. He looked back at the girl he'd been sitting beside and watched her frightened eyes. He wished he knew what that felt like.

Clark approached as the scumbag lifted his hand. Her neck was at the mercy of his fingertips. The train car was silent but for his voice, the rattling of the tracks, and Clark's footsteps nearing this pathetic existence. Clark could see the handprint on her frail neck as his eyes focused on her escalating situation. He thought Clark was headed for the door he was standing beside when the train beeped its doors open.

Clark stood still. Beep... beep... beeeeeeep. The doors closed.

No such luck you insignificant fuck. The scumbag winded his hand back. *Can you not see me? Am I invisible to you? I'm here for you. I wish I had a sickle to scare him a little. Maybe make a quip about being death or something. Could be cool... smooth. Ah whatever.*

Clark let his bag drop to the ground, sudden sounds startle scum, and this slimeball was no different. *Not so tough now are you?*

His hand jerked towards her face. Muscle memory kicked in, their biceps locked, Clark knew how to stop a fight, or start one depending on the perspective.

"What the fuck? Mind your own fuckin' business douchebag!! Fuckin' curly-hair Nancy thinks he's stronger than me!"

Are you kidding me? His bicep was three times the size of Clark's but Clark *was* stronger than him. Physical strength means nothing in such circumstances despite what convoluted Greek comics would have you believe.

Clark noticed a scar nearly covering the entirety of the left side of the jerk's face. Looked like a man had hit him so hard it left an immortal wound.

I bet it was that hand that got you that face.

Hitting a woman? I will take your life. God will forgive me if he exists and if he doesn't, if there is no afterlife, at least I've done the world a favour. One less degenerate in the world.

"Roid rage?"

Nice one Clark. Pat yourself on the back. You're a true comedian. Ha ha. Yes that is a fake laugh you hairless gorilla.

Arnold was close enough to hear. *Did he just snicker? You and your beard are next, giggling like a schoolgirl. What do you think this is, an action movie?*

Clark hated him almost as much as the Hand.

"Next stop Kontula Station. Next stop Kontula Station," Clark's bicep was shaking. W*hy doesn't he throw a circular haymaker with his other hand? Oh yeah, I've got that crazy eye.*

The infamous stare. Notorious among those who know me, and some who don't. He thinks I'm insane. I am insane. He's smarter than he looks, but he looks like a grinning idiot so that's not saying much.

Clark felt for the girl's stomach behind him with his right hand, searching for hers. She gripped his hand. Beeeeeeeep. *Goddamn it open... stupid door.* The girl grabbed his bag with her other hand.

Kind soul, he thought. *Always thinking of others, that's how you're in this mess my beaut.*

Two people walked on, taking extra care to walk around the invisible bubble of perceived space Clark and the Hand required for this disaster.

No thanks, I don't need help, don't mind our interlocked biceps or the bruising neck of the girl behind me, that seat over there by that pretty girl is free. Go sit down you pricks.

Beep... beep... beeeeeep. Clark loosened his bicep and pushed the dirtbag's forearm down with his hand. He was exposed, at Clark's mercy. Doors were closing.

I'll spare him the left haymaker, left uppercut and left jab. Just push him back into the chair. By the time he gets around the pole and the little glass screen, the doors should be closed.

The whooshing that signalled the closing doors landed on Clark's ears. He pushed him, *'I never break a promise,'* he thought, followed by *'You really are a walking cliché.'*

Scumbag neutralized.

Clark rotated the girl's hand and guided her out first lest the degenerate caught his balance on the pole and swung back.

He didn't. Whoosh, Clark snuck through the closing doors.

The man swung around, tried to open the train door with his bare hands. Clark let his jacket slip off. Maybe he'd need that haymaker after all. The stooge punched the glass. It shook and rattled the doors. The operator heard it down the car,

"What are you idiots doing?" he shrugged his shoulders as the train blew by.

Are you kidding me you baboon? Maybe he'll roid rage on Arnold next, and everyone else will watch. He'll know how it feels.

Optimism Clark? You disgust me.

The train, the people, it all made his stomach turn. He wanted to be elsewhere, with Elle, heating up the cold world, but somewhere deep down, he knew this was where he had to be.

He heard the squealing and rattling of the train wheels on the tracks. It provoked another migraine and the throbbing resumed.

Ah that old familiar feeling.

The train disappeared down the tunnel. Clark couldn't see its light anymore. He let out a deep breath. He turned and faced her. Her dark hair was in a single braid idling on her left shoulder, she looked fit enough to be athletic but didn't have the confidence. She wore small black leather loafers and a purple-coloured blouse under a big forehead that reflected infinite ideas, she was much smarter than the present scenario made her seem.

She was on the verge of tears, maybe from the pain. He stared into her eyes. They were big, turquoise, and innocent. Probably some poor lonely girl who got in over her head.

His mind swiftly rearranged her face to like the one woman he always thought about. She'd slipped away from his fingertips. Every female face started to look like hers. Faces seemed to change, subtle, imaginary changes that reminded Clark of her. It's like he'd been looking at a photograph of her and the photograph only reminded him of her absence. An absence that ate his burning heart out of her hands.

Her vocal cords were so damaged that she could scarcely say the words. She lightly brought her left hand up and touched the wound,

"Oww. How can he say he loves me when he lets his friends treat me like this? I should have never involved Nicky—oh he hates that name. I should have never involved Niccoló," she stopped quivering after two attempts. The words barely came out.

Clark recognized the look in her eye when she mentioned this 'Niccoló,' he'd seen in it in the mirror at thoughts of *Elle*.

"Love is a dream. A dream we can only whisper. Anything louder than a soft whisper and it'll vanish," Clark paused for a second, "It's very fragile. It probably won't survive our world, we are… undeserving," Clark's mild whisper seemed to intrigue her.

Nice one Clark, way to reassure the battered woman. Tell her there's no love. Why don't you tell her you saw a dead puppy on your way here and they kill seals in Japan?

She didn't know what to say.

That's fine. I don't care for words either.

"Things like this rarely happen in Sicily," she tapped her wound lightly, inhaling sharply as her fingertips made contact with the skin.

"They shouldn't happen anywhere… Where is your home?" Clark asked her. He preferred to escort her there for her safety. She can decide if she wants to call the police herself later.

"I'll just go to my friend's house, just near Hakaniemi station."

"I'd like to escort you there."

She shouldn't be alone in such a time.

"No thanks," she hesitated and looked at him up and down.

"You're like my white knight in shining armour."

My armour was taken long ago, he thought. He must have nodded slightly, because she smiled and asked,

"How about you, where is your home?"

Where is my home. What a question. My home. I live in an apartment uptown somewhere but that's not my home. That's where I 'live.' My home. Where 'is' my home? I have to think about the answer. His mind rambled and ranted as he tried to rearrange and convey the concept. He thought about a house he'd once chanced across on the hills of Tuscany. It was a vestal place. Little grey stones that grew hot from the heat of the sun. The fresh smell of dried tomatoes and herbs during sunrise and flowers, jasmine and lilies, during sunset. There stood a long, strong cypress tree near its lawn. There was a young woman who tended to the figs, pears, peaches, and apples. He could smell them all.

Even her hair smelled like lilies. He'd always been lost but someone could find themself there. He asked her for directions. She offered him black figs and as he bit into one, it tasted like a bite out of his heart. The sun seemed to be extra hot that day and it made the grass on a nearby field a yellowish brown. Long flowing, dancing pieces of grass, they resembled Elle's hair. The woman's Tuscan accent made her English sound striking. Clark could listen to her all day. She said they had black olives on the south, green olives on the north. Boars, hares, and porcupines ran on the field, dancing with the grass, he even saw a wild goat. They played with her brother. He thought he was a porcupine, like a hyper Wolverine from the X-Men comics he'd read. He was free to dance. The air was different there.

"My home?" Clark repeated. She wouldn't look him straight in the eye, survivor's code, something she must have been conditioned not to do. He tried to smile, look past the pricks on the train, past the bigoted puss-cakes and just let her know the world hadn't ended.

"I *live* outside the city," he finally smiled. It was like the awkward smile from *Terminator 2.*

"I *work* in the city," she was calm now, he heard squeals and rattles, the opposite train was coming.

"I don't feel comfortable leaving you alone after what just happened. You're in shock. You could crash when the adrenaline wears off."

The color of her neck wouldn't return to normal for weeks. It'd already bruised and turned red. He thought he saw blood drops pumping behind it from her heart to her neck.

"Here, use my phone to call someone," Clark reached into the jacket pocket lying on the floor beside him.

She took it without a word and dialed a number. She hesitated, seemed to get cold feet and didn't place the call. She handed Clark his phone back with increasing agitation. Had he triggered a flashback for her?

"I'll be okay," she pecked him on the cheek even though it must've hurt like hell and approached the train door. Beeep. She glanced back at him. He nodded slightly.

A Sicilian Kiss.

"Thank you Knight. By the way, my name's Beatrice," she slightly smirked, "So you have a name when you tell your friends the story."

Beatrice… like the woman who guided Dante through Paradiso….

Helping others is divine? Heavenly? How fitting.

Had I altered this woman's life? Had I helped her? Did I have a choice? Had I chosen to be on that particular train at that particular time? Chosen to get up and help? Or was it my nature? Had nature made the fatal decision on my behalf in ancient times?

His train was arriving too. Beeeeep, its doors opened. He sat down on the empty seat. His body still as a mountain while his mind shook like an earthquake.

He looked at the number staring back at him on the screen of his phone. *333-428-9357*. He saved it, perhaps he'd call upon her knight to aid his lady. It's what he would have wanted.

He exhaled back to reality, sitting on another train car, another pretty girl seated across him. A pair of thick black rimmed Oliver Peoples intently studying a book, held by dark purple nail polish and cheekbones that wouldn't quit. What are *you* reading he wondered? She turned the page gracefully. She was a Parisian flower.

It was a small hardcover book, the jacket was as black as night. He caught a glimpse of the cover. "Death with Interruptions."

His belief system came crashing down like Goliath in the Valley of Elah. He hadn't spent any time choosing the time of his death. He spent so much time analyzing and contemplating choices it was only logical for him to contemplate the moment of death. The idea interested him. Timing is everything.

Maybe I'll walk the rest of the way, am I able to make that choice or has fate already foreseen it?

XXIV
MIRRORED BEHAVIOR

He entered the first motel in sight and acquired a room. The entire place was empty, crickets chirped and he thought about how cliché it was.

"We don't get many visitors," the motel concierge wakened from a nap and slowly put a key on the counter.

"Smoking room," Clark put down a money clip of cash and took the key.

He walked down the hallway and approached his room. He needed a deep breath before he could turn the key into the lock. The door cringed open.

This place still uses physical keys? It will have to do. Time to move on. Bury the past out in that magical compartment in the fringe of my mind.

Clark entered the room. It was small, shabby, smelled like old wood and wet carpet.

Welcome home.

He sat down on the wooden chair placed in front of the bed. His damaged lungs welcomed the humid air. He opened the mini-bar and started drinking; he didn't need to do himself any favors. If there is one constant myth perpetuated by the indoctrinating media and entertainment outlets on our planet, it's the idea that alcohol will provide solace in times of pain. The idea that sorrows can be drowned if a person's blood alcohol level reaches a certain threshold. Clark never took any 'truth' at face value. He knew there wasn't enough scotch, migraine pills or Vicodin to ease his pain. Pains of a heart at conflict with the mind are a cancer, resilient parasites with mortal repercussions. There was no shame in searching for a cure, drinking Ardbeg to test this theory, to observe whether or not his pains would diminish. However, deep in his heart, a part of him knew that they wouldn't, he knew such things were fairy tales, that such a ready-made, simple way to ease chronic passions was certainly too good to be true.

He looked up at himself through the mirror on the desk in front of him.

* * *

His thoughts echoed back as each word left his lips.

The familiar face in there looks like my own but doesn't feel like me. It's tired of the past. My psyche is overwhelmed with fatigue. I want to show her my love, the fated passion that left a lingering puncture wound on my heart, but the cursed mirror renders me motionless.

My face weighs heavier than it should. I ask myself who is the stranger in the mirror. What's he want from me? Is he staring at me, or am I staring at him?'

I don't believe what I'm seeing. I close my eyes and tell myself that the face I see there can't be the face I feel here.

I slide my hand over my face. My fingertips tell me everything about this face. The same face in the mirror, nothing more, nothing less, nothing but the poor past.

The mirror screams, "That *is* you! They're both you! And no one else."

"What's me?" I ask, "Who am I?"

The mirror roars back, "Every lesson comes with a scar. Like the ones on your face. Look at why you desire to relive certain moments. Seek to know why you have these desires. These moments become eternal and burn themselves into your memory bank. You must remember how you got each scar, all of it stays bonded to the face in the mirror," it smiles back at me. "Now look at what's left of your face, the face in the mirror."

It must be the scotch.

The mirror shakes harder and shrieks, "You're the same face that wanted to move heaven and earth for her, why has dark calamity become your home? Why have your passion, voice, and love died in your heart?"

I pick up and smash the mirror so it'd stop reminding me of the past. The mirror falls and explodes into hundreds of pieces, but in each piece I see that face, that same scarred face staring back.

Each of the hundred faces cries out in my voice,

"Scrape out hope from the sky and from your heart. Every day is the same useless despair and pain.

The erroneous assumption that time is linear. It's not. Nothing changes.

* * *

He snapped back to his solidified identity. You can't change who you are, the nature you're born with.

So what? I stay here on a binge and drink myself to death? No thanks, Clark took out his phone and bashed the screen to write a text message,

"I've wanted to send you this message for years now but I could never bring myself up to it. I am... truly sorry, the sound of your voice falling on my ears makes me a believer, a belief in something outside of myself: in unadulterated passion, in beliefs themselves. You're my crowd in nights of solitude and my succor in crowds of decadence. The thought of you near me makes my heart beat faster. I should've never walked out on you, on your nephew. I made the wrong choice."

A deadfall. Wile E. Coyote hearing the nearing whistle of an anvil headed straight for his brain.

He swiped the screen and threw the phone at the painting above the bed without hitting send. It propped a nail off the wall. The painting flopped, a sea consuming a ship with its captain desperately at the helm. He tore a page out of his notebook and hastily scribbled something before putting the paper in his back-left pocket.

* * *

His eyes watered not because he loved her but because he recognized his weakness. He knew he'd forever be weak because of it and he knew he wasn't strong enough to apologize. The grip of his Colt was warmer than usual. He swallowed the muzzle and squeezed the silver trigger.

Click. Nothing happened. He was still here. The bullet jammed in the barrel.

Bent firing pin? Bad primer? You pull the trigger and a bullet pounces out of its dark nest, ready to obliterate anything in its way. It seemed... simple.

A bullet never lies, the don's high-pitched voice rattled his thoughts.

He cocked the gun again, the bullet flew out of the slider. He caught it and slipped it into his pocket. He wobbled away from the empty minibar and placed his head on the comfortable pillow, unable to sleep but dozing in and out of consciousness.

XXV
CONSTRUCT IV

Walking down the paved path surrounded by darkness, he finally stopped and attempted to take out the knife submerged into the right side of his back. He extracted it and the pain almost forced him *unconscious*. He had barely sat there for a few seconds before two more knives were plunged into his left and right shoulder blades. He turned around like a penguin, engulfed in pain to be facing himself yet again. That same arrogant smirk he'd grown tired of seeing. He loathed that smirk. How he wished he could wipe that smirk off his own stupid face. He blinked before his own face turned to Alex's and another knife was plunged into his heart, he let out a yelp as Alex slowly dissipated.

He envisioned being so consumed in caging his own beast that he'd been neglecting the beast of others. None of it mattered now. He was in the present and not the past. The present was the only tense that mattered. He stood up in agony, turned around and tried to walk down the path before a woman started appearing before him, walking towards him from the other end of the path. It was *Elle*, the one. Her form appeared as a ghost but slowly turned as solid and as dimensional as he was. He leaned in and touched her. She reached around him and held the knives piercing his back. Her touch turned the knives into light. The knives disappeared and his wounds were instantly healed. The knife in his heart disappeared as tears flowed from his eyes. He held her chin up and they touched noses. Reliving a conversation between them when they'd first met,

"You're the most beautiful woman I'd ever laid eyes on."

"I know," she smiled.

"You know? That's a little aggressive, not to mention arrogant."

"You look like the kind of guy turned on by aggression," she brushed the tips of her fingers against his cheeks.

"I can't think when I'm with you."

That's a good thing. I don't want to think. I want to be stupid. I want to let go. To be ignorant of truth and dense abstractions.

"Then what could you possibly want from me?" she asked with a seductive, raised eyebrow.

The synapses in Clark's brain began firing like never before. It seemed like he was asleep and still in the depths of his brain,

'*The Things I Want,* by Clark Kóróna: To relive the past with a glass of GlenDronach and a Monte Cristo cigar, people I've lost back, immortality coupled with infinite air miles, but above all of those, I want her.'

"Lyra..." even saying her name out loud gave him strength, "I... I'd bleed my heart dry for your smile," his hands on her rapturous face started to fall through; she was slowly fading away. How many more times could he endure losing her?

How many times are you going to take her away from me?

He looked at the path that appeared again, looked up and screamed,

"Let me out of here you sadist."

Instantly he awoke to the sound of the motel phone. His hangover arrived right on cue, gift-wrapped with an inevitable migraine. He could feel it sneaking around in the back of his head like a tiger circling its prey before plunging forward with its long, sharp claws.

He moved towards the phone, the thing looked like it belonged to Graham Bell himself.

"What is it?"

The voice on the other line had a thick accent, "There's a letter for you here Herr Kóróna."

Clark descended the steps from his room and stumbled to the register. He'd only slept for an hour or two and was still a little drunk. He tipped the clerk and received his letter. It looked to be an invitation. The thumping in his skull had gotten worse, he wanted to reach into his chest and rake out the pain.

He opened the letter on the small, wooden desk in his room, occasionally repulsing himself by glancing at his face in the mirror fragments on the floor under him. The letter was an invitation to a party in Paris with judges, mayors, councilors, and politicians from all nations to discuss the various issues of social inequality and exploitation in developing countries, no doubt costing a fortune to host. The invitation was from Electra, at least it looked like her writing.

How did she find you Clark?

He had ample time to brood over these questions; the invitation requested his presence in a fortnight, November 20th. He knew it was a license to indulge in acts of excess and underserved luxury but something about it peaked his curiosity enough to want to attend.

XXVI
UNITY

Jane Doe's apartment was only a few blocks from the downtown region near the central university. Upon first entry Matthews noticed that she kept a very delicate handmade kitchen table from IKEA. On the ground it looked as if the table had been replaced, remnants of a different table leg scuffed the parquet floor. He moved deeper into the apartment and looked inside one of the rooms, it hosted a big armchair and a television connected to a game system. Looked like a kid's room. He moved into the second room where a bed and a vanity table by a writing desk sat in silence. He approached the desk. It had papers scrambled and dispersed all over it. He opened the drawer of this table and reached for some complexly folded pieces of paper. He carefully unfolded one to reveal a love letter, written by her to an unknown person.

MY LOVE,

I made a decision and I must stand by it, I never meant to hurt you. This was the last thing I wanted to do. You are after all, constantly in my thoughts, and I have trouble getting rid of you.

Something had happened to this woman other than a final reckoning. The place probably looked lively and upbeat once but now it was poignant. He moved around the apartment, shuffled the papers around her desk. There was nothing notable except a cell phone bill. He finally learned the victim's name, Ms. Bergljót. A name to a face personalized the victim and made it easier to work.

He looked at the numerous books stacked under the hand-made table, among them: Dante's *Purgatorio* and *Paradiso*, More's *Utopia*, Borges's *El Inmortal*, Marquez's *One Hundred Years of Solitude, The Morality of Values*, Dostoyevsky's *Crime & Punishment*. Amongst all the books and loose paper, he saw a receipt from a prominent auction house; it was connected to a bound notebook. He extracted it and looked at the note. The note said *To 'Prince Charming,'* and housed a delivery stamp to an address the detective was familiar with, the purchased item: a 1928 bottle of Krug. The pieces of the broken jigsaw puzzle had been fitting into their respective places. Matthews contacted Durante. He'd need his help. Durante hastened to the apartment.

* * *

Durante entered the door and handed Matthews video printouts of the mob suspects: the don, his right hand man, his consigliere, and the two suspects for *The Fox* and *The Viking*. Matthews immediately recognized both men as his suspects in the Bergljót murder. All doubt had ceased from his mind that one of these two had murdered the poor girl. He noticed a high-end, watermarked envelope lying on top of the kitchen counter. Something had been taken out of it, another letter?

"No," Durante knew more than he let on, "It's too fancy for that. It's probably an invitation for a ball or something."

An invitation to what? The crime scene crew was called in to go over her apartment, to find a needle in a stack of needles, something to tie the suspects to the scene. They hurried to get a warrant for Alex's apartment, the don's estate, and Clark's apartment. The judge had no problem signing the warrant. Matthews thought justice would finally be served. Durante knew better. He wondered about the envelope, the same kind of people as the club opening?

He set his plan in motion and put the word on the street. He wanted an invite to this party. Everyone would be there. They could arrest everyone. Question everyone. Beatrice would finally see justice.

It was only a few hours before a snitch left a message for Durante at the station, a way in. For those not worthy of a personal invite but still worthy enough to merit entrance to the party, a password had been provided. No doubt the rich junkies had blabbed the password to any fool smart enough to wave an ounce of respect, that was after all, the rich's only currency proceeding money and power, in their faces. It was either respect or a snort of their magic dust. Not anyone could enter, there were doorman, bodyguards, ex-cops, retired military, but with a little luck, a lot of machismo, and the password, the duo could get in.

They tracked the rat down. He sold the password for $25 and a pack of Cohíbas. Durante was sad to see the latter go but he knew he'd have infinite Cohíbas if he brought in Don Torrino. According to this junkie, the password was a multitude of phrases,

"When asked for your invite, you're supposed to say, 'That girl in the silk dress took it, go get her and you'll have my invite.' At this phrase, the bouncer will reply, 'Okay, I'll let you in, find her and bring her here with your invite.' The twist is... there is no girl in the silk dress," the junkie was going through withdrawal.

They couldn't even see the veins on his forearms anymore. Durante knew where the $25 was going.

"It might just work, dress to kill," Durante and Matthews separated to get ready.

A dark cloud made a storm seem imminent in the horizon. By the time the doors to the party opened, it was raining ice pitchforks like hell had frozen over. The party was to start at ten. While the *really* important people wouldn't arrive until much later, undercover agents would want to be there earlier. They'd want to set up their arrest procedures if everything went according to plan and get a feel for the place.

XXVII
The Beast's Serenity

There is no redo in life, no joystick button to hold; blood can never be un-spilled.

The scotch made Clark think that this was where he would fall. This was the trap set for him. What scotch cannot cure has no cure. His practiced stoicism never betrayed a single expression but that was his nature. Internally, he was as fragile as a woman's heart. He came in through the roof of a connecting building via one of the better hotels in town. He knew he couldn't go back to his apartment.

He figured Alex had already seen his file. They'd never give him the opportunity to retrieve the folder underneath the tile of his apartment and hand it to the police. He had one advantage: no one knew the folder existed, unless John had betrayed him but that'd be a dumb move, even for him.

The ballroom was something like the Hilton lobby and den. The kind of place you read about in a James Bond novel: everyone was in tuxedos, cigar and cigarette smoke hazed up the air, rich people drank so much in hope that they'd justify their undeserving wealth. He had a lot in common with these people. This thought scared him more than death. Was tonight the night? His time to meet the man with the scythe and have his blood shed? The thought of flowing blood set his pulse on edge.

He cared little for money. Pieces of paper.... It didn't matter. He'd managed to screw up a chance at his own Garden of Eden by heaving it into the bottom of the void. He detested this place. He tried to spot the bar and nearly changed his mind because he was forced to walk through the mechanical people and the horrible music.

He gazed down at the people from the top of the stairs. The ballroom personified pretentious: Persian rugs spread over every inch of the floor, hardwood antique style stairs, purple silk curtains tied up at the center of each window. Butlers in tuxedos offered Hors d'oeuvre finger foods like fried shrimp, pigs in a blanket and other various snacks the elite could afford to indulge in. Champagne was being offered to everyone, not one person could be spotted without a drink in their hand. Clark thought about his 1928 Krug, what would become of it now? He'd waited years to enjoy it with Lyra. The person he loved, the person he loves. He thought about buying another bottle as if it had become a piece of him. The thought didn't relax him, he wanted that exact bottle, the one *she* bought. He was attached to it precisely *because* she bought it. Philosophy demanded knowledge, ignorance demanded happiness, love demanded both. It seemed like an obvious reason but sometimes truth comes in through the front door while you're waiting for it by the window.

Sentiment? It can't be, I am not a sentimental man.

A burning sensation creeping from his shoulders tormented his upper body. It started from the neck and worked its way down. Suddenly, he could barely stand. The beast wanted out and rattled the cages, his stomach and abdomen hurt. He felt like that cabin-fevered idiot from *The Shining,* losing his mind at each tick of the seconds hand watch on his wrist, destined to strike down those he loves. He hated himself for being there. Everything these people stood for was against his principles, but in the recesses of the void near the subconscious of his mind, he knew that *this* was the way out, the path to his own personal *One Hundred Years of Solitude.* He wondered who'd sent him the invite and why he was attracted to come. Fate? Destiny? Perhaps those words are too big to describe *one* life.

He moved towards the bar. He had to dumb himself down for the ignorant people and conceited conversations. The bartender recognized the look of a man who required a real drink,

"What scotch cannot cure has no cure huh?" the bartender was too smart to be a bartender.

Clark gave a slight nod before he clawed the cup and gulped it in hopes of drowning his sorrows, forgetting again, that sorrows are Olympic swimmers. The bartender smirked at the sight of a man unimpressed by the wealth surrounding him. Perhaps he recognized that Clark was trying to deafen the noise around him with alcohol. Clark caught the bartender's gaze... who better to appreciate this sight than a bartender, a man who's seen the world through the stories of other men. He seemed like a connoisseur. Clark pointed to a bottle of scotch behind the bartender; the bartender went to retrieve it as others barked drink orders at the counter, the bartender had filled Clark's cup half way,

"Be careful man, I had a guy come into my bar a couple of weeks ago, ordered the same stuff and immediately got sick. He ran and threw up in the middle of a phone call."

Clark motioned to the man to keep pouring. His ears reflexively picked out a slender whisper at the end of the bar.

"Sicilian Kiss please, with a thin slice of orange peel if you've got it."

It's the scotch talking, it can't be.

His cup was practically full. He looked down the bar but too many people were blocking his view from the origin of this familiar voice.

The pain in his chest got worse, the beast wanted to be freed. *'Not now,'* he moved towards the voice, the bartender saw Clark's cup,

"Hey boss, your drink!"

Clark weaved his way through the people, bumping into them with his shoulders. Some of them eyeballed him with disdain as if to say *how dare you bump into me... do you know who I am?*

Clark could see the outline of the woman that'd ordered the drink. She was wearing a mid-length red dress with matching shoes, a waterfall of sunlit hair streaming down her side. He could smell her hair from miles away: strawberries. She was walking away with her drink in her hand. The way she was holding it... it was Lyra. His pains disappeared, he felt like a superhero. She seemed the same: cold. Beautiful. Sarcastic. Not one glance, word or sigh of passion was wasted on her. There were only a few more people in his way.

Just like old times.

* * *

"I'll have a coffee," he could listen to her voice all day.

"How do you like it?" Olivia glared *through* her, almost too afraid to look her straight in the eye.

I'll bet you it's with no sugar. She's sweet enough as it is.

Definitely order that cheesecake Clark. You've watched too many Disney flicks.

"Three milks, two sugars please," Lyra's voice sounded lyrical and poetic to his ears. Everything she said seemed to invoke a fire inside him, fuel him to fly to the sun and bring a piece back for her.

Boom. Pay up sucker. Let me out of here, the beast howled.

"I would have taken you for a woman who has it with 2 milks."

"Why is that?"

"Because you're sweet enough as it is," the young Clark smirked.

"It's going to be a long year," she sighed. She was used to such attention. All beautiful women are.

"It'll... definitely be *fun*."

Easy hotshot... she probably deals with crap like that every seven seconds, you want to tone it down a bit... maybe tell her she looks nice, don't put her on the spot like that. Idiot, that raging inner voice scoffed.

"I should apologize. You probably get that every seven seconds. I do have to tell you though, you're the most beautiful woman I've ever laid eyes on."

And you've seen women from all around the world in your travels haven't you Clark? Models, physicists, athletes.

Shut up for two minutes you inconsiderate bastard. Since when do you talk? I thought you only roared and howled.

He who lives with beasts learns to roar.

"I know," she said softly.

"You *know*? Isn't that's a little assertive? Even arrogant?"

"I *am* assertive. Besides, you strike me as the type of man who gets turned on by aggression anyway."

"That's a fairly good read. I'm a little impressed."

"I know your type," she rolled her eyes.

"My type?"

"You're a glass half-empty kind of guy. The kind who never hears no," her intelligence made his mind howl with desire.

"Not true... it depends what's in the glass."

* * *

He moved towards her before he saw her approach another man. He stopped in between two people talking.

"Excuse me!" the stranger exclaimed with a piece of fried shrimp in his hand, "We're talking here!"

Clark's laser-vision snapped the stranger to reality, the reality that recognized the futility of money and wealth. This stranger held no real power because he possessed more things than Clark, and he swiftly backed away at this realization. Clark's stare made him uncomfortable: the eyes of a lion whose pride was in danger. The stranger would swear later he heard a growl.

She approached Alexander Torrino. He'd finally earned his name.

Alexander grabbed her forearm tightly and screamed in a whisper,

"Where did you go? You don't leave my side!"

Clark would have laughed if he remembered how. *Close…
but no cigar.*

He'd yet to be detected and it was best to keep it that way.
He recognized trouble. He'd never seen that look in her eyes. She
looked afraid and scared, not the Lyra he knew and loved. The
Lyra he knows and loves. He noticed Alex nodding to someone in
the crowd and Clark turned to see where Alex was looking, it was
a member of the family, he looked up at the stairs, another man up
there.

How'd they know about Lyra? Was she a hostage?

The whole thing was a trap taken from the most clichéd
antagonist handbook and Alex was running it page by page,
hoping to torture Clark's mind. The delicious humor of it was,
Clark had fallen in like the schmuck he was. It was no different
than the void he'd fallen into before. By now was an expert at
falling into voids and having to crawl out of them by the skin of
his teeth. Tonight would be no exception.

He detested Alex's death grip on Lyra; a lioness mustn't be
caged. She must roam free in the hills of the jungle and live for the
thrill of the hunt. He formulated a plan: he'd walk over here
blending with the crowd and choke the life out of Alex with his
bare hands and tell Lyra to run. By the time Alex's henchmen get
to him, Alex would be dead. Granted Clark probably wouldn't
make it out alive either but Lyra's safety was paramount, his was
scarcely worth even contemplating.

He wasn't some sissy Disney prince or some ideal Nicholas
Sparks superman who'd die for a woman for the sake of what it

meant in some old knighthood code of chivalry. He was a man doing what he thought was right, atoning for his downward spiral and trying to redeem himself on yet another fatally rainy night.

Albeit this was a horrible plan, it was *a* plan nonetheless. He slowly opened the cage and drew a deep breath. The beast slowly approached the open door. It was never freed voluntarily. It was suspicious.

Now you need my help?

Alex slapped her with his right hand. Clark somehow heard it over the ambient noise. He instantly opened his eyes with the intention of roaring forward with his plan. Had it not been for the hand he felt on his shoulder, he would have pounced on his prey and ate him alive. He reached inside his jacket pocket for his silenced gun...

"Uhh... Mister Króóna? I am Detective Matthews."

Matthews flashed his badge at him. Clark turned around to face him, slamming the cage door closed. The beast roared so loud Clark could hardly hear the detective.

I knew it was a trick, the dimples on the beast's face glowed like a star, its freedom was inevitable.

"Hello detective, I'm a little busy right now."

"Is that the don's son?" Matthews pointed to Lyra and Alex.

"Yes," Clark looked through Matthews, rather than at him, "I'll take him down. Just stay out of my way."

"Then how will you ride off into the sunset with her?" he pointed to Lyra through the crowd, "Your one true love. Your only hope *for* humanity, your only hope that sometimes there is truth in faith."

Clark stared at Matthews. His past had caught up to him like a bad nightmare. He'd spent years running only to fall back into the abyss.

No matter how long you spend crawling out, you can fall back down in an instant.

"Who is she?" Clark was trying to be clever.

"You haven't lied to me yet. That's why I respect you. That's why I haven't called backup in here to arrest all of you: the family, you, the men, *her...* "

"You're going to leave her out of this," the human aura around Clark's eyes dissipated. He barely looked human.

"I leave the choice to you," A false choice. It was anything but a choice. The beast circled the cage, growling as it waited for Clark to free him, it was never patient.

"I'll do what I'm here to do... stay out of my way," Clark repeated.

"If I were here to stop you, would I have approached you and struck conversation?"

Clark nodded and doubled back and disappeared into the crowd. Matthews looked at Durante, who was somewhere in the crowd chatting up a young lady, facing Matthews and Clark. Matthews nodded in his direction, *it's on*, the nod said. Durante saw the nod but didn't give way to his apprehension.

Matthews looked up near the doors to the upper rooms and caught the eyes of the Torrino man stationed at the top of the stairs.

There were only a couple of people up there. He mockingly saluted him as the henchman put his hand to his ear. Precipitously, he was jerked back and looked to be dragged into one of the rooms. He disappeared and no one noticed. The music, laughter, and loud-mouthed tough guys' voices probably drowned out his wails, at least there was one thing Clark was good at besides hating himself.

Clark silently choked the thug as he backed up into an empty room and began punching him in the face. The melancholic curls on his head twisted to form an infinity symbol. Shadows appeared around him as the man's heartbeat slowed to a halt, a black hole consumed anything Clark deemed not worthy of *true justice*. It was Lyra, seeing her had triggered a luxation. A mania crept into the depths of his brain and routed his brain waves. He felt euphoric, with a fear that past evils had attached themselves to this jubilation and were waiting for the perfect moment to slither out of their Trojan horse.

He was composed as he turned the goomba around and choked him again.

"You brought *her* here? I'm coming for you. All of you, I'm going to kill every last one of you. The entire planet if it means sparing her from half a second of inconvenience."

He wanted to save Lyra. He *had* to save Lyra. He was a clichéd literary character who thought saving her would be his redemption and his hope of capturing an elusive moment of solace, an eternal moment of light instead of this dreadful nightmare humanity found itself in.

Clark's scowl turned to a fury. He was a different person. Unrecognizable to the few acquaintances he had and even to *her*. She wouldn't have recognized him if she walked in at that exact moment. The gangster fell to the ground writhing. Clark had fallen to the commands of the beast.

The dolt on the main floor near Alexander put his hand to his ear. He heard everything through the earpiece. With a fear that consumes a man prior to death, he looked at Alex,

"It's him."

"Why are y'all staring at me? Go!" Alex screamed.

Lyra smiled.

"What-are-you smiling about?" Alex yelled in her ear, narrowly escaping the hearing of the other partygoers.

"It's him isn't it?" she asked rhetorically. Her eyes lit up like Times Square on New Years Eve. "You screwed up now... he won't stop, he never stops. It's a gift... and a curse."

"You think—(pronounced *tink*)—you know him don't ya?" Alex chuckled.

"I know he doesn't live in the same world as us. We imagine things and say why? He does them and shrugs *why not*. He believes, no, he *knows* that nothing is beyond him. You know what I learned?" she asked again rhetorically.

"You're gonna tell me," Alex said trying to appear unfazed, a snake catching a glimpse of the soaring eagle about to descend upon him.

"It's all a façade, for all his charm, intelligence, and dry wit, he's an unwavering, calculating machine. He does what he wants when he wants, and never gives it a second thought."

Alex looked at her. It was a frightening foreshadow marking the inevitability of his doom hanging over him like a thunderous cloud. He tightened his grip on her and viciously guided her through the crowd. She dropped her drink, shattering the martini goblet. The few people who noticed the broken glass only did so to note whether or not their shoes were damaged and didn't noticed the woman being pushed into the private area.

He took her into one of the many rooms on the main floor and threw her in, "Sit down," he demanded.

She didn't move until he extracted a gun from his belt and told her again.

"He's coming for you. I've never met anyone with his determination, his commitment. When he wants something, he gets it," she said admirably.

He cocked his gun,

"One more word… and," he moved his index from ear to ear, to signal cutting her throat.

Clark came out of the room with his mind in pieces like the shattered glass he saw on the main floor where Lyra had been standing. He didn't deserve her but he had to save her. She was here because of him.

He looked through a nearby window. The sound of the howling sky did nothing to calm his throbbing heart, if anything it made things worse and rejuvenated forlorn emotions that wouldn't benefit him in the slightest given the circumstance at hand. More Torrino chumps approached. He'd stolen the henchmen's earpiece who was lying in the left-most upper room. He could hear every word above the sound of raindrops colder than the devil's heart sloshing against the window. His hands brushed against the soft purple curtain as a drenched raven cawed at a man who was granted entry by a Torrino faithful.

He thought he was thinking it, but Clark in fact spoke the words that appeared in his mind, a poem he'd read in his youth,

"And the silken sad uncertain rustling of each purple curtain
Thrilled me - filled me with fantastic terrors never felt
before;
So that now, to still the beating of my heart, I stood repeating
`'Tis some visitor entreating entrance at my chamber door... "

"Nevermore! ... Edgar Allen Poe," the voice behind him caught Clark off guard.

Clark turned around trepidatiously. The man immediately followed up with, "I am Niccoló Durante. Matthews's partner, we've haven't had the honor."

Clark kept his gaze and extended his hand. They shook hands, Niccoló's handshake was firm. Clark knew a gentleman when he saw one.

The world was too small for comfort. Niccoló. You've heard this name before.

"Have we met before?" Niccoló asked, "You look strangely familiar."

"I must have one of those faces."

"Ahhh, of course, although it's not everyday you bump into someone at an existential moment quoting Poe."

Clark's fingertips played with the curtain, "Ecce Deus fortior me, qui veniens dominabitur mihi."

"*Vita Nuova* by Dante, 'Behold a God more powerful than I who comes to rule over me.'"

Clark looked at Durante with an inquisitive gaze. It was the *Longfellow* translation.

"You know..." Clark exhaled, "Poe and Longfellow didn't get along, Poe thought he was a fraud, a translator and a mediocre poet, and Longfellow of course, thought Poe was deeply disturbed."

"I did *not* know that my friend, it's interesting, that's to be sure."

"It's also not everyday that you meet a stranger who understands Dante in Latin and recites its Longfellow translation."

Durante chuckled, "I spent some time in Florence," he referred back to the Dante quote, "She is more powerful than you?" he asked Clark.

"Beautiful woman often are."

"Yes of course, as we say in Italy, a man's only goal is to find the woman of his dreams." Niccoló's accent thickened as he completed the sentence.

"Niccoló? Does anyone call you Nicky?" Clark knew that any man who understood Dante references in Latin could be trusted.

"I hate that name but yes, two people did."

"Was one of them a pretty petite woman named Beatrice?" there was no time for games. Clark had to move fast, build rapport and make a friend.

Niccoló's eyes answered in the affirmative. Clark recognized that look. He'd seen it before, in the reflection of his espresso at the university café.

Get this Clark, the guy's name is Niccoló 'Durante,' also known as Dante, and he loves a woman named Beatrice? I didn't take Fate for a comedian.

"Pretty horrible odds," Clark thought the silence was becoming uncomfortable and he didn't need an uncomfortable Interpol agent who might suddenly free his beast in order to get to his Beatrice. The party wasn't big enough for the two of them. He needed to get to Lyra.

"Yep... they don't stand a chance," Durante unholstered a 44 magnum. He realized what Clark had done for him, it was only fair to return the favor and help get to his own Beatrice and save her.

Clark looked at the gun. Durante had watched too many *Dirty Harry* movies.

"I work better alone," Clark pointed to the crowd. "Things are going to get heavy soon, when they do... when you get my signal, unleash the *Inferno*."

"With that look in your eye, I have a feeling you'll do that by yourself," Durante recognized that look, his reflection in the small bar window the day Beatrice went missing.

"If we never meet again, go to my apartment, remove the small rug from the top of the den. Count three tiles from the right corner, the fourth is a false tile, I've kept records of everything. If by chance some of them survive, those files will ensure they don't. I trust you will do the right thing," he didn't think for one second that putting these men behind bars would be his redemption. He didn't want to save the city like a misguided DC comic book hero with a false sense of justice, to rid a metropolis of criminals or gangsters and make life easier for the *leeches* so they could boast about declining crime rates in an upcoming re-election. He didn't want to save the *innocent*; no one is innocent. He wanted to save *her*, not because she was innocent either but because she stood for innocence in his mind. He wanted to save her because he realized he loved her, because he *chose* to love her.

He took out the empty ink-blotted piece of journal paper and wrote Beatrice's last known whereabouts. She'd told Clark her 'friend' lived "Near Hakaniemi station," he relayed all the necessary information onto the paper and handed it to Durante.

"I hope we will meet again… but if we don't," Durante went into his pocket and came out with two cigars, "A token of my gratitude."

Clark took the cigar, "… Cohíba Corona Especial, Castro's preferred cigar, how very…. I will have to save this for the opportune moment, thank you," he placed the cigar in the inner right jacket pocket. It wasn't a Monte Cristo but Cohíbas are a sign of exquisite taste more often than not.

Durante concealed the cannon and descended the stairs, blending with the crowd. Clark watched him as he whispered something in Matthews's ear. He was a natural. Perhaps he'd help after all this, not that he wanted it but he seemed like an honorable man. *Things are not what they seem to be, nor are they otherwise.* As he had this thought, he noticed Electra amongst the partygoers. She was wearing a long black dress, walking through the crowd as if she were looking for someone. Was *she* the one who invited him?

Clark took out the second last Monte Cristo from his pants pocket and sat in front of the curtain. It tickled his hair. More second-rate thugs blended in with the partygoers by the second. It progressively became more difficult to tell the henchmen who were there to kill him from the naïve partygoers. Plus, Lyra had disappeared, he knew no doubt that she was in one of the private rooms on the bottom floor but he had to get there stealthily. He couldn't risk being discovered, captured or killed, lest they kill Lyra. His death was inevitable upon capture and so was Lyra's. They wouldn't leave a witness alive for no reason. She would be dead by the end of the night if he couldn't save her. For the first time in a long time, he wanted to live. He stood up through the haze of his thoughts and cigar smoke and entered the room he'd killed the Torrino clown in. The dead body was still staring up at the sky, waiting for some deity to take his soul to the next world. The clock in the room started ringing. It was midnight, Cinderella's chariot awaited. In his case, Cinderella's chariot was a walk through the park in this unrelenting storm and her slipper was her hand wrapped about his. He looked down the window of the room and saw a '72 Cadillac. He appreciated the tenacity of a man who'd restore such a car. He could see Lyra staring out of the window of the room next to his, directly below through the windshield reflection of the car. He stepped out of the room into the party. More people were on the upper floor now. He brushed past them, two of whom he suspected were made Torrino scumbags. He entered the following room. He saw shadows of footsteps outside the door of his room. With his back to the door, he locked it and placed a small table and chair in front of it. After a few attempts, the men outside gave up. Through the earpiece he heard,

"He's trapped up here, no way out."

Come he slow, or come he fast, it is but death who comes at last.

He was directly above Lyra's room now. He looked towards the reflection of that crystal ball of a windshield. Lyra stood there staring out the window. He thought he saw her mouth words to the window. Had she seen him through the reflection as well? He froze staring at her, he felt like his arms were injected with icicles. Her perfect hips connecting to her slim waist, her seductive lips moving up and down, touching each second. Eventually she moved away from the window in slow-motion, *relativity*. He caught his own reflection in the window. His scars, wounds, and pains as visible as a light in a tunnel of darkness. It no longer disgusted him.

Smart move would have been to call Matthews and Durante. All three of them could enter the room with the duo's badges, and safely procure Lyra from the clutches of that tyrant, using the files as leverage but he'd already played his ace, moved his knight into enemy territory.

No thanks, I'll tie the pieces of this thin duvet together and dive through the second-story window, rotate around and break main floor window in, tearing up my body and face in the process, a stupid move but you don't fight your nature or deny your true self. I'm a stupid guy.

He was tying the sheets to the duvet when an idea flashed across his mind. He didn't have to live inside an action movie. He could simply open the window, slip out, and if Lyra approached the window once more and Alex was facing away, he could slip into the room undetected. A lot of variables... a lot of luck but he liked his odds. It didn't feel like his time. A couple of quick puffs of the dormant cigar on his lip aided his relaxation. He unlatched and opened the window, he saw Lyra approaching the window through the windshield.

He only looked up to the sky this time, *thank you.*

His foot nearly slipped on the small edge of the window still, he held the sheets harder, the farthest right bedpost shook. It'd support his weight. His cigar was drenched immediately. It was freezing cold. The storm wasn't going to die down, visibility was barely a few meters. He was wet from head to toe in a matter of seconds. He reached into his jacket and took out his silenced Colt 1911. It'd never been this wet before but hopefully it'd fire. He looked at his gun, what they'd been through together. He watched the rainwater stream down from the edge of the barrel. He cocked it.

He wanted to be there, he had to be there, he felt the rise of the old familiar feelings, he hated them, he welcomed them.

He remembered the fatal bullet from the motel room and eventually took it out of his pocket and put it at the top of the clip, the first bullet blasting out of the mouth of his barrel. He cocked the gun again.

A bullet never lies.

* * *

Alex paced up and down the room, calling people on his phone and asking them to the party. Eventually all the bouncers were Alex's men. The whole place looked like a mob gathering, the vibe of the party had been altered.

"Any word?" he said into a walkie-talkie.

"Standby," another voice responded, "Target spotted. I'm approaching now."

Lyra's face filled with anguish. Was this truly the time, was she never going to see Clark again, never hold his hands in her own, never feel the cracks and burns of his lips against hers? Her heart sank lower than Clark's sorrows.

"He's trapped up here. No way out," a voice finally returned.

"This is your hero? HA!"

Lyra got up and began walking around the couch, going to the window and back. She promised herself that no matter what happened she'd make amends. She didn't care what Clark had done in the past. She just wanted to see him one last time, she'd never felt like this before, the feeling of fear, the feeling of losing someone you'd die for. Through a reflection in an odd looking car, she thought she saw him in the room above and to the left... *it can't be*, she mouthed, "Is that you my love?" Her ears whistled so loudly and her heart throbbed so fast that she convinced herself it was her mind playing tricks. No way Clark answered her invitation, no way he walked into this calculated trap, he was smarter than that. He was probably in San Francisco by now. Her eyes watered up, she walked back towards the couch to ease the pain.

"Stay here bitch," Alex snarled as he opened the door and she saw six or seven men through the small crevice left by the keyhole. There were so many of them. How was Clark going to get out of this one? How was he going to survive? Did he *want* to survive? Alex stepped out to talk with the men. She was alone on the couch. She opened her clutch, which was sitting beside her. Her license, ID, lipstick, and cell phone were in it. She took the charm off her phone and wrapped it around her pinky finger. She glanced up at the mural ceiling and tried to take a deep breath. Her breaths weren't drawing on air, like she was inhaling nothing. She began to choke and was in dire need of fresh air. The sound of the thunder grew by the second. She walked to the window and unlatched it. Taking in the storm breeze and the smell of rain calmed her. She could breathe again. She stood there for a few seconds before she turned around and walked back towards the couch.

She'd taken two steps when a white sheet descended through the air followed by a foot that grasped the edge outside the window. Clark climbed down his makeshift rope and entered the room, wet as a shark.

Lyra had her back turned and was walking towards the couch.

Walking away, you're always walking away from me, he thought.

"L, L," she pretended not to hear him, thought it was her mind playing tricks again. "Lyra," he whispered loud enough to get her attention.

She froze in her tracks. She recognized the voice. His sweet, sonorous, timbre voice; she turned around slowly, savoring each second. It took an eternity for her to face him. She saw Clark completely drenched, holding a pistol in his left hand, and extending his right hand towards her.

"Oh my Go—" a single teardrop formed under her puffed eyes, it streamed down and around her left dimple.

"A canvas of perfection," Clark caught the teardrop as it left her chin and kissed it.

She extended her hand to him. He reeled her in and kissed her. She put her hands on his wet face and their lips met with the passion of love's engulfing flames. The storm behind them thundered hell's inevitable victory. He felt like a Zen Master recognizing his place in the universe.

Their moans served to infuriate the storm. Their lips touched, separated, and touched again in rhythm with the wind like the dancing trees outside FACE. They both wanted to freeze time in that moment, to live in that second with no fear of an imminent *Dahaka* chasing them but such things are reserved for fairy tales of yore, for *fictional* stories of love and redemption.

He backed away against every instinct in his body. His muscles ached with a ravenous pain. She was desolate. Murderous fury consumed him when he noticed the left side of her face was red and bruising. The thunder wouldn't stop howling. His heartbeat rose drastically. He was ablaze with a fierce coveting every time he thought of her and there wasn't a single moment when she wasn't consuming his mind in some way. He closed his eyes and inhaled softly when she placed her hand on his heart. He was elevated to paradise. His pupils constricted as he loosened his grip on her waist to the point of letting go.

"You have to go," he whispered in her ear. "I'll catch up," his eyelashes tickled her earlobe.

"No, I'm not leaving without you," her face aged in the silence at the thought of losing him again. Every part of her wanted him. She wanted all of him, including the heartbreaks, grazes, and scars. She knew it was what gave him depth, what made him who he was, what made him *unique*.

He put his hands back on her waist, "Lyra, don't argue, you have to leave, I have to take care of them or they'll never leave us alone... go."

He turned her around and guided her out of the window. It was a small jump to the little grass lawn that then led into a road away from the compound. He helped her down. She stood on the grass. The storm immediately wet her face and her lips shimmered under the rain, she looked back, *come with me*, her eyes said. Her gaze brought a tear to his mind's eye.

"Go," he whispered. "I'll be right behind you... wait, take these."

He reached into his right pants pocket and extracted a large stack of folded papers, which unfolded from the lack of pressure from his pants. She reached for them, the soaked papers made both their hands feel colder than it was. Neither of them cared, Clark held her touch longer than he needed to, he held her hand until it slowly slipped away as he backed behind the window frame.

The visibility of the storm made it impossible to see her as she took three steps towards the path. He couldn't even make out her silhouette. She stopped and looked towards him and he was still behind the window frame, staring out.

He looked up at the sky, then straight ahead, *you don't owe me anything... fine, we never got along... fine, but let her be. Punish me when you need to quench those sadistic thirsts you get too often. Let her go... please... please let her be safe.*

A deafening thunder followed by lightning lit up the road for less than a second. He saw her looking back.

He reentered the room with the gun still in his hand. He looked around for a vantage point. With an eye on the door, he moved towards the drink table, opened what smelled like scotch, and poured a little into the glass beside it. The drink in his right hand, the gun in his left, he sat in the seat Lyra was sitting in moments ago. He saw her clutch, he hid it under one of the couch cushions. He'd come back for it later. There was no reason for anyone to know who she was or where she lived.

He sipped the drink.

Hmm. Johnnie Walker Blue... not a bad way to go... not bad at all.

He was there to die. A life for a life: his life for Lyra's. There'd be no reason to chase Lyra and kill her if he was dead. The 'family' would have nothing to worry about if he were dead. He was happy to abide. It was time. It was one good thing he thought he'd do on this miserable planet for the one person he cared for.

XXVIII
La Donna

Clark spun and tightened the silencer onto the muzzle of his 1911. He was hidden outside an apartment in complete black gear: black jacket, ski mask, track pants, and work boots.

A Torrino assassin who's killed four innocents so far. One of them was a woman, I'll be damned if there's a fifth.

He was outside James Aerios's house. Aerios was an assassin for the Torrinos and unlike Clark didn't discriminate among targets. Women, children, *innocents*, it meant nothing to him. He never cared for anything or anyone in his life, a dead man walking.

Might as well make it official.

Aerios had no code. A person without a code is not a person. Civilized people require *some sort of* code. It's what separates them from the barbarians. He'd recently botched a job for the family. The contract was for a made Calvano man, an essential cog in their narcotics machine. Clark had confirmed that there were two witnesses: the man's niece and daughter-in-law who were visiting him. They came out of the guest bedroom as he was putting two bullets into the Calvano man and Aerios killed them too. Understandable, but they were innocent. Innocents are sacred. He should have done a better recon. Clark knew that Aerios secretly enjoyed his life, playing some makeshift God by taking people's lives, no different from a banker who takes away a man's castle and starves his family just because he can. They enjoy the blood.

He bent down outside the door and started picking the lock. Tick tick tick, click. He quietly cocked his gun. He opened the door and entered the pitch-black ambiance inside the house. The darkness was advantageous to him. He mounted the first two stairs when he noticed a small light emitting from the next room. He crouched towards the light. It was the kitchen. Aerios was taking food out of the fridge. He was a fat, gluttonous man, thinning hair with a small light-brown beard. This sight disgusted Clark. He could see Aerios's face through the fridge light with his tongue hanging out as he looked in.

You've killed innocents, how are you smiling? What's so damned funny?

He felt like the world had told a hilarious joke and everyone had heard the punch line but him. He snuck up behind Aerios, as he neared him, Clark stood up. Aerios heard his footsteps and turned around, a piece of toast dangling out of his mouth. He continued chewing as Clark raised his gun towards his chest. He slowly chewed the last piece of bread in his mouth and gulped it down, getting down to his knees.

"Please... don't do it, I was only following orders... please," he cried like an abandoned baby on a church stoop.

Clark was disgusted, "The woman and child, why?"

Aerios choked up, barely being able to speak the words, "They saw me, saw my face. I'm a professional. With the way you got in here, I assume you are too..." he sniffled, "I couldn't let them live if they saw me."

Why didn't you do a better recon, his family was only visiting, you'd have known that, and could've postponed the hit by a day or two, you were sloppy and now a child is dead. When you take a life, you're not only taking a present life, but a future one, you cease what the person *might* and *can* be.

Clark pulled the trigger. Aerios blobbed to the ground as his blood morphed with his tears and sweat. Clark walked out of the house and took off his mask, holstering his weapon. His heartbeat hadn't risen a single beat. He imagined the old stories of bravery and justice he'd read in his youth, stories now long descended to the realm of fabled mythical creatures like dragons, unicorns, and trustworthy people. Such stories no longer served as fact but were confirmed as fiction.

* * *

Knock knock.

"5:04 in the morning. It's late. Who the hell could it be?" a voice returned on the other side of the door.

Lyra opened the door in her pajamas. She was the most elegant woman he'd ever laid eyes on even in her pajamas. The familiar smell of strawberries overwhelmed his nostrils and tingled his fingertips with a sort of warm sensation. Her eyes were like flames burning hotter than the core of a supernova, his heartbeat rose so fast he nearly went into cardiac arrest.

"Hmm," she smiled, "No suit?" she eyed his big black sweater up and down, "How... disappointing," she rubbed under her eye with her index finger.

"Hello beautiful," Clark stood in the doorway. He wouldn't enter without an invitation.

"Don't call me that," she replied.

But you are beautiful... —

Stop it Clark, are you... feeling? A stoic sage leaves no room for trivial emotions. You just took a life! What's the matter with you? You're not supposed to feel anything. Don't tell me you're falling for her. You're pathetic. Bury the feelings like you bury the past. It's what you do best anyway.

He stood there staring at her.

"Well are you going to come in or are you waiting for me to invite you in?"

The smile on his lips lasted for half a second. She caught it. *Love* was too small a word to describe what he felt, a mere four-letter term denoting some obscure form of affection but it was the only one he knew and respected.

She rolled her eyes, "Would you like to come in Clark?"

"Nothing would make me happier."

She opened the door and extended her hand out, *mi casa es su casa.*

What is this thing in my heart? It's not pain. It doesn't hurt. A peculiar thing. I don't know if I like it.

It'd been 6 years since Clark last entered her abode. She'd moved things around and rearranged them. The serenity of the place was intact. He could breathe here even better than that house in Tuscany. He looked towards the kitchen, there a late teen/young adult raiding the fridge. The man was blonde, tall and handsome. Very... tough-guy looking. He came out with a sandwich and a glass of milk, not dissimilar to Aerios but worlds apart. It was Vero.

"CLARKKKK!!!" he screamed in elation. It'd been a while and Clark was somehow still one of Vero's role models after their sole encounter.

Clark flashed to a memory of receiving a text message from Lyra asking him when he'd drop by. She said Vero wanted to see him. She said he was his hero. *I'm no hero*, he thought. He never replied. That was the last time they communicated. He didn't want to corrupt Vero, corrupt Lyra. String her along and pull her into a life of despair and death. He'd shed tears at this mistake.

So many mistakes, so few correct decisions, do we make our own choices? If we don't, it means some of us are doomed. If we do, it means some of us are doomed because we've made bad decisions.

Vero was ecstatic. He lifted Clark off the ground with a bear hug and squeezed him. Clark was not short but Vero towered over him anyway.

Lifted by Truth.

Lyra turned the coffee machine on; its memorable smell pranced in Clark's nostrils. He was at home. His assumption that truth was pain had been erroneous, the truth was he was in *love* with her and it wasn't painful. *Vero*, was anything but painful.

"You've... grown," Clark said as Vero put him down. Clark liked Vero, most eighteen year olds would fall in love with their own saga and act like a 'tough guy' and feign stoicism. A neutrality or a carelessness at the entrance of an old friend they hadn't seen in a long time. Clark knew that's what he would've done. They'd feel betrayed that their friend had forgotten them. Vero wasn't like that. He didn't act like something he wasn't. He lived in the present. He was glad Clark had shown up and wasn't afraid to express it. He poured another glass of milk for Clark.

"Now I know how you've gotten so big," Clark took the milk.

"*Leon the Professional*, it's all he drinks."

A quip about a hired gun? Who is this kid? Vero's presence triggered old mystic feelings. You can't choose how you feel. It was as if he was conversing with his younger self, holding that joystick button down and traveling backwards through time. Vero had always been special to him.

"I'm so happy to see you," he told Clark. Lyra watched the exchange in the background near the kitchen, peering towards the men in the main room. She had papers and letters scattered on the small coffee table in the middle of the living room. Most of them crumbled, it looked like she was writing a letter but it wasn't coming out right.

"And I you, old friend," Clark suddenly felt empathic and a rush of something he'd never experienced crowded his mind and body.

Vero turned to Lyra, "'*And I you, old friend?*' See what I mean? No one talks like that. No one has the *balls* to talk like that. You truly are one of a kind Clark!"

Clark remembered thinking the same thing about Vero the first time he met him.

"Beat Prince of Persia yet? Or do you need my expert help again?" Clark couldn't wipe the stupid smirk off his own face.

"Prince of Persia? How times have changed. No I'm playing something else, come, I'll show you."

They took their glasses of milk into Vero's room. Nothing had changed about the room except the TV and game system were now newer and there were pieces of letter-sized paper with quotes on them taped up to the wall. Clark sat down in the familiar chair and Vero unpaused the game.

It was a shootout, a bald man with a big black beard wearing a torn shirt fought airport officials on a private runway. He'd taken cover behind some luggage and Vero shot them as they approached the bags.

Clark could see Lyra from in between the small gap of space left open between the door and its frame, she was looking in, smiling while waiting for the coffee. Clark turned his head back towards the TV, a quote taped to the wall caught his eye.

> If the sun and moon should doubt,
> They'd immediately go out.
> To be in a passion you good may do,
> But no good if a passion is in you.

"Blake?" Clark was thinking out loud.

Vero paused the game and turned around, he saw Clark looking at the quote,

"Yeah, she'd read it to me all the time, said a friend quoted that part of the poem to her once. She was moved by it or something. I think she loved the guy."

Loved the guy?

"She read it to me every other morning at the breakfast table. Told me to remember it and hold onto it."

Clark wanted to weep hysterically. The submissive vibrating of his tear ducts whispered inevitability.

What are you doing you sissy?

Men aren't supposed to cry. That's what we've been told anyway. Who said men shouldn't cry? I want the name of the person who made this rule because it's a stupid rule. I must be true to my passions, my emotions—

What a sissy, you going to cry little girl?

Shut up! You did this to me! I will have my revenge of you, in this life or the next.

The clamoring beast tried to cage his thoughts back into the realm of stoicism.

Bury it.

A man in the game was elevated on a mobile stairway. Clark presumed this to be the boss: the bad guy. After a tiresome gunfight with the airport officials, federal agents, and hired guns, the boss fired a grenade towards the bald man Vero was controlling. Vero slowed time down at the press of a button,

What is it with this kid and time?

He took aim and fired at the grenade in mid-air. The grenade exploded. The bad guy flew backwards and fell onto the runway.

The bearded hero followed, the boss was lying on the floor, torn to pieces but still alive. Clark could see inside his wounds, his left arm was missing and half his face was burned from the blast.

"Those graphics... it almost looks real, what game is this?" Clark asked.

Vero turned the volume up, "Max Payne 3," he whispered. Clark had shifted his gaze to the Blake quote above the TV until he saw the bearded man approach the bad guy, pointing his gun at the mangled man on the floor. His monologue was about being a hired goon, a man with no depth realizing he was nothing more than a second-rate bozo. It disturbed him.

Vero was given the option of letting the man live or putting him out his misery. Clark left the room.

Too many coincidences.

He walked towards Lyra who was taking cookies out of a tin can. He spun her and kissed her. Her cheeks were as red as the blood pumping through his heart. Their interlocked lips reminded Clark of the infiniteness of the universe, the abstract world where perfect love is presumed to exist.

Do I love her?

Clark stroked his left hand from her waist to her nape. Their lips separated after a minute.

"I'm... I don't..."

Lyra wanted to tease him. *Use your words Clark.* It would have been sweet. She decided not to, she could see he was conflicted and she didn't want to push him, he was already a man on the edge.

"What are you afraid of?" she asked him.

"I thought…" he couldn't breathe. "I thought I'd never been afraid, that I was naturally fearless. I've never been afraid of anything in my life, not even death, and God knows that's all I deserve. I thought fearlessness was my nature, but when *you* ask me what I fear…"

"Clark, you can tell me anything… I hope you know that," she put her hand where his heart was, rubbing it with her fingertips. She moved her nose close enough so that it wasn't touching his but he could feel it.

He thought he saw her start to choke up she snuffled, of all the wishes he'd screamed onto the empty air, only the mortal one was granted: seeing an angel cry.

You're worse than me! You're doing this to her again? Jesus Clark, you should see someone, and he calls 'me' the beast! The nerve on this prick.

A migraine loomed in the right part of his head. He could hear the sound of gunshots from Vero's room. It was as if the gunfire was behind him, always barely audible but there nonetheless, like the past. The symbolism nearly made him walk out of the apartment to never return, to try again to catch the lying bullet in a bluff.

"You ask me what I fear, I've been afraid since the day I laid eyes on you, your beautiful eyes," he stared deep into her eyes, moving his nose slightly closer so they finally touched. "Your perfect lips," he ran his thumb on her mouth, "Your mystical smile," he traced a smile on her dimples. "I am afraid that I am not enough for you. You are a goddess, an angel. Angels deserve saints, and I'm far from a saint…"

He shut his eyes as tightly as he could to ease the torturous headache in the back of his head. There it was, the vulnerable blink she'd been waiting to see.

"I am afraid that you'd see who I really am… and hate it."

She put her hands on his face—

A whistle went off. The coffee was ready.

Timing is everything. Life is lived one second at a time. What a concept: time. One half second here and you don't make it, one half second there and you don't get it. To live without despair, you have to make the correct decision in half a second and then perform the corresponding action. The gag is, it's all impossible. You can't live without despair without making bad decisions. Why is it then some mistakes hurt more than others while some choices blindly lead to success?

They both looked down towards each other's chests, he slowly let her go and she moved towards the coffee machine.

There are two tragedies in life. One is to lose your heart's desire. The other is to gain it. Maybe Shaw was onto something.

He knew what he wanted, he always knew his heart's desire and knew how to get it. Getting it meant fighting his nurture and accepting his nature. Accepting your nature takes years. From the second you're born you're taught to reject your nature, your true self and accept what you're being told. *Do this, eat that, see this, believe that.* It's all bullshit. All nurture. It's nature that's to be nurtured, not nurture that's made to be natural.

You got the wrong quote Clark, it's 'There are only two tragedies in life: one is not getting what one wants, and the other is getting it,' and it's Oscar Wilde, not Bernard Shaw.

What are we, friends now?

He wanted to kiss her again, hold her and never let her go. *Can I leave everything behind? What if I didn't get it, what if I don't want her, what if what if what if.*

The *what ifs* were making him weak.

Everything he'd read and analyzed was coming back to haunt him. His ideas took him hostage and crucified him for all to see like soldiers standing at the gates of Troy. Ideas stand ready to give their lives for a higher abstract. Even Clark didn't understand *true* sacrifice until that moment. It was as if he knew too much, had read too much, too much information flowing in his intricate neurological system weakening his passions. His mind was in complete control of his heart and this diminished his motivation for action if the logical process didn't permit an acceptable degree of success in correlation to risk. However, he knew in his heart that a man has to risk everything, including his life, to attain an angel worth dying for, and this thought overrode any 'logic' or 'equation' proclaiming to some nonexistent variant of truth.

XXIX
SERENITY INTERRUPTED

—The door whooshed open, the repetitive audio-track of shrilling thunder whistled in his ears like Lyra's coffee machine.

"I'm telling you, if you don't find him— just get more guys! He's one man," Alex was still facing outside into the hallway. He stepped into the room and shut the door and nearly began weeping. His shoulders bounced up and down rapidly. He'd yet to see Clark.

Clark clacked the ice in his cup. Alex's eyes were closed but it was as if he knew the sound wasn't coming from Lyra, after all, she could've been the one drinking. Something deep within him knew he'd been bested. He didn't want to open his eyes, wishing this was a nightmare his dad would wake him from before some mild insults about his manhood. Clark calmly drank the remaining portion of his scotch and placed the cup on a table to his left. Alex finally opened his eyes. Clark was wiping his mouth with a handkerchief, the gun sat close to his left hand. He was looking straight at Alex, who practically trembled. He dropped the walkie-talkie on the floor and stayed frozen with his back to the door.

"I was going to leave... Don *Fiddy*," Clark's primal stare forced a fear in the made *man* he didn't think he was capable of.

"Listen... bradere... I," Alex muttered as he tried taking a step towards Clark, Clark put out his hand to signal him to stop moving. Alex abided.

Alex suddenly reached behind him and came out with a silenced gun of his own. He pointed it at Clark with a shaking hand.

Special relativity. Einstein is right. All things are relative, including time. When you're staring down the black hole at the wrong end of a gun, your life flashes before your eyes. Your wounds, battle scars, memories, loved ones. You can see them all. Play your cards right and you can live a life in that half second alone.

Alex didn't like Clark's boiling stare, he lifted his hand and fired in a panic. He conflated stillness with apathy and ruthlessness like the witness's husband in Scandinavia.

A bullet never lies.

He'd missed. Clark drew his gun and fired three bullets, center mass. The first bullet sounded like a symphony orchestra and pierced Alex's chest like hot steel on butter. Alex couldn't breathe, he slipped to the ground. A pool of blood immediately surrounded him.

"I'm not your brother, I *was* going to walk away... then you brought *her* here. I can't let that go. I'll never let that go.

Don't fight it, it's time," Clark reached into his pocket and shook his cigar box, "It's a Cristo, I know your family's brand is *Don* Tomàs," he emphasized the word 'don,' "But dying men never get what they want, and we're all dying... aren't we?"

Blood squirted out of Alex's chest. Clark offered his final cigar to him, Alex wheezed and managed a puff before he expired with the cigar on his lip.

"A cigar's life..."

He stood up and walked towards the window. He couldn't exit through the party and he had no intention of waiting for the police. He'd given them everything they needed. He disappeared into the storm. A few goons broke down the door. Matthews heard the racket and took this as the intended signal Durante had whispered to him about. They found Alex's dead body on the floor with the cigar burning on his lip and rainwater dancing on the windowsill.

Durante called backup. He told Matthews to start arresting people. Undercover officers poured into the party. Backup was on the way.

XXX
SICKLE-ING INEVITABILITY

Lyra's glances towards the compound were wasted. She expected the night air to part and reveal Clark's gait. The way he walked, the way he talked, she realized she loved everything about him.

I've lied to him, I tore out his heart and he still loves me with the pieces that remain.

She loved him almost as much as he loved her. She heard a car approaching, her worries were at ease. Clark *had* come for her. The car progressively slowed down behind her. She knew she could count on him. She thought she heard a wolf howl or a jungle-car roar. *There aren't any of those here,* she thought. She stood there like an angel ascending to grace, breathing in the night air. She turned around, clutching the letters and the cell phone charm firmly.

"Clark, I love—"

A knife penetrated her Elysian flesh. She stared into the eyes of the man that killed her, shaking like the last petal of a wilting rose.

Does he love me? How did he choose me? What have I done to deserve him? I love him. I know I do, I chose him. I made this choice.

"I told him to stay away from you, he was never good at following instructions was he?" Ventoni's reptilian stare shook her delicate frame as he turned the knife in her heart, her yelp would've sent Clark over the edge he'd been tiptoeing on since they walked away from each other. A river of blood flowed down to her abdomen, tears rolled down her eyes and the storm took possession of the letters in her hand. Ventoni had gotten fat, his once-athletic prowess was no longer comparable to Clark, his gelatinous belly flopped over his designer belt, a greasy beard made him look like a modern 'action' star with nothing to lose, a slimeball easily confusable with a homeless man begging for change.

"He's a better man than you," she whispered in his ear. His porky nostrils widened with rage and he violently twisted the knife in her again for a second time. Her ribs crunched. He looked down at himself; he *had* gotten fat. How disgusting. He thought he should retrain, wake up at the crack of dawn and exchange mind and body banters with a nice fellow at his local stadium.

"He's…" she gargled and swallowed blood, "Smarter than you!"

A murder of crows dispersed from the trees beside her. She fell back into the pouring puddle and held her wound. The headlights of the man's car stared back at her. She saw the driver; there were two of them. A faint silhouette of a man could be seen walking towards them, the driver looked at his side mirror and peeled out. Ventoni disappeared into the forest beside her, leaving behind the sound of rustling leaves and howling wind. She looked at her hands. The charm was partially covered in blood. Her hands fell by her side. She stared into the infinite crevasse above her where the storm had formed. Raindrops smacked her in the face harder than Alex. Her tears went unchecked. Her eyes remained open as her breaths became shallower.

* * *

She approached Clark and another man playing chess at the park, catching an ongoing conversation between the two.

"Clark, come on. Take off that hat. It makes you look ridiculous. Like an outlaw who rides into town with no beliefs or passions."

Clark lifted his head from under the brim of a white homburg and caught his opponent's eye, "Maybe I don't have any passions," the cigar smoke blew outwards from the edge of the hat.

Lyra grabbed the hat and put it on her head, "It's an *injustice* to hide hair like that Clarky…" she curled a strand of Clark's hair onto her finger, "Looks better on me anyway."

"You're certainly right about that," Clark stood as she sat down.

You've been reading too much Cervantes Clark.

"What a gentleman," the man said, thinking about her lasciviously. "Clark, you're like a knight. That'll be your nickname: Knight," and the man picked up a white Knight from the chessboard and threw it at Clark, who was unfazed by it, staring into Lyra's sizzling eyes.

"It's my move right?" the man said.

Lyra noticed a pair of Oriental men beside them as Clark placed the knight back on the board. The strangers were playing a game that looked like checkers but wasn't. There were so many pieces and the design was different.

"What's that?" her irises darted to the peculiar board.

Clark quickly shifted his gaze from her eyes to their neighbor's,

"It's Wei Ch'i, Chinese chess or checkers. Arguably the most difficult board game ever conceived. Mao demanded its mastery from all his generals."

"You know so much... so many... *things,*" she shifted her gaze to his right hand, which was meshed with his left resting on a copy of Longfellow's *Inferno* translation, the corner of the cover flapping in the wind.

"I love Dante," she said, "But only the *second* English translation is good, it's archaic but flows nicely, can't find the hardcover anywhere though."

She squinted towards the flapping cover, "Wait. That *is* the second English translation isn't it?" she stood over him and reached towards the book. Her hair brushed Clark's face. He didn't move a millimeter.

"Yes," Clark said amongst her hair.

Knight takes Queen, his opponent thought.

She saw her hair in Clark's face, "Oh... I'm so sorry."

Don't be, Clark thought. "I assure you, it's quite alright."

Clark's opponent finally moved a piece. Clark shifted his gaze once again from her eyes to the board and in seconds moved the thrown knight forward into enemy territory.

His opponent studied the board, stealing glances at Clark and Lyra, who rarely looked away from each other.

"Screw it. I know your nickname."

"We've moved off Knight?" Clark asked sardonically.

"Yep, I'm going to call you…" he moved his hands through the air to create suspense, acting like a showman, "… The Viking."

Clark felt that familiar smirk creep its way onto his cheeks, the same one he'd seen in the mirror, in his dreams, always staring back at him; he hated that smirk.

"Viking? Yes my long flowing blonde hair and white skin is quite pronounced," his sarcasm bordered on patronization.

"It's not about what you look like, it's about passions."

"Come on Rook, don't be absurd."

"Hear me out," John said while Lyra observed this exchange, wondering how she'd use her knowledge on Norse mythology to prove John wrong.

"Your passions must be genuine. The physicality, or what you look like has nothing to do with it. It's about where your passions lie, where your heart lies, what you love, who you love, and how you express it."

Lyra tittered when John said 'express it,' he turned to face her, afraid to look her right in the eye.

"I know I know, he doesn't express himself too much but that's part of the reality of it, his passion. He expresses himself, but he's no more expressive than his true nature," he ranted. "He respects his *true* self, he's not a soft man. Buttered with objects like those who the devil deceives with his silvery tongue."

Clark estimated John's IQ at about 160.

That sounded like Zen. What's a man like John doing with Zen? He must be up to something.

"*True* self?" Lyra interjected.

"I think he means, 'If the sun and moon should doubt, They'd immediately go out. To be in a passion you good may do, But no good if a passion is in you.'"

Lyra's heart sank lower than a freshman's standards after two Bellinis at a frat party.

John looked at him quizzically, *yes, that's what I meant dumbass. Always trying to impress the women with poetry. What a fairy.*

Lyra *was* impressed. She gazed at the sky, the sun gleaming behind her and shadowing her profile over the dusking horizon. She looked contemplatively at Clark's knight on the board.

"And this relates to 'Viking' how?" Clark asked.

How stupid. I know what he's going to say, Clark could see his doom in the distance, Wile E. Coyote seeing the cliff but unable to stop because of the malfunctioning jetpack.

John's envy could boil an egg. "Your heart lies with a Norwegian woman. You love her. Logic dictates your heart is Norwegian, ergo you're the Viking!"

Lyra was Norwegian. They all knew what Ventoni meant. Betrayal never surprised Clark but the timing was horrible.

Clark noticed her blush and her cheeks turned rosy, she stood up and walked away abruptly.

John moved a piece on the board hoping he could expose Clark's game,

"Open sesame," he whispered, referring to Clark's defense. That's why he did it. Because he wanted to win a chess game. A chess game. Human hubris…

Despite the delusions he possessed about his own superiority, John's intellectual poverty amused Clark. John loved to say, and Clark assumed he'd also said it numerous times in his head whenever his life granted him the opportunity, 'open sesame.' He never once looked into the origin of the phrase. He was a sheep browsing BrainyQuote for something to make himself sound cleverer than he was and had stumbled upon it somewhere. He didn't know it was from *Ali Baba and the Forty Thieves,* from *Arabian Nights*, about the princess Scheherazade perpetually deceiving the murderous king by telling a never-ending story in the purpose of her own survival. That the deeper meaning behind this phrase could be that even kings, the arrogance that John fancied himself a king was all but sure, could be fooled. Status means nothing. Clark realized John's intelligence was never curious, he never sought to be wise or to be better. He only wanted to be wiser or better than the next second-rate idiot, which made him a first-rate one.

Their friendship came to a screeching halt as Clark stood up to follow her. He glanced at the board and moved the other knight into enemy territory,

"Checkmate."

A final screw-you to the 'prodigy,' Clark had paid John the worst insult there was, an intellectual one. He'd been beaten at his own game. He made John feel like an idiot. Payment for angering Clark was his ego and pride. The checkmate was an exclamation point to everything that preceded. The disrespect he'd paid to Clark.

"Impossible!" John gasped. He looked at the board. He *was* beaten.

Touché you prick. Knight takes Rook.

Clark chased Lyra. It should have taken him a few seconds to catch up to her. Each second felt like an eternity. She was only pacing away from him yet Clark felt himself sprinting.

Time is relative.

His thoughts became scrambled. He couldn't think and could barely see, feel, or even hear. The abstruse system in his brain responsible for emotion was malfunctioned in the crater of his mind. He couldn't process what he was experiencing in those moments. He caught up to her out of breath like he'd run across the world. She was rubbing her eyes, he grabbed her hand and turned her to face him. She *was* crying. The sight almost made *him* fall to his knees and sob like a child. Their hands meshed together; her hand was like a sea of scolding lava and burned his.

"I can't... I can't..." she had trouble saying the words; she was nervously shaking her head, trembling with sobs and weeps, averting his eyes.

For the third time in his life, Clark had trouble holding a gaze,

"I love you... *I* love... *you*. You make me see light where there's only darkness, you're my only solace in battles against demons.... Don't leave, my heart could not endure it," he *thought*.

"Lyra..." The words wouldn't come out, he knew what he wanted to say, he knew how he wanted to say it. The beast wouldn't let him.

Oooooo. Look at her, I think you just broke her heart. She was waiting for you to say something. What's wrong tough guy? Cat got your tongue? How does it feel, tearing out a woman's heart... I wish I knew.

SHUT UP SHUT UP SHUT UP! You did this! Be sure to tell me how a warm bullet feels against your flesh.

You can't kill me. You'd kill yourself!

Don't tempt me.

"Clark, I don't want to see you again, you're confusing me. Sending mixed signals, I can't figure you out," her voice broke.

His mind went blank, "I won't... bother you again; I don't want to force my morbid soul into your heart. It wouldn't be fair," these were the words that came out of his young, arrogant mouth, not realizing what he'd condemned himself to. He'd engineered his own demise. It was for the best anyway. Like he would later realize, he wouldn't want to string her along to a life of despair and pain. He wanted her to be happy and mistook her overwhelmed emotional response for rejection. Conflated stoicism with apathy. The fatal mistake mirrored through his own behavior.

Her tears worsened before they got better.

"Why are you crying?" and Clark had never understood such things.

"You're... like a delicate shadow, I chase and you run. I run and you chase, what do you want?" the tone of her voice escalated as each word left her rosy lips, churning an erupting mountain.

The things I want.

She understood him so well. He knew how rare it was. The coin had landed on its edge.

I hate Ventoni.

It was as if she'd blown the dust off his cold, unused heart and it began pumping as it from the moment he laid eyes on her. He wished he could tell her all he felt was contempt, disgust, and scorn, except when it came to her. He wished he could make her understand that he'd give his life, that further, he'd *take* a life to protect her. He wished a lot of things. Wishes are for children who don't know better.

Man loves woman, man doesn't get woman, man broods in self-loathing misanthropy and excess carnal affairs. Hahahahah. Clark... even your life's been said and done before. You 'are' a walking cliché Clark. Some bozo is probably going to read your story and feel sorry for you, pity you and your stupidity without really understanding the depth of your pain, the intensity of your passion for this... what do you call her again? ... Goddess? ... Oh give me a break.

Too much time had elapsed in silence, her shoulders stopped jerking up and down. She held his hand and nearly collapsed in his chest but he backed away. Their hands slowly parted. She handed him the hat, he'd never wear it again. Lyra walked away from him; the beast screeched so loud it nearly shattered every window in a five-mile radius.

He sat down across Ventoni and began organizing the pieces for a new game.

John had watched them from afar. He got the gist of it. He couldn't believe Clark's stoicism.

What a jerk. Breaking a woman's heart like that?

"Nothing less than a sophisticated badinage I assume." John regretted the words as soon as they left his mouth, Clark's glare was a fearful sight, he thought he heard a roar as if Clark would've broken the wooden chessboard over his head in a rage but instead Clark just clenched his jaw.

He failed to see that he was the catalyst in a fragile situation, that he might have caused these two pains to last a lifetime, the sort of raw chronic aching that never dissipates. A dark beast stalked them everywhere like a forest fire. No flames could burn this away. It'd only make the beast angrier, more eager to pounce.

Clark only then realized what he'd done, *Viking it is. I am my nature. I accept this. I will not fight it. Let it go Clark... let 'her' go.*

Yeah Clark, let go of what I've done. I'm looking out for you.

The ruthlessness and aggression of a Viking matched the beast but the beast couldn't be allowed to roam free lest it consume him as it nearly did moments before. It lusts for blood and for darkness; it *is* darkness. It must be countered, tamed. What counters darkness? Light. Lyra is the light.

Lyra is gone.

What else you got? it roared

Cages. Cages also tame beasts; he built a cage and forced the beast in, vowing to never allow it an infinitesimal ounce of freedom again. He'd break this vow in the future but young minds often say things that old minds would later laugh at.

* * *

"Ma'am? Ma'am?" A hero emerged through the storm. He must have been the one who scared the assassins away.

She felt paralyzed but managed to lift her head and look through the blood on her dress towards the direction of the compound. She could see the faint outline of a gold shield. The man's screaming demeanor was out of focus. She stared at his detective's badge but couldn't quite make out what he was saying.

The storm fell silent,

"I think I'm dying," she said calmly.

They taught Matthews at the academy to never cry but he couldn't help but project the image of his cancer-stricken mother onto Lyra.

"What's your name?" Lyra realized it wasn't Clark.

"Charles Matthews, everyone calls me Charlie."

"Nice to meet you *Charles*," she tried her hardest to get her hand up to shake his but didn't have the strength.

"It's been a long time since someone called me Charles," *please don't die* was all he could think about.

"It's funny, did you know Poe and Longfellow didn't get along? Two creative minds like that. Two... geniuses let's say for the sake of argument... and they didn't get along?"

"No, I didn't know that..." *please don't die.*

"Is that our nature? To be consuming and combative at all times? Is that what we've been reduced to?"

Matthews thought about his father's last case, "I… think… so."

Lyra's eyes flickered, "The place is a mess. I told Vero to clean up. He'll be here any minute."

Matthews gripped her hand as tight as he could, "You… have someone?"

"If the sun and moon should doubt…"

"Breathe," Matthews couldn't hold back the two tears amongst the raindrops on his face. She was so young and so beautiful.

"I'm cold. It's so cold," she chuckled a little before coughing violently, "He'd say that was a cliché. That it's what any second-rate damsel would say as their last words."

"It's okay. I know it's cold. It's freezing. Let it pass over you. It'll hover over you, let it stay there."

"The coffee should be ready any minute, he knows how I like my coffee, 'An artist's heart twice beat… '"

"Do you love someone?" Charles couldn't help but think the worst, she already wasn't making any sense and his hope had never been rewarded, not after the months of chemo his mom went through, not after the doctors told his dad that the cancer was in remission, why hope now?

She blinked away the tears, "I," she sniffled "Do," the words barely left her paling mouth.

"Think of him, let your thoughts go,"

"It wasn't—"

Matthews knew what it was supposed to feel like, his mom had told him on her deathbed, "It'll feel warm. You'll make it. Think of your loved ones. Let your thoughts warm your body."

She extinguished the flames in her irises one, last, time, with her thoughts roaming to Vero and Clark, the two men in her life who'd never betrayed her.

XXXI
LIES IN PURGATORY

Clark extracted an old cigar he found at the bottom of his pocket as he walked through the grumbling storm. It seemed like a miracle to be able to smoke in such harsh conditions but he seemed to have no trouble and thought that maybe his luck was turning.

The storm had other ideas. He didn't think it could get any worse and could see the clouds dispersing in the distance ahead of him; the blue sky ran from one side of the horizon to the other. He could feel the breeze and warmth of the sun minutes in front of him.

Is that where she was? Had the clouds parted for her? Was I going to catch up to her? Are we going to watch the sunrise together? Drenched from a storm?

There must be darkness in order for light to shine.

He hated himself for having such hope.

No. Life isn't a movie defined by genre.

Hawks with broken wings; lions with broken paws; *men* with broken hearts, they all have one thing in common: they're all as sure to die as those unbroken.

He turned onto another road with some houses on the side to avoid detection and looked back. A goon car followed by a police car was slowly driving away from the compound. He slumped towards the street. He realized he needed luck to get out of this one. Luck and him weren't on speaking terms; the irony was almost amusing.

He saw a man sitting on a porch with his dog. The thunder was so loud he could barely hear himself think. The man appeared to mouth something to him. He could have said it but Clark wouldn't have heard it and although it sounded and looked like "Be patient," Clark stopped in his tracks and stared at the man.

Be patient? What a joke. Do I look like the Count of Monte Cristo? I've been patient for years. Patience is brother of agony and son of pain. I'm a samurai without a sword. My soul is missing, steps ahead of me but I can't seem to ever embrace it. There's a curse of life and a gift of death in every breath and its shape was my body and my mind.

He thought perhaps he could find support on this man's porch just long enough to evade his pursuers. He approached the man and mounted the porch steps, the dog looked up but Clark's gaze tamed the animal.

"Thank you for your generosity," Clark's gratitude was infinite. He thought he'd be reuniting with Lyra in a few moments. He felt hope coupled with warm elation.

* * *

Eventually a black sedan sped through the street and both men heard the distant sound of sirens. It was the opportune moment, the time, if not the place to move on. Clark looked at his watch, nodded to the old man for the shelter during a storm and continued towards Lyra. He'd barely walked inches before his heart began pounding out of his chest. This not uncommon when it came to Lyra, it felt like it was going to tear out and land in his left hand. He saw police lights ahead.

He spotted an alley and turned down to escape. He didn't look back. He seemed to have gotten away.

Hey 'Luck,' this doesn't mean anything, we're still not friends.

Thunder crackled.

"You!" an officer shouted.

Clark looked into the distance *ahead* of him, *right on cue.*

The rain was coming down harder than when he touched Lyra's sunlit hand. He turned back slowly. He wasn't going to run and attract unwanted attention to himself, not now.

* * *

Clark moved down the alley, his heart doomed to tear out his ribcage and present itself to his hand, something he'd happily pledged to Lyra. He leaned against the alley wall to collect himself.

Oh. He didn't miss. He looked inside his jacket amongst his flowing blood. Luck was a banker who'd taken his credit simply because she could. Alex's bullet had struck him in the left abdomen.

A bullet never lies.

He pulled out his phone.

How do people believe, and even pray to be loved by a sadist?

It can't end this way, life is not to be ossified just when you're about to attain your dream.

He highlighted Lyra's name and looked up at the divided sky: the dark, black clouds above him contrasted with the clear, blue oceanic sky only steps ahead. He wouldn't make it that far.

He shook his head as if to rid the pain but agony is not so easily banished. He didn't have the strength to press the 'call' button. He didn't know what he felt. His memories lapsed and meshed together, he knew Lyra didn't have her phone, he saw it in her purse in Alex's room but he didn't care, he wanted to hear her voice one more time even if it was only her voicemail greeting.

No pain is equal to the pain of a harmonic body and mind aching for an action that borders on the impossible. When both forces decide you've failed. No stabbing, shooting, or beating could compare, 'Some are born to sweet delight, others born to endless night.' Perhaps I was born damned, and I've been stupid to think I could change that.

The phone slowly slipped out of his hand and fell into a puddle on his left side. To his dismay, Clark was unable to do anything about it. He stared at the screen through the puddle and rainwater dousing it with the weakness of the *Dahaka*. The phone's brightness decreased until it was fully submerged in a sea of liquid and showed only darkness. Lyra's name flashed back and forth on the phone until he couldn't see it anymore. He reached into his jacket pocket by gathering all his might and extracted Durante's fine cigar.

"Look for it," that charlatan was right.

He put it to his lip but didn't have the strength to get to his matches all the way on the right side of his body, and so the Cohíba withered on his wet lip unlit until it dropped to the ground in slow-motion; Special Relativity at its best.

It makes me laugh, life. My last thoughts are of Lyra just like my phone's last thoughts in highlighting her name. For all my utter remarks, my stoic gazes, my passionate despair for her affections, I never told her I loved her. Perhaps she knows. Perhaps my actions showed her, or perhaps I'm deluded. There's solace in that I guess. His thoughts were becoming as black as space.

At least I did one good thing, made one right decision: I saved her.

His ignorance was bliss.

His vision deteriorated, there was a bright light on the right side of his peripheral on the wall, the light got bigger and brighter with each second. He turned his body forward towards it, towards the blue sky and tried to claw his way out of the storm with the tips of his now serrated fingernails. He could no longer see. He fell down into a puddle and paralysis set in, and as soon as he realized he couldn't move his arms, his legs gave out.

All he had left were thoughts of Lyra, until those too, diminished into darkness like his phone. The beast bawled in the cage for the final time and laid down, its barred door swinging back and forth... until its squeaking ceased like Clark's quasi-rhythmic heartbeat.

XXXII
DURANTE'S CIRCLE

Although the canvass of the scene after the murder turned up Clark's name as a person of interest thanks to Officer's Johnson's *razor*-sharp intellect, there was also a car registered to the late Alexander Torrino. Obviously, having died earlier, he could not have been the one driving the car. Durante tracked it using the LoJack system in place for all high-end luxury cars. He caught up to the ridiculously overpriced 760Li, complete with spinning chrome rims and tinted windows on the highway moments after Lyra's body had been found.

Flashing his police lights behind the car, he pulled the car over.

He could see the man in the car remove gloves through the back window as he approached. He enjoyed the reverse role since he had just put on his brand new leather gloves.

"License and registration please," he asked the driver as the window rolled down.

"Officer, listen…"

"Sir, step out of the vehicle," Durante demanded of the driver with widening eyes and a sharp exhale.

The storm had died down. The icicles had melted into a light drizzle. The sun was beginning to rise in the horizon. Two crows swept down and landed on the trunk, scratching the matte paint with their talons.

"Now? Officer… please."

Durante opened the door and forced the man out; the crows cawed.

"Okay okay Officer, take it easy."

Durante pushed the man against the back driver-side door of the car. He took a step back and drew his gun faster than Clint Eastwood in a Mexican standoff.

"Hello Dev," Durante's last jigsaw fit into the puzzle like one of his father's tailored tuxedos.

"Have we met?" the don's top enforcer asked Durante.

"You took someone from me long ago," the crows' songs were too loud not to be symbolic.

"Listen man…" Durante tightened his grip on the trigger, "I don't know what I did."

He was negotiating for more light from the darkness and change his destiny. Durante was the *Dahaka*.

"For Beatrice," Durante pulled the trigger. A gaping wound dissevered Dev's forehead from his face and he fell beside the car. Durante dropped the gun beside him and walked towards the sunrise, clutching the paper Clark had gifted him.

XXXIII
Paradiso

Electra pressed her phone tightly to her ear. It rang to no avail.

Come on Clark, where are you?

She'd seen him at the party the night before and was a little offended he didn't even say hi.

"This is Clark Kóróna. Leave me your message and I'll call back when I acquire the time."

"Clark, this is the fourth message I've left you. Where are you? By the way, change your voicemail. You can't *acquire* time."

She sat down on her bed and turned on the television just in time for the news.

"And in an obscure crime spree, Alexander Torrino, the notorious Don Vitaly Torrino's son, was killed at the annual Paris Ball of Justice. Don Vitaly Torrino himself was arrested this morning for multiple counts of extortion, kidnapping, murder, and narcotics racketeering. Don Torrino has allegedly been the head of the organized crime family for decades.

A young woman was savagely murdered blocks away from the ball. Lyra Bergljót (her DMV photo flashed across the screen) was found stabbed once in the heart two kilometers from the party.

Another unidentified man was found heavily injured from a gunshot wound in the alley near Mort and Grave. He is in critical condition at an unnamed hospital.

The final victim, Devo Neimetti, reported to be Don Torrino's right hand man, was also found dead. Reports suggest he was lying beside a car not registered in his name with a single gunshot to the head.

The police have no suspects in any of the murders but assume that it is probably a mugging spree and the connection of the victims is coincidental...

In other news, the mayor decided to vote for tax breaks for the higher-income individuals in an effort to accelerate the development projects he hopes will create more jobs."

Electra turned the TV off and laid in her bed trembling with fear with the weight of the world on her shoulders. *This is what Atlas feels like.* She curled into the fetal position and cried a little before eventually mustering up the courage to move. She went into her dresser and packed a suitcase. She collected all the bare necessities, not forgetting of course, the Dante note she wrote just before Clark's disappearance. She stepped outside the hotel.

"Excuse me," a voice said to her.

She could narrowly pinpoint where the voice was coming from, it sounded like the person was right beside her. She spotted a man: vest, a small-brimmed hat, dress pants, shoes, and worldly eyes.

"Yes sir, I have some change for you."

"Very good," a devious smile formed on the man's lips.

Electra hastened to grab some money from her purse and she came out with her Louis Vuitton wallet and checkbook.

The man laughed, "Everyone always assumes that. No, I don't want money. I assumed you meant you have change. As in generally. Which I thought was odd. *Change* in your purse. If only."

"I... don't understand," Electra's bewildered eyes answered the man.

"My daughter. Do not worry. He is in a better place. At peace. At rest. ... At last."

"Who are you talking about sir?" Electra queried with an eerie chill continuously running up and down her spine.

"There is a time. A man cannot change his destiny, nothing can change its destiny, not even this rock," and a rock appeared in the man's hand.

"It was his time, and he went, as we all will, understand this, know this, accept this."

Electra closed her eyes to hold back the tears that were sure to come flowing as soon as she opened them. She'd get over him. He was only a man. Her eyes sharply opened at this thought seconds later but the man was gone. She looked around but saw no sign of him. She looked down at her hands. He'd placed the rock in her hand and she was tightly grasping it, she hadn't noticed until now. After a few moments, she composed herself and flagged down a taxi.

"Where to ma'me?"

She entered the taxi and sat down, falling back into the used black leather smelling of cheap cologne, body odor, and alcohol. She handed the driver her credit card, "Hamill and Espace," the feeling would pass. It was only a crush anyway, at least that's what she told herself, it was all she could afford. She had a *family* to lead now.

* * *

Clark thought his mind was playing tricks on him. He couldn't feel anything.

I'm dead.

His subconscious fired synapses of what he yearned until his thoughts glided to eternal focus. He was sitting across Lyra,

Who needs Apple Maps when you can get lost in eyes like that?

Their stare-down went longer than he liked. Her eyes were as deep as the ocean, sinking his heart lower than the Titanic. His glass overflowed with passion and he knew it would. No cup will ever be big enough to fill his heart. He could have a freighter full of the stuff and it still wouldn't fill this crevice doctors condescendingly study as an "aorta," seemingly a one-way river of passion flowing towards an ocean of ecstasy, neglecting to mention that waves of pain will erase the passions left in their sands with but a single touch. His heart felt like Swiss cheese, pieces missing from the prior women who used their serrated claws to surgically leave holes where blood used to pump.

He stared down their past at the bottom of an empty whiskey glass at a new hipster bar he hadn't heard of with a name he stopped trying to pronounce. The bartender refilled his cup. He could see people outside through the glass windows, three of the four walls in this godforsaken hipster wasteland were glass, goons inside could see the idiots outside and the idiots outside could see the goons inside.

Probably something to do with envy, they want what you have, vice versa, etc., he thought.

The storm became a reflection of his life. A fateful linear sequence of events, rain turned to hail which turned to sleet while little droplets of each sloshed the ground like an explosion of mindless consumerism. It made him wonder if everything was preordained in an abstract world external to his intellect.

"Would you bring me soup if I was sick?" Lyra teased the beast and tried to tame it.

He looked at the others in the bar as he contemplated her question: a couple talked by the counter, a nervous double date unfolded in a distant table. Clark always seemed to see everything.

Hyper-sensation kicking in big boy?

You're really getting on my nerves... bitch.

Very... Winston Churchill of you.

"You have a boyfriend for that."

Good one Clark, where do you come up with these?

"I'm asking *you*," her pupils dilated, she licked her top lip as she bit the bottom one. He wanted her more than Poseidon wanted Atlantis.

"Yes, I'd bring you soup."

Wait, the soup was a symbol wasn't it? We have to route the path in her head. Figure out what she meant. This is probably a test of emotional capacity, a gauge of passions.

Oh do shut up!

Both their hearts were beating so loud each was afraid the other would hear it.

The heart is always more rational than the mind.

"I'd bring you more than soup."

"Very selfless of you Clark. You're in danger of becoming a moral man," she thought he was being sarcastic.

She's so beautiful.

Focus Clark. Remember why you're here.

A perfect example, in all matters contingent on free will, options decrease to a singular course.

She hadn't let up her gaze. She's lasted longer than most, "You know what's funny?"

"What?"

"I noticed that you don't have a code. Ironic isn't it? You study moral philosophy don't you?"

The top of the glass wall furthest to the main door was slightly ajar.

The breeze cooled his lungs, "I've been… enlightened in their flaws."

"Nothing's perfect," she ran her fingers through the right side of her hair, which was resting on her breast.

Except you, he thought.

"Except you," he said. Only a tight t-shirt wearing steroid bound mama's boy doesn't say what he thinks.

She scoffed. The bubble of tension would have burst if that same breeze blew too hard. Clark stared at her until she seemed to catch the trail end of a fleeting thought.

She was in a playful mood, "Do you love me Clark?" her delicate voice fell to a whisper as each word left her lips. She was as subtle as the champion's haymaker in a heavyweight title fight.

Of all the questions he'd set out to answer he never considered the one that mattered to him most.

Do I love her? Do I have a choice? I feel what I feel and see what I see. How can I change that? The world lies alone in the middle of the cosmos surrounded by darkness. We're barely a pixel compared to the universe, a black hole could form and end our meaningless existence at any moment, but loving her, that's a whole other matter.

He noticed a piano as dark as space across the room.

The flashback skewed the current *reality*, merging the dream world with the real world. Was any of it real or was it an existential mind-body thing? He could think things and they would come to be?

That's a Parmenides paradox Clark. Something can't come from nothing! Come on, you know better!

He wanted to scream for tech support like Tom Cruise in *Vanilla Sky*. Could *a* omnipotent man come and make things right by fixing the glitches in this experiment everyone calls 'life'?

Clark… did you just compare yourself to Tom Cruise? That's as low as a man gets, and I'm not making a height joke.

He suddenly remembered the reality of her fate, her inevitable doom before his own and she faded away. He stared at the piano. This was as good a place and time as any to play his dirge. He approached it as a man approaches a tame tiger, unworried but fearful of its potential. He practically glided to the leather bench. The smell, a mix of oak and piano wire intoxicated him more than the drink he'd set down on the coaster. He pushed back the fallboard covering the keys and propped up his shoulders half an inch as if he were drawing a deep breath. He put his fingers on the keys, they were smooth and polished; the contrast almost made him want to slightly smile... and the pianist played on.

The ground shook like an earthquake. He closed the fallboard and shot a glance at the door because he wanted to know what was happening. The floor split open and ate him, throwing him back to his seat across her and the memory returned in full force. He couldn't escape it. No one can escape the past.

"Cllllllark? You're going to leave me hanging like that?" the Ls hummed in his ears like a vestal foreboding of a Paradise Lost and Returned.

Do you love her Clark?

"I..."

She smiled, "Whoa whoa whoa. Don't answer it. ... I'm joking. Besides, you barely understand the need to smile and laugh. You know something though? A study found if you smile and laugh, it will actually contribute to your happiness, something about the muscle reactions and your brain reacting to the muscles," her tongue slightly stuck out the right side of her lip.

There's nothing to smile and laugh about other than you.

Don't say that. She's an angel and we're evil and even evil has a limit.

Did you happen to catch how quickly she changed topics? It actually made her uncomfortable to consider the possibility that you love her. She hates you Clark. She could never love you. Who could love you? You don't feel. You don't... live.

Curious though, that she thinks you're capable of such trivial emotions.

"I'm glad such informative studies are so handsomely funded."

She broke her gaze when she reached into her bag and came out with her iPhone 3GS. She only did that when she was nervous, she knew how much Clark hated such 'boorish behavior by self-indulging jerkwads with too much money to throw away' but she couldn't contain herself. The wallpaper was interesting though. *'Starry Night,'* by Van Gogh.

They say he cut off his ear for a woman he loved but they also say he did it because he had auditory hallucinations.

He liked the first reason better; he thought he might cut out an eye and gift it to her. He valued his eyes so they'd be the most appropriate. He'd give her an all-seeing eye and be her guardian angel.

She has perfect eyes Clark. Think before you think!

Why in the hell would she want your tragic eyes? Why would you want *her to see what you've seen?*

I can't think in her presence. I like it though. There's a certain... tranquility in ignorance and mindlessness.

"Van Gogh?" he asked.

Her gaze penetrated his soul, the Maps app crashed.

"Your wallpaper. It's *Starry Night* by Van Gogh."

"How do you know these things!? No one knows these things! Why do you laser in on details no one else would notice?"

"It's a gift… and a curse."

He focused on her. She couldn't be perfect. Perfection is an impossibility. A conceptual apparatus of the unattainable created to point out inferiorities of the physical to the abstract. He looked for flaws. He couldn't find any.

"I like him," she finally said.

"Really? Dutch Impressionism turns you on?"

"Not really, but he cut off his ear for a woman he was in love with. Can you imagine that?"

You thought that before didn't you, does she understand you that well Clark? Maybe you do lov—

"How are the drinks?" the prescription Ray-Ban wayfarers of the hipster waiter triggered a migraine. He thought about quantum physics or whatever the discipline is called nowadays, about the multiverse, and wondered if the other Clarks got migraines and whether they were as bad as his.

"Fine, thank you," she hadn't noticed Clark's inability to keep his eyes open from the agony. His temples pounded, the only thing that diminished the pain was the thought of conceptual perfection across from him. "Where were we… oh yes, Van Gogh, cutting out his ear for someone he loved."

Truth is pain. His migraine forced the words, "I'd cut out my heart for you," he tried his best to say it nihilistically, attempting at the sardonic or satirical to rid it of any meaning but it came out more serious than he wanted. His ulterior motive that she know how much he valued her as a goddess made him sound sincere.

"What's that supposed to mean?" she was onto him.

You're in trouble now. Hang on let me get the popcorn. This ought to be good.

"Everyone shows their affections differently."

Her pupils constricted and dilated, "Like glancing at the wallpaper of their friend's phone for conversation pointers?"

"Guilty," a man admits when he's been caught with his hand in the cookie jar; his forehead weighed a ton.

"A rather smooth conversationalist too," a half smile developed on her cherry lips, he could see her left dimple. "Hey Clark, are you okay?" she finally noticed him looking odder than usual.

"It's nothing," he couldn't remember if he got all the words out. His vision blurred. She saw the vein on his temple pouncing up and down. She fumbled in her bag, dropped her phone, her keys jingled, the lid of her lipstick propped loose, the sounds turned his head into a ticking time bomb. He exhaled to push past the pain. She came out with a painkiller and put it in his hand across the table. She held it in his palm longer than she needed to.

"I don't need it," Clark was tougher than he looked.

"Another migraine? You should really see a doctor."

"Doctors are walking paradoxes," her touch eased the throbbing. It'd been too long since he'd had some peace, hardly a moment when he wasn't battling some dreadful headache. He looked over to her and watched the trees dance through the glass wall behind her. The breeze blew her hair a little to the side and he could smell her shampoo. It was a Polaroid moment engraved forever in his mind. Clark relaxed for less than a second. He was lucky to have such a moment but the second anyone has the thought it changes their luck; like asking for the check at a restaurant, a looming foreshadow of the hit on their wallet, or in this case, their soul. Luck always carries a heavier price tag than anyone can afford.

Lyra's friend walked in. Her name was exotic enough to remember but her personality was boorish enough to want to forget. She always seemed to be in a hurry, constantly angry at everything, stomping her feet on the ground as she took each step, craving attention at all times, a textbook case of a pretty girl with father and abandonment issues. She was a treasure trove for the clubbing enthusiast-loser-bro with contrived proclamations of dominance who values such things. It was practically unbelievable that Lyra and her were such good friends. The way Lyra entered a room was a complete contrast: with the aura of a queen, the face of an angel, the gait of a princess, with her hair seemingly harnessing the power of the sun emitting a sort of natural light that blinded Clark every time he looked towards it. She would walk over and greet her friends with what always sounded like an aria over a blossoming flowerbed, but that was Lyra, and then all at once, Clark was confronted with his *present* circumstance.

He stood up anyway. A gentleman never breaks his own principles.

"Hello," he pointed to the seat beside his own.

"Yeah? Hey," she muttered and sat somewhere else. Felicia was hotter than Dutch love in harvest, which was amusing since the slight European accent she carried made her sound sexier than she actually was. She had a near perfect body coupled with a naturally tanned face but she was far from *beautiful*. Clark assumed it was due to the fact that she had her heart torn out half a dozen times because she thought *boys* wanted her for more than her body.

She irked him, reminded him of Cruella Deville.

"Licia, be nice," while Lyra reminded him of Belle, or Cinderella; he hadn't decided yet.

"No, he's like a tiger, give him an ounce of weakness, show him a *little* fear, and he'll consume you without a second thought."

Whoa. She's almost as dark and morbid as I am, almost.

My miry thoughts never liked her, but then again, they can't stand anyone but Lyra.

"That's very… amusing," Clark arched his eyebrow, mirroring what Lyra had done to him one time.

"What… *amuses* you?" Felicia condescended back with her palms facing up.

"Your name… Felicia. It means catty, feline, and yet you're rather quick to label *me* a hungry jungle cat."

Felicia collected herself momentarily, "You're far too smart to be here right now."

Clark couldn't tell if she was mocking him but thought it was a safe bet.

"You think too much of me Cruella," a Freudian slip.

"Did you just call me 'Cruella'? The evil bitch from *101 Dalmatians* that wanted to kill the puppies?"

She's getting angry. Good. "She drives a cool car," he enjoyed this more than he liked.

"Are you serious?"

"Always, she's Cinderella, or Belle, I haven't decided. You're Cruella, that's just the way it is; the way the paper folds."

"And who are you in this little fantasy?" she drew a makeshift circle with her hands, "Prince Charming?" she barked, "Wouldn't you like *that*?"

"No," Clark never hoped for anything in his life. Hope *always* leads to disappointment.

I'm The Beast, the closest thing to truth these indoctrinating bastards at Disney got right: man as an angry and consuming beast.

Beep. Bring. Boom. His pocket vibrated; a text message from Lyra. *I'm right here, why is she texting me?*

'no clark, u aren't the beast, u are prince charming <3'

Did she just read my mind? He looked into her eyes in awe. The universe couldn't even come close, her eyes were vaster, more complete, and far less savage. That Maps app he was running would never give him directions out of there.

"Why are you here?" Cruella had a knack for ruining such moments; biting on a long expensive cigarette filter holding a North State, and lighting it in the silent gap.

"Well, some argue an evolutionist theory but others lean towards a creationist narrative," Clark's dry wit wasn't for everyone.

Cinderella's half-smile turned into a full one. The dimples on her cheeks formed the Moon, two perfect crescents.

"Well aren't you a clever prick?" she took a drag and puffed it in Clark's face.

Clark breathed in the smoke, "How very Oscar Wilde of you."

Ha. Ha. Ha. If only you came up with that yourself Clark.

"Don't you have other friends? She's taken," she thought he was like the dozen guys who'd torn out pieces of her heart with a meat cleaver.

He wasn't going to play her game, "I don't need other friends. I have you!"

She didn't know, couldn't understand that it hurts much more when women tear out your heart with a scalpel.

"I don't know how you stand him!" Felicia turned to Lyra with animated facial expressions, putting out a quarter of the cigarette on the apple shaped ashtray.

"He's only like that to you!" Lyra would've screamed if her elegant voice permitted her such uncouth behavior. She cared more about Clark than she let on or she wouldn't have defended him to a friend she knew longer.

"NO!" Cruella roared, "He's only *not* like that to you! It's like you're the only thing he cares for. And I hate him. *She's* taken!" she pointed to Lyra.

She keeps saying that.

"You're not giving him a chance. You ought not to judge. You know better. You study literature; there isn't a book, no matter how obscure, he hasn't read, if you come out guns blazing, you have to expect to be shot."

"Fine," she turned to Clark, "What do you know?"

Let's have some fun Clark, "Hmmm. You know Bruce Willis? ... Ghost all along. Harry Lime... not actually dead. What else do I know?"

"Okay that's it!" she lifted her martini and was about to throw it at him. It was mystifying even to Felicia herself why she held Clark with such an intricate disdain. It seemed like she was jealous that he'd picked Lyra but it could've been simply that he annoyed her.

"Don't ruin the night Felicia," Lyra put her hand out in front of the drink. Clark didn't flinch but Lyra locked eyes with him and orated a speech of empathy and compassion. Clark's slight nod answered in the affirmative; the beast was tamed... for now.

"Tell us a poem Clark," Lyra pointed up to the ceiling with an open palm, "He's good at these."

"Who do you ladies like? Felicia, I assume literature means you know poetry."

"Oh, what? Not smart enough to make up an original poem?" she raspberried mockingly at him and gulped a shot of her drink.

"Make one up? Okay," Clark's eyes zoomed on his muse. Their gaze locked harder than the Federal Reserve.

Lyra's face emitted a sort of youthful radiance while at the same time appearing as wise as an aged master's. Clark's eye for detail failed him in deciding exactly which she was. She couldn't be both young, passionate, and adventurous while simultaneously being mature, tranquil, and wise. She was, after all, only human... *or was she*?

Felicia's increasing agitation at Clark, despite having yet to hear the poem, grew as Clark spoke each word.

"Let's see," he continued, "Women enjoy love elegies most. I'll start. You guys help."

Felicia rolled her eyes while Clark took a sip of his scotch,

"A thief's heart once throbbed," he animated a throbbing heart on his chest,

"He eventually got it robbed.

An artist's heart twice beat. Now he'll surely paint a defeat."

Lyra breathed in each word. She tilted her head towards the side her hair was parted to, "Now a philosopher's heart *must* think. How tragic, since it'll surely sink!"

"That's amazing," Clark smiled inadvertently before he could control himself.

"What kind of crack have you two been smoking together?" Felicia demanded.

"Got it: 'A gentleman who cries for hope

Will only find solace in dope.'"

Felicia laughed a little and sat down on the seat Clark originally pointed to, their legs touched. She didn't need to sit so close but was starting to warm up to him. She wanted to play now, she looked up at the ceiling and closed her eyes,

"Often a man lies to win a heart,

But his success is an illusion,"

Clark and Lyra both laughed, "This is kind of fun," Felicia turned to Clark, who responded,

"Since he's been torn apart

And forced into seclusion."

The trio erupted in laughter, Clark couldn't remember the last time he laughed like this.

Lyra looked straight at Clark,

"The heart she wants *appears* cold

But *this* man respects ways of old."

Clark knew this was clever double talk; it was time to answer the question he'd been eluding since he met her,

"All men are warned," he lost his train of thought when his heart pounded harder than a drunk frat-boy on his dorm room after a sorority party.

Felicia chimed in,

"'Hell hath no fury like a woman scorned.'

BOOM!" she hadn't laughed like that far too long either, "I'm not being cocky... but we're awesome."

Ooooo, oooo! Can I play? Clark I want to play!

'There is nothing but the void.

Everyone hopelessly waiting to be redeployed

To eventually die a horrible death

By rich old men who've no understanding of pain,

Whose sons and daughters are all addicts of crystal meth,

Forcing those better than them to a life of bane.'

Clark tried to ignore the vexing inner voice only Lyra could deafen.

"What should we call it? A poem like that can't be untitled!" Felicia's anger was curtailed by good-natured poetry, her eyes lit up like Paris on a moonlit autumn night.

"Elegy of a Rhythmic Dirge," the words had barely left Felicia's mouth when Clark answered.

"That's… a little dark, no?" Felicia's eyes seemed to change color when sorrow circled around her pupils.

"We were just talking about this," Lyra pointed to herself and Clark, "Having fun, even pretending to can actually result in happiness, something about human brains and muscle reactions."

"I guess he's not too bad," Felicia pecked him on the cheek.

"I kissed thee ere I killed thee, no way but this, killing myself, to die upon your kiss."

Is that Shakespeare Clark? Nice! That's always a good bet with damaged women… and damaged women who study literature! Clark you really are a genius. I think I love you!

"Not too bad at all," Lyra blushed seductively. She assumed Clark was really talking about her. She was correct.

Clark retained only the outline of this experience. He knew he was there. He knew others were there, but couldn't discern whether or not he was alive, inside the *Inferno*, the *Purgatorio*, or the *Paradiso*.

Felicia put the brim of the goblet to her lip and slurped the rest of her drink, "Hmm, it's empty now," she giggled, "I'll get the next round," she retained her balance on Clark's knee as she stood up.

"That's one Sicilian Kiss. A Dry Martini, and..." she looked at Clark,

"__"

She interrupted before he could even utter a syllable, "Wait, let me guess, scotch. Top-shelf. Neat."

He nodded contently. *Such a cliché.*

She walked over to the counter. Lyra and Clark locked eyes for the trillionth time and it still wasn't enough. He was eternally famished when he thought of her. He imagined the two of them facing a mirror, unzipping her red dress from behind while staring deep into her eyes. The dress slowly slips off as she reaches around and touches his neck and her angelic body stares back while she turns towards his shoulder.

Wake up Romeo, reality calls.

Huh? Leave me alone for 5 minutes you prick! Can you do—

He looked towards the entrance where five loud-mouthed, salon using, house-music-loving, Guido scumbags welcomed themselves to the bar. The universe lies in balance. Clark and Lyra's harmony; violent ferocity. This *would* be the kind of crappy pseudo-hipster-or-bro bar that'd attract wannabe macho goons who wouldn't know a fight if a guy walked up and punched them square in the face. Too much UFC and YouTube clips deluding them into thinking they're Bruce Lee.

The *bros* had by now made their way to the bar; they noticed Lyra's long flowing red dress and Felicia's overwhelming vulnerability. Clark looked at her with eyes she'd never seen before. A side of him she didn't know existed, she stole a glance at the oafs by the bar counter and immediately knew what he was thinking.

Harmony in thought.

Clark's composure made it obvious that he'd gotten into his share of bar fights. He was never afraid of bigger numbers. To him, more enemies simply meant more weaknesses to exploit.

Felicia was aloof to such things. *More idiots who watch too much 'How I Met Your Mother,'* she thought. She walked back and set down their drinks in front of Clark and organized them accordingly while Lyra pretended to check something on her phone.

Just as she rotated around towards her seat, one of the scumbags, the fatter one with a shirt tighter than Katy Perry's concert dress, put his hand on her shoulder and opened his mouth to say something. Clark didn't hear what he said to her because he'd abstracted himself from the scenario and adopted a birds-eye view. He knew the beast was trying to break out of him but he was resilient in his quest to keep it internal. This rendered his senses moot. He reentered himself with his ears ringing so loud they seemed like they'd explode any second. Lyra shot a glance towards her white knight. Her eyes screamed of discomfort. It sounded like Clark growled. A lioness wasn't meant to be touched and although Felicia wasn't *his* lioness, she'd become a part of his pride, which meant he was responsible for her. Like an eagle hunting a snake, he soared in the sky without sweeping down. He truly believed aggression wasn't needed. Chest-puffing macho behavior that'd show these *insects* they weren't prey ought to have been enough.

Resolve the situation amicably.

He wanted to let it go and thought he could take the their hands and guide them away. Violence always begets more violence. A gentleman never fights in the presence of a lady; a knight kneels in front of her. Another of the males stood in front of him while a third sat beside Lyra.

I guess the one they sent to block you off from them is their wingman. They're like a pack of hyenas. Hungry stray dogs of some sort. They're no match, let's do this Clark.

Clark shouldered past the co-pilot with only a stern look and walked next to Lyra. He slipped his hand inside hers and stood her up towards him. The tranquility of an entire universe in her small, slender hands. He pulled her towards his chest. He'd planned to hold her by the waist and whisper words of passion to her.

The question always hovered over his psyche.

Plans rarely work out, the tight-shirt prick held her shoulders with both hands, shaking her frame towards his face and screaming,

"Come be with a real man toots!"

The monster knocking his chest freed itself. Clark opened the cage and let it out. It roared out and deafened everyone. He seemed in control but losing it each passing second.

One small jab should do. It doesn't need to be too hard. Just enough to let this utter excuse of a person know this is not the

place and certainly not the woman he ought have touched without her permission.

No onomatopoeia would suffice to accurately depict the sound exuded as Clark's fist left the clown's jaw.

What was that noise? Something cracked, a snap. I heard a pop of some sort. That was a small jab? Such anger Clark. Such brutality.

He'd dislocated the guy's jaw, in all probability fractured it completely. Lyra looked into his eyes.

What are you doing Clark?

She found the scene strangely erotic. It was sexy how Clark presented a perfect balance between virility and chivalry almost effortlessly. She wanted him. It wasn't the *Inferno*.

Clark looked at the others with the eyes of a predator. The one closest to Felicia walked away from her after apologizing. He was outnumbered but his eyes boomed with confidence. He looked as if he longed for pain as long it spared the ladies in his presence and he had the look of a man who had years of experience in the field of ruined dreams and constant despair, the look of a man not wanting to be trifled with.

The one backing up from Felicia suddenly moved towards his injured friend, Clark snarled and he froze. None of them moved an inch. They'd seen enough, the half whimpers and cries of their *bro*, unable to talk because his jaw was across the room, deterred them from any action. They shook in their boots at the sight of a *pride* unlike others they'd encountered, and like the snakes they were, they ran from the talons of an eagle. He hovered towards them,

"I'll still be here when the shock wears off," two of them flinched back.

Just then, Clark felt startled. A hand grasped his chest near his heart. He was shocked; his defenses were lowered and thought that one of them had flanked him. Snakes aren't known for their honor.

He was wrong. It was Lyra. She was pushing him back, taking him away. His eyes spoke a thousand words.

Yes. Take me away. Far away.

She looked in his eyes and smiled and her smile seemed to do just that. It wasn't *Purgatorio*.

* * *

He wanted her more than life itself. The passion in his heart burned the pain away. Every second he spent with her was a second he spent in the Garden of Eden. Was it fate? Had he chosen her? Did he have a choice in his passions? Does anyone?

The familiar grinding of his key unlocking the giant door to his penthouse was a plague upon his ears. He opened the door and entered in a mystifying fog. Lyra leaned against his kitchen island attentively reading the copy of Dante's *Inferno* she'd lent him. His life had been a nightmare, another idea he was trapped in. Everything that had preceded was a dream. Hell, life could be a dream and we wake up when we die. She saw him come in and dropped the book. He froze in his tracks as if he'd seen the ghost of an angel. His neutral expression faded like a war scar. She wondered why he looked at her like they hadn't met in years. He gripped his abdomen. His wound had healed, no scar, no evidence of the past.

She was wearing a thin robe. The clock had barely struck 6:00 A.M..

Their eyes exchanged cantos. Clark took a step towards her, forgetting the elegy he'd been composing for her. Had a black hole consumed the earth at that moment, neither of them would've noticed. Their eyes locked harder than Fort Knox. Lyra countered each step Clark took towards her with a seductive step backwards until her back was against the wall of his den. She tilted her head up while he stroked one finger through the dimples of her neck. He put his hand on her neck and ran his finger down the middle of her chest. He pulled the string on the robe and it slid open. Her body epitomized the sublime. Their noses touched but they didn't kiss. He put his hands on her waist and reeled her in, rubbing his cheek against hers like a lion until she finally devoured his face, unable to contain herself any longer. Their lips met like fated lovers who hadn't seen each other in years. Neither broke eye contact. He ripped off his jacket and carried her to his bedroom.

He woke in his bed gasping for air. He couldn't remember having sex with her; he never believed in such details. His love for her transcended mere physical lust for something beautiful. In our nominally post-modern maniacal existence, sex is trivial, meaningless, and empty. An hour of fun with no deeper insight other than a bubble of hedonistic behaviors consuming the minds of youth and adults alike, an aging portrait of a subject not worthy of its sophistication.

Lyra was a symbol, something more than a mere Disney fairy tale, more than a perverted sense of love and a quixotic rescuing of a princess in distress by some gallant knight. She was his absolution for the crime of ideas he'd imprisoned himself in.

The faint smell of strawberries and freshly grounded coffee progressively filled his nostrils.

Lyra lay sleeping beside him.

It somewhat made sense. It is a cheap copout but to be honest the entire plot seemed unbelievable anyway. Humans dream over thirty times a night but an intricate process in our brains forces us to forget them when we wake. Why? Are dreams that painful? Are they so dark and mournful that a defense mechanism in our brain has the specific job of deleting them? What process protects us from our conscious destructive thought or our consuming natures?

All literature and philosophy has a common thread, all believe 'humankind is smarter or less savage than all other creatures.' These are both false. If logic creates cognizant apathy, we have forfeited all aces in the deck of consciousness: empathy, compassion, love, and sacrifice. We have folded a decent hand. How can we understand passion without first understanding our nature? How do we know whether we are appropriately divined to go all-in with the highest four-of-a-kind? How do we know our thoughts are reliable? That another doesn't hold a straight flush? We have no proof other than a misguided sense of pride. There's only one way of gaining access to the truth and that's to serve those we are passionate about. If these passions aren't pure, we become the monsters we seek to fight.

Clark stared at her sleeping face. She was a superhero without powers, an angel without wings, a politician with honesty. It was as real as a leprechaun hiding a pot of gold, a pirate treasure, or an honest businessman. He *felt* it was real, he knew *she* was real. Her subtle smile opposite the dark monster that'd consumed him long ago. He wasn't desperate for love, he was desperate for hope. He wanted a relief from the psychological pains he couldn't avoid. She was so elegant, so eloquent.

How can you 'see' her eloquence Clark?

The eyes. She could recite a canto of Dante's Paradiso with her eyes.

How long had he been asleep? He'd lived another life in that dream. It was a life without Lyra. He didn't enjoy it one bit. He was a killer, a rent-a-clown with a gun, a second-string thug with a pistol.

It's over. What a nightmare. I think for the first time in my life. I'm happy.

Looks like your luck is turning around Clark.

Oh great... you're still here, I wish 'you' were a dream.

No such luck.

He couldn't look away, her skin beguiled him. He brushed his nails against her cheek. She smiled; it was the smile he'd readily die for. She glided closer and rolled on top of him with those gorgeous hazel eyes staring back at his.

Clark knew better. It was too perfect.

Am I still dreaming?

He wasn't some desperate Dostoevsky protagonist looking for existentialism in some obscure religious text or dream, nor was he critiquing social aspects in matters of right and wrong and searching for *The Morality of Values* in a haze of cigar smoke. It's easy to analyze the ignorance of shortsighted zombies lining up for the best-marketed *thing* and eventually becoming iProducts themselves. No, he didn't care that he killed people in that life, didn't mind his status as a desperado. He wasn't afraid of his conscience like suicidal Russian novelists. The chronic migraine scraping in his brain stemmed from losing Lyra. An outlaw without a babe and a rebel without a code. He knew now he had to do whatever it took to never let her go, to never lose her again no matter what it meant in abstruse relativistic moral codes or values society placed on its podium.

He looked up at her and closed his eyes to savor the moment. Something dripped onto his right pec.

Weird.

He opened his dilating pupils. It was blood. He looked up at her and it seeped through her black bra and fell in drops onto his chest with increasing speed.

Why is there so much blood?

"My love, what's happening?" he felt panic and couldn't help but show it.

He swiped his hand out from under the blanket faster than a speeding bullet. He was the farthest from the neutrality required of a stoic sage as he realized he was firmly grasping a hunting knife in his right hand. It certainly wasn't *Paradiso*.

This is not happening. Her head slumped onto his chest into the pool of blood that'd formed. It rolled from his heart to his abdomen.

"Lyra...? Lyra...?" he shook his head, "Lyra..." his mouth trembled, "ELL-WHY-ARE-EH," he spelled her name. Her stillness on his body could only be understood by his death.

You can say her name as much as you want. It won't change anything.

He blinked and she disappeared. He was lying in bed again but this time, it was Electra who laid beside him, awake and watching *him* sleep.

Had I chosen Electra? Killed Lyra for her? Electra is the more logical choice, the mindful choice since Lyra is gone. Mind has nothing to do with passion and the heart... do I love her?

He disgusted himself again; the old familiar feelings. He *had* killed Lyra; metaphorically, abstractly. She'd still be alive If she hadn't met him. They were after *him*; he *was* responsible for her. He loved her; he was responsible for her for eternity. He was a failure.

His choices weren't made in solitude like he was used to. No choice is made in solitude. Choices ripple outwards, form waves, and crash back on the beachfront.

Hourglasses turn and with each turn a grain falls out until eventually those grains become the moments of your life living outside the hourglass of time.

XXXIV
ARCHITECTURAL DARKNESS

The hospital equipment beeped louder and louder as Clark woke with an unwavering headache. He'd lived even though he didn't want to. The universe was nothing more than a middle-school prankster playing a bad joke on him. He lived when he wanted death and would probably die just when he'd catch a glimpse of yet another improbable dream.

Too long had his questions gone unanswered. He didn't care how weak he was; he checked out of the hospital wounded and bandaged against the advice of *'established'* experts. M.D.'s who place more value on the results of a computer test of what something is rather than listening to the information provided first-hand by their patients.

There are variables in your life you do not choose: your feelings and passions. Clark had been swimming in the waters of the void long enough. He walked for hours with a deteriorating body. She was the answer. He caught glimpses of her in his peripherals. Her presence seemed to follow him everywhere he went like a swinging pendulum gliding from one side to the other with no real goal. He was trying to recreate her route while wanting to understand the winding course of the tempest in his head. He was looking for her but not really. He was looking for something more, for *Vero*.

He couldn't find her and for a while he searched for a decent piano to play his dirge but it wasn't the proper time or place.

He traveled outside the city in the direction she'd hinted at years ago to a man that specialized in such answers.

Her father's estate had its origins in Scandinavian darkness and Victorian Gothic. It was a quaint house with gargoyles and sharp edges, the kind of place you'd fear in a horror movie.

"We meet at last Mr. Kóróna," he said as Clark approached the front door past the security gate.

Clark walked inside.

"There is only one true reason we go to war," he was trying to identify with the young man.

We? Clark thought.

"Passion. Passion of blood, lust, whatever it may be," he quipped as he handed Clark a glass of 1968 GlenDronach. Clark liked the man's taste.

"I fought many wars in my time," her father took a sip of the magic elixir, "Few were for land. More were for glory. Most were for power. But fighting for my passions, whatever they were at the time, was the only worthwhile reason."

He picked up a picture of Lyra's mother. Their resemblance was uncanny. He looked like *he* wanted to fall to his knees and sob.

Maybe 'we' is right, Clark thought.

The cage disappeared but the beast didn't move. It stood up and waited for a command. For the first time, it stood obedient to Clark rather than demanding submission from him.

Clark's mask of stoicism slipped, in danger of being consumed by his grief, to mourn the death of his love. No glass was big enough for the amount of GlenDronach needed to forget his mistakes and his past failures.

He looked at a painting of Lyra behind her father, reaffirming a truth he'd known for too long.

'Death is inevitable.' We are afraid of it and this fear forces us to play the odds. We are apathetic so we don't get hurt and so we don't feel the pain. Over time this mask of apathy becomes our only remaining face.

The odds were never in his favor this way. Without love he was already dead.

Her father composed himself, "Have you seen *Seven Samurai?*"

"The film?" Clark had an idea where this conversation was heading.

"Yes."

"I have."

"The samurai in that film are warriors; they're all honorable, honest, and capable men. But they are rōnin. Do you know what this means?"

"Yes. They are master-less samurai," Clark's only master had been Lyra. He approached a series of framed family photos on a credenza and picked up one of Vero pecking Lyra at what seemed like his birthday.

"Vero," Clark whispered, tracing the little blonde curls on his head in the photo forming eights across his scalp. He must've cut it short prior to needing Clark's help in outrunning the *Dahaka.* Clark ran his fingers through his hair, "Vero?" He watched the beast fall into the void along with his dysania.

Her father sighed, "It's funny, Hemingway despised Dostoyevsky... I've always wondered why."

"He felt he was always serving Dostoyevsky. Always second to him and living in his shadow. Hemingway was a jealous prick. And thus Dostoyevsky..." Clark paused, "...Was secretly *his* master. Hence why Hemingway was never considered the greatest writer of *all* time."

"She was right. You *do* know a lot of obscure things. But I guess *things* like this are often interchangeable with *wisdom.*"

Clark scoffed and looked outside the big window by the armoire where a thin layer of snow covered the pavement. Truth was a burden.

"And who do you serve now?" Her father approached from behind.

"I tried serving... I don't know what I served," Clark said, *until I met Lyra, then I served her.*

"A samurai without a lord. An outlaw without a revolver. A mariachi without a guitar," her father tried to understand Clark's mind.

"I guess so," Clark returned. *Like father like daughter*, he knew what Clark was thinking.

Her father smiled, "A *rōnin* without a lord..." he repeated, "Is impossible. Even if you have no physical master, no *one* person to whom you serve, you still serve something. Some*thing,* you serve your passions. Otherwise, in this society at least, you run the risk of *karoshi.* Are you not brave enough to admit that?"

Lyra's father was clearly well-versed in Japanese vocabulary, cinema, art, and philosophy. *Karoshi* is a term used to describe death from being overworked. In other words, *any* blue-collar death in this *just* society.

Clark saw a picture of them framed on the credenza just beside the one of Lyra and Vero. Lyra was eight or nine years old. They were clutching each other's chests tightly.

"Vero," Clark whispered lightly, "What happened to his parents?" the pain in his abdomen worsened.

"His father doesn't know, ...and his mother..." he had to compose himself before he could say the words, "His mother is dead," he sniffed into a handkerchief.

"Doesn't know..." Clark's pupils dilated. He couldn't help but think everything *had* been for Vero. He looked at the picture again as a lone tear escaped from his left eye and suddenly realized how alike they looked. How Vero was the spitting image of Lyra's beauty mixed with his own hair and inquisitiveness. He'd been waiting for truth near a window while *Vero* had been waiting at the front door the whole time.

"She truly... understood you?" her father asked with bloodshot eyes.

Clark smiled, "She was the only one who did. I committed *koi na yokan.* The fatal sin."

Bergljót chuckled, "You speak a little Japanese?"

"If you can call it that."

"It's *koi 'no' yokan. No yokan,*" the phrase is defined as that elusive feeling of falling in love at first sight.

Clark's wound suddenly started bleeding. He hadn't noticed the pain creeping up his neck from his abdomen.

Everything was contextual, tied to space and time, love and passion, life and death. All things became subjective: decisions, answers, morality, good and evil.

"Oh, I'm supposed to give you something from Lyra. Hold on… I'll get it," her father disappeared above the spiral stairway.

Had he found her and lost her? He'd been dead until the moment he laid eyes on her but by then it was too late.

Einstein was dead on; Clark noticed the fresh red stain on his white shirt. Time *is* relevant to the observer. He stared down the Grim Reaper, sickle and all, and knew he'd eventually blink. He took out the final piece of paper left in his pocket and chuckled.

Last piece of paper, last thoughts.

He borrowed a pen from the telephone desk beside the round drink table and hobbled down to the floor, falling faster than a heart in love. At the very least, he could avenge her. He *hoped* he had one friend left in the wasteland labeled 'Earth'.

"Mr. Bergljót, get the following message to the man at *333-428-9357*:

'His name is Ventoni. Jonathon Ventoni. If you're looking for *true* justice and wish to return that favor.

CK.'"

His life flashed by as the pen rolled off the paper. Every graze, heartbreak, and scar just existing, nothing more. His abdomen felt like it was giving out. He'd felt like this before:

looking down the muzzle of Alex's twenty-two and in the alley near *Grave* and *Mort*. It felt like dying.

Life is like kissing a porcupine, its thorns biting into the void of your mouth, your eyes tear not from the pains of a cut tongue but at the thought of your love and the source of your passions. A *potential* solace in an arid swamp deluded with myths of success and lights at the end of tunnels.

He saw Lyra again. Every encounter. Every word. He felt like he could reach out and touch her lips. Her beauty was perfect. He hated its flawlessness. He *loved* her perfection. His fingertips felt cold.

It was love. She'd dragged him from the debris even though he'd given up, wanting to lie there and blink. She made the ultimate sacrifice and disregarded the consequences to herself and showed him it was all right to live. She showed him that there was hope, a choice, that he could put down his sword and stop fighting. Even a rōnin could find serenity in her eyes.

It wasn't *just* love but its abstraction from the physical, the form in its purest. The form only possible in death, in *Paradiso*.

The pain crept from his neck to his brain. His heart felt like it was clawing out from the inside.

He thought about the last time he saw her: wet from the storm with her hay-colored hair damp with a natural glow that incepts a dancing tree in Parisian spring.

A cold breeze sprinted up his back. The past is an abyss, your only chance is surviving a fight to the death with it, but it's like kissing the crimson lips of your love and a cosmic hole consuming the fire in her irises.

He stumbled back and knocked over the pictures on the credenza and most of the frames shattered. The glass slipped out of his hand baring resemblance to her goblet back at the party. He laid on the ground staring at a thin river of scotch penetrate the frame and soak the picture of Vero kissing Lyra: the picture of his family.

He was willing to suffer the aches in his bones and die for the things he cared for. For passion, for her. She'd made him stronger; and like Superman in front of the sun, she became his solace, his milky way, his galaxy, and his whole universe.

He closed his eyes, his bloody fingertips reaching for her portrait above him.

Every single encounter they'd ever had continued to flash in an intricate system of firing synapses. He caught himself *hoping* that there *would be* an afterlife. That she was there waiting for him. The moment was eternal. He would not be.

* * *

If he could do it again, he'd choose to die sooner: in that motel room or lying behind the witness's couch so he could spare her pain and save her life. If he could do it again, he would, no matter how many times, for eternity. He'd give his life for her. This was the choice he made. A final smile formed on his scarred lips and his death was a black hole.

* * *

Bergljót came rushing down the stairs with a wireless phone pressed to his ear. He saw the picture frames on the ground next to Clark down on his side. He turned Clark's face and slapped him lightly, pressing his ear to Clark's nostrils and mouth, hoping to feel his breath.

"Come on son! I have it! I got it!" Ethan Bergljót unfolded a letter, "Listen! Just listen!

'CLARK,

I'm truly sorry I kept this from you. Knowledge is pain and I knew the burden on your shoulders would be vicious if I told you.

Your search for truth has no place for family. Ideals are perfect and immaterial, I am not, despite your efforts to convince me otherwise.

I am sorry.

Vero is yours,'" Bergljót crumbled the paper and ran his hand through his face, he didn't see a point in reading the rest, but he thought he felt Clark move his fingers so he straightened the paper and continued reading,

"He is your son. I kept this from you because I guess I knew deep down that you'd be against bringing life into a world filled with venality, consumerism, death, and anguish. That you wouldn't know what to do.... But as time progressed, I realized how similar he was to you and I could not bear to see the infinite distance between you two. It was when I realized how much his long hair reminded me of you that frightened me in your similarities.

I don't know why I didn't tell you the second you met him. A part of me thought you always knew. That you'd know the second you saw him and he'd know the second he saw you. You were the only person he ever hugged so I assumed deep down, he knew too. Perhaps it was the nature you always speak of, that because he was your son, you were attracted to each other like two magnets.

Such ideas fly right over me but I hope that wherever you are, you will come back and find Vero and finally attain that which you pursue with such dedication.

Take care of our son. Hold him close to your chest, and never let go.

> *AMORE,*
> *LYRA.* "

Ethan's attempts were futile. He found a picture in the envelope Lyra had put the letter in, a photograph taken of the two of them at some restaurant or bar. Lyra goofily sticking out her tongue at the lens while Clark stared at her with an ever subtle smirk on his right cheek. The contents of the envelope would've been indelible in different circumstances.

Her father buried his head in his chest and noticed Clark's hand reaching for his left back pants pocket where a corner of a small piece of paper stuck out. He extracted the paper and unfolded it. A small card fell out, it read:

"Account no. 3784678890. Bank of Geneva. Password: 'Lyra is the tragedy of the divine.'"

He put the card down and skimmed the letter. The young man's forlorn elegy for his late daughter was simply…

DEAREST LYRA,

If you are reading this I have ceased living. Your celestial touch will no longer animate me to life like it did every time you gazed into my soul with your warm eyes.

I was dead until I laid eyes upon your Olympian beauty, your seductive charm, and Queen-like demeanor.

I realized immediately after I'd met you that I was not worthy of your affections. I have seen and done things that no man ever should and my anguish is simple atonement for the acts I've committed. I've accepted this.

I would readily give anything, including my life, for nothing more than a bare glimpse into the past I shared with you.

I've contemplated my existence and it is nothing without you. I do not exist.

I have watched the moon rise and the sun set; I have listened to the trees dance and the fields howl. I see, hear, and touch nothing but suffering. The future holds nothing but sorrow without you. The silence and reality of this thought deafens me, blinds me, and numbs me to everything else.

I give you my heart like Van Gogh gave his ear.

All I wanted since I laid my eyes on your perfect beauty was your love. You tamed the beast in me. The monster dwelling in the recesses of my psyche I could never keep out. You were its master.

I thank you. I understand now and I know that my search for truth is over.

I'd hoped we'd be a crappy romantic comedy rather than a tragic love affair but only fools and lawyers see life as black and white.

I ask of you only one thing: if you believe I've ever caused you pain, whether intentionally and unintentionally, I want you to condemn and spite me for it. I will take this punishment gladly.

I believed that nature is nature. We cannot fight it for we would be fighting ourselves, and that is always a losing battle.

If we were doomed to never be then I surrender my belief of fate and question it to the grave.

Everything I have done has been for you and 'Vero.'

P.S., I urge you not to worry about me.
It's nice down here: warm and LOTS OF CIRCLES.
MY SOUL IS YOURS.
CLARK.

END.

Enjoy the present; nor with needless cares,
Of what may spring from blind misfortune's womb,
Appall the surest hour that life bestows.
Serene, and master of yourself, prepare
For what may come; and leave the rest to Heaven.

Oft from the Body, by long ails mistun'd,
These evils sprung the most important health,
That of the Mind, destroy: and when the mind
They first invade, the conscious body soon
In sympathetic languishment declines.
These chronic Passions, while from real woes
They rise, and yet without the body's fault
Infest the soul, admit one only cure;
Diversion, hurry, and a restless life.
Vain are the consolations of the wise;
In vain your friends would reason down your pain.
O ye, whose souls relentless love has tam'd
To soft distress, or friends untimely fal'n!
Court not the luxury of tender thought;
Nor deem it impious to forget those pains
That hurt the living, nought avail the dead.

~ John Armstrong
The Art of Preserving Health;
Book IV: The Passions;
Lines: 129-149

BRUCE CROWN studied Philosophy at the University of Toronto. He's lived in Florence, Paris, New York, and currently resides in Toronto with his sister.